FLAW IN THE DEFENSE

THE LEONIDAS CORPORATION
BOOK THREE

TARINA DEATON

TARINA DEATON LLC

Dear 'Rona,

Eff you.

~The World

FOREWORD

Dear Reader,

This book has been almost three years in the making. I had originally planned to release it in April 2020. Well, we all know what happened early 2020.

Personally, I had retired from the military, was homeschooling my kids, was hired into a new job and spent a few months training for that (virtually), and then moved back overseas. Needless to say, a lot was going on. Unfortunately, it all took precedence over writing.

But now it's finally here. I hope you love Paige and Ash as much as I do.

Tarina

PROLOGUE

CHARLESTON AIR FORCE BASE, SOUTH CAROLINA - 2005

"Sergeant Davis. Line unsecure. May I help you?"

"Did you see it?"

Paige sighed. Carrie's love for drama seeped over the phone with her breathy question. "Did I see what?"

"Lexi's picture!"

"I have no idea what you're talking about."

"You have to see it!" Her excitement was palpable. "It's on MySpace."

"Carrie, I don't have MySpace."

"I don't understand why you won't get an account. Everyone has MySpace."

"I have better things to do with my time. What's the picture?"

"Hang on," she said. "I'll send you a screenshot."

Paige switched over to her unclassified computer system and waited for Carrie's email.

"Did you get it?"

An email notification popped up in her inbox. "Yeah. Hang on."

She clicked on the email, then double-clicked on the picture. A woman's left hand, adorned with a large, round solitaire diamond, appeared.

"What am I looking at?"

"He proposed!"

Paige wrenched the phone away from her ear. "Christ, Carrie. Quit screeching in my ear." She tucked the phone back into the pocket of her shoulder and tilted her head to hold it in place. "Who proposed?"

"PJ. He proposed to Lexi!"

Paige's breath left her in a whoosh. "What?"

"A day after she got out. Turns out they've been dating forever but hid it because he's an officer."

A deafening moment of silence, then her heart shattered into tiny, jagged pieces that burst outward before collapsing back in on themselves like a supernova. She'd known he'd been seeing someone else—had even asked him about it, but he'd said they were *just friends* and it wasn't anything to worry about. Turned out she was the one not to worry about.

Carrie's voice continued to drone over the phone as a tear escaped and rolled down her cheek.

God. She'd been stupid. So fucking stupid. She'd known better. Told herself time and time again to break things off, not to fall for his excuses, not to fall in love with him, but she'd done it anyway.

So stupidly stupid.

Fuck that. No more. No more waiting. No more hoping. No more lying to herself. No more being someone's doormat.

Paige swiped at the wet trail on her cheek. "Hey, Carrie. I need to go. I have a meeting in a few minutes."

"Oh, yeah. Sorry. Are we going out this weekend?"

"Sure. Give me a call later."

"Okay. Bye," Carrie said.

"Bye."

Paige tossed the headset into the phone receiver, then pulled up the global address list in her email and found the number she needed. Snatching the phone up, she dialed.

It rang twice. "Force Management. Sergeant Johnson."

"Sergeant Johnson, it's Sergeant Davis."

"Hey! What's going on?" he asked.

"Is that assignment we talked about before still available?"

"Yes..."

She took a deep breath. "I'll take it."

"Wow. You sure?"

No. "Yes." *Yes.* No turning back.

"What changed your mind?" he asked.

Paige closed her eyes. *I'll never escape him if I stay here, and this is the only way out.* "I've been here almost four years. It's time for a change of scenery."

"Okay. I'll put the paperwork in."

"Thanks," she said.

"No problem. Good luck."

~

Heat enveloped her like a clingy lover. Every pore in her body opened in an effort to cool her skin, which was covered in a sheen of sweat. It ran freely down her temples from under her helmet, between her breasts, and along the hollow of her back. Beneath her body armor, her uniform was soaked, and the slight bit of air wafting in from the gunner's window did nothing to relieve her discomfort.

She was going to melt before she ever touched the ground. They'd have to medevac her in a mason jar.

She stared out the window as the helicopter circled the landing pad, the touchdown surprisingly gentle given the speed of their descent. The doors of the UH-60 Blackhawk slid open, and she released the harness holding her in place. Hopping down, she took a deep breath before muscling one duffel bag over her shoulders and dragging the other from the floor of the bird. It clunked to the ground, and she grabbed one end, thankful it had wheels. She squared her shoulders and walked in the direction the soldier crouched under the spinning rotor blades pointed to with his knife hand.

A tall, wide-shouldered officer, clad in a rumpled and faded Army Combat Uniform, waited on the other side of the waist-high concrete barrier. His cuffed sleeves, hands in his pockets, and overly relaxed posture made her think he was not "regular" Army.

"Staff Sergeant Paige Davis?" he asked.

"Yes." She raised her voice to be heard over the helicopter's engines as it took off.

"Major Aidan Graham." He held his hand out and Paige shook it, noting the extensive tattoos on his muscled forearm, then saluted. A good reminder that he was an officer and therefore off-limits. She did not volunteer for Iraq to repeat her poor life choices.

He waved her off. "Don't worry about that—we're in a no-salute zone."

"Yes, sir."

"Let me grab one of those." He took the bag off her shoulders and walked to a Gator utility vehicle, placing her duffel in the small cargo area.

She hefted her other bag in and removed her helmet. Pushing the damp hair back from her face, she dropped it next to the bags.

"You can take your vest off too." He climbed into the driver's seat.

"Are we going far?" she asked.

"Three or four minutes, maybe."

She settled on the passenger's side. "I'll keep it on. It's easier to carry on my body."

"Good point." He reached under the bench seat and held something out to her. "Here."

She took the proffered water bottle, chugging half of it.

He started the engine and released the brake. "First time in country?"

Still swallowing, Paige nodded.

"How long is your tour?"

"A year." She took in the dirt, the large tents, the concrete barriers, the concertina wire, and the armed towers. Brown. Everything was brown, and she was definitely a long way from Charleston.

He glanced at her in surprise. "Wow. Long tour for Air Force. Who did you piss off?"

"I volunteered."

"Huh." He stopped in front of a squat, tan concrete building, set the brake, and turned off the engine. "I'm going to drop you at your room. Your roommate's off today and knows you're arriving. She said she'd hang out, get you set up tonight and show you around the camp, then bring you to work in the morning."

"Okay." They grabbed her bags and helmet from the back of the Gator.

He banged on the brown metal door before opening it and shouting, "Male entering."

They waited a few seconds for a response before proceeding down the hall. He stopped at the third plywood door and knocked.

It swung open to reveal a woman about Paige's age in Army PT gear and black flip-flops, her dark blond hair pulled up in a messy bun on top of her head.

"Hey, sir." She stepped back and opened the door fully.

Major Graham stepped back and set down Paige's bag in the doorway. "This is where I leave you. Sergeant Reynolds, she's all yours."

"Later, Major," her new roommate said.

Paige crossed the threshold into the small room, awkwardly dragging both bags behind her. No more than ten feet by ten feet, it held two twin beds against each side wall. Two metal wall lockers stood side by side against the far wall, and two small nightstands were wedged between the wall lockers and the beds.

She dropped her bags at the foot of the unmade bed and

peeled off the heavy vest, careful not to let it drop on the floor to avoid cracking the plates. Taking a deep breath, Paige filled her lungs for the first time in hours, now that she wasn't weighted down by an additional forty pounds.

"Here."

She took the bottle of water the woman held out.

"I'm Denise." She kicked off her flip-flops and sat cross-legged on her bed, leaning back against the wall.

"I'm Paige." She sat on the edge of the other bed. Exhaustion pressed down on her and seeped into every muscle. Between the heat and the last three days with little sleep, she was ready to pass out. For the five million and eighth time, she wondered what the hell she'd been thinking.

"What's your MOS?" Denise asked.

Paige gulped water, not sure how to respond. "My what?"

"Military Occupational Specialty—your job. What do you do in the Air Force?"

"Oh. I'm in intelligence."

"Ah. That explains why they sent you here." Denise folded forward and reached under her bed, pulling out a bottle of Gatorade. "Here. You need to hydrate."

Paige capped her water bottle and took the sports drink. "Thank you. Why does me being intel explain why I'm here?"

"There's a lot of information coming in, but not enough analysts to write it up for it to go out. There's at least three months' worth of backlog, if not more."

"This is my first time doing this kind of intel. We don't really do analysis in the Air Force. At least not of raw intelligence," Paige said.

"Don't worry about it. Unless you've been here before, no one has done this kind of analysis. It's overwhelming at first, and there's a steep learning curve, but once you find your groove, you'll be fine."

Paige gave her a grateful but weary smile. She'd worried

people would judge her for her lack of tactical experience. This was all new territory.

"You look like you're about to pass out," Denise said. "But you at least need to eat, and chow isn't for another hour, so how about a shower? It may help wake you up a little."

"A shower would be great." Without a doubt. Sweat was drying, forming a salty crust along her hairline and in other places where there should not be a salty crust.

"Okay. I'll give you a quick tour and show you where the shower and latrine trailers are. We'll get you some sheets and then go to chow."

In the not-too-far distance, there was a thud, followed by a muffled explosion. Paige sat up straighter. "What was that?"

Denise looked up at the ceiling. "Mmm…mortar, if I had to guess."

Paige jumped up from the bed. "What? What do we do?"

"Nothing." Denise shrugged.

"Nothing? We're being attacked! Shouldn't we go somewhere? Take cover? Man the battle stations? Something?"

Denise waved a hand. "They're probably taking potshots at the guard towers. Happens all the time. By the time we got to the bunkers, it'd be over. Besides, we're safer in here than we are running around out there."

Probably? Slack-jawed, Paige stared at Denise. She just sat there. Completely relaxed and calm.

BOOM!

Paige flinched and covered her head with her arms as the walls and furniture in the room shook.

Denise grinned. "Welcome to Abu Ghraib."

CHAPTER 1

SEVENTEEN YEARS LATER

"Here are your room keys, Ms. Davis, Ms. Garcia. Your other guests checked in about thirty minutes ago. Go through the doors behind you and turn left, then follow the signs that point to the villas. You're in building twenty-two."

Paige took the key cards from the reception desk clerk. "Thank you."

"You're welcome. Enjoy your stay."

Handing one of the keys to Angie, Paige grabbed the handle of her suitcase. "Let's go."

The sultry air of St. John was a sharp contrast to the almost arctic air conditioning of the resort lobby. god , she loved this place. This was her retirement plan. Not the resort, but a small cottage close to the water in the middle of the Caribbean? Hell, yeah. She'd already bought a property in Costa Rica. She tried to visit it at least once a year, if not more. Everyone could have joined her there for her birthday celebration, but she liked to keep it hers. Besides, this resort was all-inclusive, and she didn't want to worry about anything this weekend.

"Oh my god ! The pool is gorgeous!"

Paige grinned at Angie, whose excitement shone from her heart-shaped face. "Wait until you see the beach."

"How many times have you been here?"

"Only once, a few years ago, but it's by far one of my favorite resorts."

"Thank you again for inviting me."

"There's no need to thank me. It was completely selfish on my part—I wanted a single friend with me as well."

"Then I'm your girl." Angie's voice held just a little bit too much eagerness. "There—building twenty-two."

"I think we're on the backside," Paige said. Sure enough, their villa was the corner unit, facing the beach.

Angie gasped. "Oh my god ! It's so blue!"

"I know. I never go to the beach in Charleston because this is what I always compare it to."

"Well, thanks for ruining it for me."

Paige laughed and pressed her key card against the reader, pushing the door open when the lock tumbled and the light turned green.

"You're here! You're here! You're here!"

Bree enveloped her in a tight hug before she fully entered the room. Paige dropped her tote and hugged Bree back, closing her eyes and holding on to one of her oldest friends. Damned if she didn't even tear up a little bit.

Helping Denise a couple of years ago had hit home that she missed her sisterhood. She had friends in Charleston, but none who knew her. Not really. They knew the her she presented now —smart, independent, and would go out of her way to help her friends—but very few people found her soft spots.

Bree sniffed and pulled back. Her nose appeared bright pink against the rest of her pale skin. "Sorry. I'm feeling very emotional lately."

Paige laughed. "You've always been emotional."

"I know, but I cried over a toilet paper commercial yesterday, so I'm way more emotional than usual." She looked over Paige's shoulder. "You must be Angie. I'm so sorry! I didn't mean to keep you out of the room—I'm just so excited to see Paige."

"Careful," Paige said. "Bree's a hugger."

Angie dropped her backpack. "That's okay, so am I."

The two women hugged each other as if they were long-lost friends. Paige smiled and dragged her bags farther into the room, breaking into a huge grin when she spied Denise. Not much had changed in the seventeen years they'd known each other. A few more laugh lines around her blue eyes. Although in Denise's case, they might have been scowl lines.

"Hey."

Denise returned her smile. "Hey."

Her hug was just as tight, surprising Paige, although not nearly as long.

"How have you been?" she asked.

"I'm good," Denise replied.

"I'm Angie." She approached with her arms open.

"Denise isn't a—" Paige gave them a confused look when Denise welcomed Angie's hug. "Hugger. When did you start hugging?"

"Domestic bliss has softened me up."

"I'll say. You're almost a squishy marshmallow, you're so soft."

"I will cut you."

Paige laughed. "There's the Denise I know and love!"

"Oh my god ! I know I keep saying that, but oh my god ! This place is ridiculous!" Angie darted from room to room, her brown eyes sparkling with exhilaration, exclaiming over the things she found. "There's a bidet!"

Paige looked at Bree and Denise, who wore identical amused expressions. "She gets a little excited."

Bree laughed. "Not gonna lie, I did the exact same thing when we arrived. We took the room with the twin beds. You should have your own room and we weren't sure how comfortable Angie would be sharing a room with a stranger."

Angie returned to the living area and threw herself onto an armchair. "Paige, this place is bananas. You have to let me chip in for the cost."

"That goes for us as well," Denise said. "This resort can't be cheap."

Paige flopped onto one of the couches. "Ugh. It's part of a timeshare I got swindled into a long time ago. Other than the booking fee, it was already paid for."

"Then let us chip in for the booking fee." Bree sat on the other end of the couch.

"You can buy me drinks at the bar this weekend," Paige offered.

"I thought the drinks were included," Angie said.

Paige grinned. "They are."

Someone knocked on the front door and Angie jumped up. "I'll get it."

They all stared toward the entrance. Angie returned carrying a covered platter and a bottle of champagne. "Compliments of the hotel. They said happy birthday."

"Sa-weet." Paige lifted the cloche, revealing a small cheesecake. "Yum. If this is the same cheesecake they served when I was here the last time, it's delicious. Not too sweet but still decadent. So good."

"Well, now I want some," Denise said.

"Let's pop that cork and start celebrating. Then we can go hang out at the pool and get drunk," Paige said.

Angie brought glasses from the sideboard while Paige opened the champagne and poured.

Bree sniffed the contents and grimaced, setting the glass down.

"Bree, you okay?" Paige asked.

"Yeah. I think my stomach is still upset from the flight—we

had a pretty rough landing. And I've never been a big fan of champagne. Sorry."

"Don't apologize," Paige said. "I'm not a fan of champagne myself, but I'm not turning down free alcohol either."

Denise frowned at Bree. "You've been complaining about an upset stomach for a while."

"It comes and goes. I think it's a mild stomach bug that just won't go away."

"Or you're pregnant," Angie said.

Everyone lowered their glasses and stared at Bree expectantly.

"No. We aren't trying," Bree said.

"But are you not *not* trying?" Paige asked.

Bree shrugged. "We aren't doing anything. We were, but…now we're not." She shrugged again.

Everyone continued to stare at her.

Bree blinked. "Shit."

Paige leaned over the side of the couch and picked up the phone handset, pressing the button for the concierge. "Hi. This may be a strange request, but is there any way I could get a pregnancy test?"

"Yes, of course. We'll have one brought right to you."

"Thank you." She hung up the phone. "The concierge is sending up a test."

"How embarrassing," Bree said.

"Why?" Denise asked. "It could be any of us who're pregnant."

"Yeah, but I know it's me."

Angie shook her head. "That doesn't make any sense."

"Let's change into our bathing suits while we're waiting." Paige dragged her suitcase to the main bedroom and set it on the end of the bed to dig out her blue bikini. Changing quickly, she pulled her cover-up on right before someone knocked on the door.

A young man dressed in the hotel uniform held up a small brown bag.

"That was fast," she said.

His gaze flitted to her abdomen. "It happens more often than you'd think."

"Probably happens more often a few weeks after guests leave." Paige winked and closed the door.

Walking into their bedroom, she held out the bag.

Bree took it, opened it, and stared down into the contents. "Okay, I can do this." She disappeared into the bathroom and closed the door.

Paige sat next to Denise on the edge of the bed and held her hand while they waited for Bree to come out.

Denise stared intently at the door. "They've been talking about kids for a while. I really hope she's pregnant. If anyone should be a mother, it's Bree."

Paige squeezed her hand. Finally, the door opened slowly, and Bree walked out, staring down at the white stick in her hand.

She looked up. "I'm pregnant."

Paige grinned while Denise and Bree hugged, even as a twinge of something close to envy settled deep in her stomach. She shoved it down—hard.

"Yay!" Angie jumped up, clapping.

Bree covered her face with her empty hand and burst into tears.

"Not yay?" Angie asked, her voice thick with worry.

"No, it's yay. It's a huge yay." Bree sniffed and tried to wipe the tears from under her eyes. "It's just...we quit trying because I was so tired of being disappointed month after month, so Jase convinced me we needed to take a break and try again in a few months."

She took the tissue Paige offered and wiped her nose. "And now I've ruined your birthday weekend!" Bree burst into fresh sobs.

"What? No." Paige pulled her into a hug. "Honey, this is the best news ever. I'm so happy for you." No matter what that annoying coil of something in her stomach said, she was ecstatic for Bree and her husband.

"But now I can't drink."

Everyone laughed and Paige pulled back, brushing hair away from Bree's face. "That just means you can be the responsible one and tell us all when we're being too obnoxious."

CHAPTER 2

"When do you think it'll be ready?"

Ash sighed and tucked his cell phone into his shoulder while he dug through his suitcase. "I told you, Patrick, I'm working on it. There's something wrong with the tail end of the worm—it's not repairing itself like it's supposed to. I need to fix that before we can do the test run for the demo next week."

"Ash, there are a lot of people interested in this program, beyond the initial investors. I have people calling *me* asking about it. Everything is riding on a successful test run of the program for the next phase of funding."

"I understand that, but I promised Natalie I wouldn't work this weekend so I can be in the moment. I'm not going to break my promise to her."

"A few hours working on it won't hurt anything," Patrick said.

Ash rubbed his forehead, thankful when someone knocked on the hotel room door. "I'm not going to disappoint my sister on her wedding weekend, Patrick."

He turned the latch and opened the door, going back into the bedroom to continue looking for his goggles.

"You ready?" Conor, his soon-to-be brother-in-law, asked.

"You better not be working or Natalie is going to string you up by your toes and beat you to death with her veil."

"I'm not. I'm in the middle of telling Patrick I'm not working this weekend."

"Okay. Fine…fine," Patrick said in his ear. "Just call me when you get back."

"Will do. Bye." He ended the call and threw the phone on the bed.

"You know Natalie doesn't like him, right?" Conor asked.

"Kind of hard to miss when she tells me at least once a week." He found his goggles tucked into the bag with his dress shoes for the wedding.

"You're going to do laps at the pool?"

"Yes."

"You know it's more of a float and relax pool than a do laps and exercise pool, right?

"Yeah. So?"

Conor shook his head. "You're weird. Let's go."

Ash grinned. "Thanks." He'd stopped getting upset when people called him weird, or a nerd, years ago. Now he took it as a compliment. "Nat already at the pool?"

"Yes. Just so you know, Suzie started drinking about two hours ago."

"Okay?"

"She gets handsy when she's drinking."

They started down the stairs.

"So?"

"She's already made a comment about wanting to put her hands on you this weekend."

Ash side-eyed Conor. That would be a definite no. He hadn't really hit his stride in the looks department until his sophomore year of college, when he finally started filling out instead of up. Suddenly, girls who hadn't given him the time of day a year before were throwing themselves at him. Natalie told him it wasn't fair since he would continue to get better looking as he got older.

He usually wouldn't consider it an issue since most of the time he was oblivious to a woman's interest in him unless it was blatant. Even then he had a tendency to question why they were talking to him. But Suzie, his sister's maid of honor, had been one of those girls who never spared him the time of day throughout high school. Not only that, she'd gone out of her way to tease him about how skinny he'd been, his braces, his preference for computers instead of football games. Most guys wouldn't care, but he wasn't about to encourage a selfish and shallow woman.

"Thanks for the warning," Ash said.

"No problem. I need to stop at the restroom."

"You could have used the one in my room, you know."

"Didn't need to until we hit the stairs."

"Okay. I'll see you out there." Ash meandered through the paths lined with thick foliage to the pool, easily spotting his sister and her friends near the bar, unsurprisingly.

Natalie was sprawled on a lounge chair, soaking up the sun and adding to her tan. "Are you wearing sunscreen?" he asked, by way of greeting. "It would suck if you got burned two days before your wedding."

"Hi, Sebastian," Suzie said in a singsong, flirty voice from next to his sister.

"Hey, Suzie." Even if Conor hadn't warned him, the way Suzie smiled at him would have done it. No one who knew him well called him Sebastian—they would've known he didn't like it. Not since fifth grade when Steve Wakowski had started a rumor that he was named after that stupid crab. It was just another thing she'd teased him about.

Natalie looked up at him and shaded her eyes, even though she was wearing sunglasses. "You made it. Did Conor have to pull the cord on your laptop to get you to leave your room?"

"Ha, ha. I'll have you know I didn't even bring my laptop."

She shoved her sunglasses to the top of her head and rose up on her elbows. "Are you serious?"

"Yes, little sister. You asked me not to work, so I'm not working. I knew if I brought my laptop I'd be tempted, so I left temptation at home."

"Are you…are you okay? Are you nauseous? Shaky? Do your fingers move as if they're typing?"

"Baw ha ha ha ha. You're not funny, brat."

Natalie smirked and replaced her glasses, laying back down on the chaise. "I'm hilarious and you know it."

"Keep telling yourself that." He pulled his shirt off and tossed it on her face. "I'm going to swim."

She grabbed his shirt and threw it into the foliage behind her. Shaking his head, he walked around to the far end of the pool. It wasn't very long, but he'd swum in worse.

The sound of a laugh caught his attention, and he glanced at a group of women settling into lounges on the other side of the pool. One of the women grabbed the hem of her cover-up and raised it. He couldn't look away as the fabric slipped over her hips, the dip of her waist, and finally the curve of her breast before she pulled it over her head.

The simple blue bikini provided full coverage and accentuated the softness of her curves without resorting to strings and scraps of fabric. Her sun-kissed skin had enough color to tell him she spent time outside but probably didn't intentionally tan.

He was very grateful he'd opted for board shorts instead of his usually tight swimming trunks. He wouldn't mind her attention at all. How bad of a brother would he be if he ditched his sister for the afternoon and hung out with a beautiful woman? Of course, that would mean walking up to a stranger and introducing himself.

Heat flushed through his body at the idea of making small talk and amped up the restless energy coursing through him. That settled that.

He rolled his shoulders and tilted his head side to side. Settling his goggles over his eyes, he executed a shallow dive into the pool and powered his arms and legs through the water, quickly reaching the other end of the pool. Turning, he swam almost half the length before surfacing for a breath and swimming to the other end. He flipped again and settled into a rhythm, soon forgetting everything except the feel of the water over his skin, the easy strokes and kicks propelling him across the pool. He lost track of the number of laps he did before something hit him on the head, literally stopping him in his tracks.

He surfaced and slicked his hands over his head. "What the hell?"

Natalie stood on the edge of the pool, a fist on one cocked hip. "Come be sociable."

Glancing around, he found the small ball she'd beaned him with. "Why?"

"Because it's what people do, Bash. And it's my wedding and you have to do what I say."

"I'm pretty sure that only applies on the day of the wedding." He snagged the ball and swam to the edge of the pool.

"No, it applies all weekend," she said over her shoulder as she walked away.

Ash remembered the women on the other side of the pool. He glanced over his shoulder and found them paying absolutely no attention to anything.

Sighing, he hoisted himself out of the water. Figured. The one time he wanted a woman to notice him, he was still invisible.

~

"*L*ook. Look, look!" Angie smacked Paige's arm.

She pulled her arm out of striking distance. "Ow! What?"

"He's getting out of the pool."

Paige looked where Angie was pointing, then pushed her arm down. "Don't point."

The man set his hands on the edge of the pool and lifted himself out of the water. The muscles of his back bunched, then water sluiced down his body as he stood. The red swim trunks hung low on his hips, and it looked like the high curve of his ass was the only thing keeping them from falling off.

"Sweet baby Jesus," Bree whispered.

Paige couldn't agree more. They'd missed him getting in the pool but had noticed him swimming laps. Always one to appreciate the male form, she'd watched what little of his arms and shoulders she could see. The way he swam back and forth had been mesmerizing, and she'd bet good money in a Leonidas betting pool he was a competitive swimmer…or had been at some point. He was muscular but lean in the way swimmers tended to be, with broad shoulders and narrow hips. Which made sense with the way he'd swum laps for the last half hour.

She kept replaying his exit from the pool in her mind but in slow motion. Like an advertisement for something she wanted to buy RIGHT. NOW. Take *all* her money.

"Look at that, the hotel got you a birthday present to go along with the bottle of champagne," Denise said.

"He looks like he's in his twenties," Paige said.

"So? What's wrong with that?" Angie asked. "They say women in their thirties are more sexually compatible with younger men."

Paige looked at her. "I'm in my forties now and not into cradle robbing."

Denise scoffed. "Please. He crawled over the side of that crib a long time ago."

"I don't think it matters," Bree said. "I think he's with that woman."

Across the pool, he stood over a woman shaking his head, sprinkling water on her while she squealed.

"Yeah. That makes sense," Angie said.

Even though she'd just said he looked way too young, Paige felt an irrational sense of jealousy. She shook her head and took a sip of her drink. What the hell was going on with her? She didn't get jealous of strangers' relationships. Hell, she didn't get jealous at all. It was one of her mantras.

"Not unless they're in a polyamorous relationship," Denise said.

Paige looked at the group again. Another man had lain down on the woman and was shimming on top of her while she laughed and the swimmer faked dry heaving next to them. He must have said something because the guy pushed off the woman and tackled him into the pool.

The woman sat up and rushed to the edge of the pool, yelling loudly enough for them to hear. "If you give him a black eye before the wedding, I'm going to kill you!"

"So the guy she was making out with is the fiancé?" Denise asked.

"The other guy is the best friend?" Bree added.

"Or a family member," Paige said.

"What about that one?" Denise nodded toward a woman with a too-new spray tan sauntering toward the pool. She eased down on the edge and put her legs in the water, but acted like she didn't want to get wet, even squealing when water splashed in her direction.

Paige and Bree said at the same time, "Maid of honor."

Angie leaned forward to look at them all. "Do you guys always do this?"

"Do what?" Paige asked.

"Figure out what roles people play in a group."

Bree cocked her head. "Come to think of it, we do."

"It's an occupational hazard," Denise said. "Once an analyst, always an analyst."

"I don't think I've ever looked at a group of people and tried to figure out who they were," Angie said.

"Have a plan to kill everyone in the room," Denise said in a low voice.

Paige and Bree grinned.

"I don't know if I should be horrified or impressed," Angie said. "You're like the female version of Graham."

Paige laughed. "Oh, she's much worse than Graham."

"Horrifically impressed? Impressively horrified?" Angie tilted her head back and forth, considering both descriptions.

Bree chuckled. "That'll do it."

"Well, this weekend should be interesting." Angie raised her glass. "Cheers!"

*A*ngie slid into their booth, another Bushwacker in her hand.

"Hey," Paige said. "You should be careful with those. They sneak up on you."

"But they're so delicious!" She slurped on the thick chocolate shake-style drink.

Paige shook her head. Angie was definitely going to regret sucking them down like...well, like chocolate shakes tomorrow. "Where have you been?"

"Talking to this guy. You have to hear this story. He's a tugboat captain out of Miami, and he comes down here once a month for a tax break."

Paige pressed her lips together to stop the bubble of laughter that rose.

Denise covered her mouth with her hand.

Bree nodded her head. "That's...interesting. Did you ask him to tug your boat?"

Angie laughed. "I did! I don't think he understood what I was saying because he started asking about the size of the boat and where I had it anchored. I felt so bad when I had to admit I don't actually have a boat."

Paige cleared her throat. "Was his name Skipper?"

Angie shook her head. "No, it was Brian. Why?"

Paige couldn't hold back a laugh, and once she started, Denise joined in.

"Stop laughing!" Angie said. "Do you know how long it's been since I've been laid? By a guy? Too long!"

Paige wiped under her eye. "I'm sorry, honey, but you have to admit it's funny."

Angie rolled her eyes. "Okay, yes. I can admit it's kind of funny. But! That's not why I came back. Grab your drinks. We got invited to the VIP area."

"We did?" Bree asked.

Paige grinned. "Go, Angie."

"By the tugboat captain?" Denise's question sent them into another fit of giggles.

Angie rolled her eyes. "No, not by the tugboat captain. Remember the woman from the pool earlier today? It's her bachelorette party. I bumped into her on the dance floor, and we started talking. You guys were right—the guy who rubbed on her is her fiancé. They're getting married on Saturday. The swimmer is her brother, and he is single." She grinned at Paige. "The guys are at their bachelor party thing, but they'll be here later."

It was weird that her heart sped up a little upon hearing that. Seriously, what was going on with her? Was it a minor mid-life crisis? The idea of turning forty and being "over the hill"? Her heart did not flutter at the thought of seeing a guy. Especially a stranger on vacation. Other parts of her might flutter, but not anything in her chest.

Oh, god . Maybe it was a heart attack or an undetected murmur. Now she knew she was being ridiculous—the military would have caught a murmur a long time ago.

"She should have been an interrogator. She got all that information in fifteen minutes," Denise said.

"No kidding," Bree said.

They grabbed their glasses and followed Angie toward the steps to the VIP section. Once they cleared the top of the stairs, the bachelorette jumped up and hugged Angie as if they were lifelong besties, not someone she'd just met minutes prior. Which didn't surprise Paige in the least—Angie rarely met a person she wasn't immediately friends with.

Natalie, the bachelorette, hugged each of them as she was introduced, then waved over her future sister-in-law and her bridesmaids. Paige and Bree exchanged a look as they met Suzie, the maid of honor. The same woman they'd clocked at the pool, who did not appear happy to have them join the party.

"We need shots! Lick My Pussy, bitches!" Natalie shouted.

"I seriously hope that's the name of the shot," Denise said.

Paige nodded. "You're not the only one."

The maid of honor returned with a tray laden with shot glasses filled with bright yellow and red liquid. Paige took one of the glasses and toasted the bride, throwing the contents of the glass back in one swallow. She shuddered and set the glass back on the tray, sipping her gin and tonic to wash the taste away.

"That was disgusting." Denise sat on the couch next to her.

"Yes, it was." She watched the bride and her friends for a few seconds. "I feel old."

"Forty isn't old," Denise said.

"It's not even about age—it's about...life experience. They're—what? Late twenties, early thirties? Maybe? Think about what we were doing at their age."

Denise followed her line of sight. "You have a point. We aged before our time."

Paige watched the bride and her friends laughing and hugging each other. "Are you happy?"

Denise stared off into the distance for a moment. "You know? I am. You?"

"I think so. I'm not *un*happy. More…unsatisfied in some way, but I don't know how."

Denise shifted so she faced Paige more fully. "I'll be honest. If you'd told me a few years ago that being married and having two kids would make me happy, or in some way fulfill me, I would have punched you in your throat."

Paige grinned because she could see Denise doing it. "That's not in the cards for me anymore."

"Maybe. Maybe not. I didn't think it was in the cards either and look at me. My sage advice is to keep your options open. Like, for instance, giving a hot, sexy, younger guy a go." She pointed toward the VIP entrance.

Nicole's fiancé, the hot guy from the pool, and several other men filed into the space.

Paige gave him a slow once-over, taking in the way the cream-colored shirt hugged his shoulders and tugged at his arm when he bent it. His dark hair was either styled haphazardly or he'd run his hands through it.

He laughed at something, and his eyes crinkled at the corners. Maybe he wasn't as young as he first appeared. Maybe he was one of those men who aged disgustingly well and would get more ruggedly handsome the older he got.

She smirked. "You know what? It's my birthday. Why the hell not?"

Ash followed Conor into the VIP area. He had a nice buzz going from the rum tasting Conor's dad had arranged for them rather than the best man's strip club suggestion.

Ash had nothing against strip clubs or people who worked in

them. If a woman had the confidence to strip, more power to her. But he had questions.

Where did he put his hands? Where was he supposed to look? Was the woman doing it because she wanted to or because she had to? Did she enjoy it or was it like waiting tables at a restaurant, but the tips were better? Should he talk to a woman as she was dancing? What should he talk about?

Thankfully, Conor had shot down Joe's suggestion quickly and they'd settled on the distillery tour.

Ash swallowed hard and stifled a groan at the crowd in the VIP lounge. There were a lot more people than he expected. It was supposed to only be the wedding party, most of whom he already knew or had met that day. He had a hard enough time faking being sociable with people he knew.

Glancing around for a friendly face, he noticed a blonde and a brunette sitting on one of the couches. The brunette looked slightly familiar. She pushed a lock of hair over her shoulder and it clicked. She was one of the four women at the pool earlier in the day—the one he'd noticed in the blue bikini. Did they have access to the VIP area for another reason or had Natalie invited them?

Natalie probably invited them. She was the exact opposite of him—outgoing, social, and never met someone who wasn't a friend. Whereas he was none of those things.

The brunette glanced over and their eyes met. Her gaze traveled down his body and back up.

He ran a hand down the front of his simple button-down shirt, smoothing it to his chest and abs. Her gaze met his again, and she smiled, displaying a dimple in her left cheek.

Natalie's screech drew his attention as she jumped off the couch she'd been standing on and leaped at Conor, wrapping her legs around his waist before plastering her mouth to his.

Thankfully she was wearing shorts and not a skirt. He was happy for his sister but really wished she wasn't as demonstrative with her happiness in front of him. There were just some things he didn't need to know about his little sister, especially since he thought he heard her say "suck," "cock," and "later."

Conor's cousin appeared at Ash's side, holding a beer for him, and he took a healthy drink. Lowering the bottle, he looked back over at the brunette. Her friend had left and was talking to Joe, the best man. The brunette tilted her head toward the empty seat next to her and raised an eyebrow.

Just to be certain, Ash glanced over his shoulder to make sure she wasn't motioning to someone behind him. When he turned back around, she was outright grinning and crooked her finger.

In most situations, he wouldn't have done it. He never knew what to talk about after asking someone's name and what they did for a living. It always ended awkwardly with half-mumbled words of "nice to meet you" or "good talking to you, I'm going to go talk to someone more interesting." They never actually said that, but that's probably what they thought.

And women…it never went well. He'd had a few hookups, but all his long-term relationships had been with women he met through work. Even then the relationships ended when they accused him of being hot and cold. He'd either disappear into his computer for days at a time or he was too clingy.

But what the hell? It was his sister's wedding. Wasn't there some kind of moral obligation as a groomsman to hit on the single women? He had nothing to lose, and a little bit of liquid courage went a long way.

CHAPTER 4

$\mathscr{B}$ree smiled when he took her very obvious hint and sat close to her on the couch. He leaned even closer to speak in her ear, even though the music wasn't so loud in the VIP section that they had to shout.

"I'm Ash."

"I'm Paige." She held out her hand.

"It's nice to meet you, Paige." He slid his fingers across her palm, gliding his hand into hers before grasping it firmly.

f"You too, Ash. Is that short for something?"

"It is, but it's pretentious and only my mother uses it."

Paige grinned. "Ash doesn't like to be pretentious. Noted."

"What do you do, Paige?"

"I'm an operations officer for a small private security company."

"So you're someone important?"

She laughed. "Well, I make sure the bills get paid, so I suppose I am." She always played down her role and what she did. She'd found it made men less intimidated than saying, *I manage million-dollar international contracts and sometimes play mercenary.*

She'd learned on more than a couple of occasions that men

lost interest if she came across as too smart or capable. If men wanted to assume she was a glorified secretary, who was she to tell them otherwise?

"What do you do?" she asked.

"I'm a computer programmer."

"Really?"

His brows pinched together. "Why does that surprise you?"

She shook her head. "You know what? It shouldn't. Our IT person doesn't fit the stereotype in my head either—I should know better."

"What's the stereotype?" he asked.

"You know…disheveled, dozens of mugs half full with the dredges of coffee surrounding a computer, glasses…typical stereotype. Which doesn't fit our IT person at all."

He laughed, a low, easy chuckle that resonated deep in Paige. She hated fake laughs. The ones people forced. Ash's reaction felt real, and she found herself smiling in response.

"Except for the glasses, that description actually fits me when I'm deep in a program. I lose track of time. Forget about meetings and appointments. My business partner takes care of the day-to-day aspects of the company while I do the programming. My sister even made me promise I wouldn't work this weekend. I think she's afraid I wouldn't show up to the wedding otherwise."

"The wedding's tomorrow?"

Ash shook his head. "Saturday."

Paige nodded and sipped her drink. She was kind of out of things to talk about. He wasn't doing any of the things she was used to guys doing and responding to. His gaze was intense, but he wasn't touching her, wasn't leaning into her more than neces-sary, wasn't asking leading questions to gauge her interest. Could he be *not* interested?

He was handsome in a classical sense. Strong jaw and profile. Thick, dark hair. Most guys who looked like Ash knew their appeal. He, on the other hand, seemed like he was waiting for her to leave.

The bride came over and grabbed Ash's hand. "Come on! We're dancing."

Panic flashed briefly across his face. "Nat—"

"I don't care! It's my wedding weekend—you're dancing! Don't make me come back and get you." She led the groom out of the VIP section, followed by most of their group.

"How do you feel about dancing?" he asked.

"In general or specifically with you?"

His grin was hesitant. "With me?"

Was it an act or was he really that shy? "I'd love to dance with you." She'd give it a few songs, but if he still had the platonic brakes set, she'd call it quits.

He drained his beer in one swallow and stood, holding his hand out for her. Taking it, she set down her glass and followed him to the dance floor.

With a large group of people, there wasn't any pressure to dance only with each other, and she found herself dancing back-to-back with Angie. The DJ turned on Dua Lipa's latest song, and more people rushed to the dance floor amid a chorus of cheers.

The bigger crowd on the small dance floor pushed her closer to Ash. He moved easily to the music, and she couldn't help but think about how he'd move in bed, sending a tingle of anticipation through her. Their hips and thighs brushed against each other as they danced. Someone bumped into her from behind, and he pulled her closer, moving back toward the dark edge of the floor, keeping her close when they cleared the crowd. They swayed to the music but no longer danced.

His gaze dropped to her lips, and hers did the same. There was no mistaking his attraction now. She could feel it pressed against her lower belly. Her hands were on his upper arms, fingers wrapped around that sweet spot right above his bent elbow on the back of his arm, and his hands rested on her hips. Not tight, but she could feel his thumb rubbing back and forth across the top of her hip bone.

It was strangely intense. They were barely touching. Hadn't kissed or traded thinly veiled innuendos, yet desire throbbed heavily between her legs.

This was her favorite part of the game. Would they? Wouldn't they? How long would they drag it out, and who would make the first move?

She licked her lips, and his Adam's apple bobbed as he swallowed. She tilted her chin, bringing her lips closer to his.

He brushed his lips against hers. They were warm, soft, but the kiss was unexpectedly brief.

It was nowhere near enough.

He pulled back, and their gazes met. His eyes were full of heat and desire. That was what she expected.

Except…it wasn't.

She anticipated quick and rough. A hot and heavy night-club hookup make-out session. Instead he was slow and methodical, as if memorizing the shape and feel of her mouth.

His tongue brushed the seam of her lips, and his mouth whispered against hers again before he parted his lips, and their tongues tangled slowly together. Her whole body vibrated with tension, but she followed his lead even though she wanted him to hurry up.

His hand grasped the base of her skull, directing her head where he wanted as he deepened the kiss. It was teasing and languid and so fucking hot, she squeezed her thighs together to put pressure on her clit. She lost herself in the sensual glide of his mouth until he lifted his head from hers.

Her chest rose and fell as she tried to catch her breath. His fanned across her moist lips.

"We should go back to the VIP room," he said.

Paige blinked to hide her disappointment. She thought for

sure he would say they should get out of there and go somewhere more private—not less.

"Sure."

He took her hand, lacing his fingers through hers, and led her back to the VIP suite. A lot of people had given up on the dance floor, and she spotted Bree on one of the couches, looking as if she were about to fall asleep.

"What are you drinking?" Ash asked.

"Vodka tonic with a lime."

He brushed a hand down her arm as he headed to the bar, and she joined Bree.

"You look like you're fading fast," Paige said.

"I am. I'm such a wuss."

"No, you're not. You're pregnant."

"True, but I don't think I should feel this tired, this quickly."

"I have no idea, but if you're tired, go back to the room."

"You don't mind?" Bree asked. "I feel bad—it's your birthday."

Paige laughed. "The whole point of this weekend is to have fun and relax. I don't expect you to spend every minute with me."

Bree wiped the back of a hand across her brow. "Whew. That's a relief. It'd get awkward when you bang Pool-Boy."

Paige laughed and glanced toward the bar. Ash was walking their way.

Denise joined them on the couch. "I'm peopled out."

"I kind of figured," Bree said.

Ash handed Paige her drink and wiped his hand on his pants, then held it out to Bree. "I'm Ash."

Bree smiled wide. "I'm Bree. This is Denise."

He shook both their hands, then sat on the edge of the couch perpendicular to theirs. "Can I get you two something to drink?"

"I'm good." Bree held up her almost empty water bottle. "Thank you."

"I can get you a fresh one," he said.

"No, that's okay. We're leaving," she said.

Ash's gaze whipped to Paige. "Are you leaving too?"

Paige looked at Bree. "Do you want me to go back with you?"

"Of course not. You and Angie stay here and have fun," Bree said.

Paige glanced around the room. "Where is Angie?"

"I saw her on the dance floor when I came back from the bathrooms," Denise said.

"Okay, I'll look for her in a few minutes."

When Bree and Denise stood, Paige joined them. She hugged both of them and promised not to make too much noise when she got back to the room.

"You better not come back to the room tonight," Denise whispered in her ear.

Paige grinned. "We'll see." She joined Ash on his couch once they left.

"You guys are staying at the Emerald Bay Resort, right?" he asked.

"We are. How did you know?"

"We're staying there as well. You were at the pool today."

Paige hid her smile against her glass. He'd noticed them earlier.

"Are you in the main hotel or the villas?" he asked.

"The villas. You?"

"Most of us are in the villas. The parents and extended family are in the main hotel."

"Guess that makes us neighbors," she said.

"Well, neighbor. Would you like to come over for a nightcap?"

She smiled. "Do people still say nightcap?"

Ash shrugged and looked down briefly. "It sounded better than what I was thinking."

"What were you thinking?"

"Whether you'd come back to my villa and have hot, sweaty sex with me."

Paige barked out a surprised laugh.

A blush rose up his neck, and he tried to pull away.

She grabbed his hand. "No, I'm sorry. I wasn't expecting your response to be so blunt. It caught me by surprise." She rested her hand on his thigh and moved closer, her mouth a hairsbreadth away from his. "I'd love to have…a nightcap with you."

Ash smiled slowly and touched her knee. The soft glide of his fingers on her skin sent goosebumps racing up her leg. "Do you need to find your friend and tell her you're leaving?"

"Yeah, I'll be right back." She purposefully brushed her lips against his when she leaned over to set her drink on the table.

She found Angie on the dance floor with the bride and several of the bridesmaids.

"Hey, I'm leaving."

"With the hot swimmer guy?" she asked.

"Yes."

Angie jumped up and down and clapped. "Yay!"

Paige shook her head at her. "It's not like I never get laid, Ange."

"I know, but he's cute."

"He is." Even if *cute* didn't begin to cover it. "Are you staying here or do you want to walk back with us?"

Natalie's plastic silver tiara and short veil slipped sideways on her head as she grabbed Angie's arm. "No! She can't leave yet."

Paige looked at Angie for confirmation.

"I'll stay for a while."

"Okay, but take a cab back to the hotel. Don't walk back by yourself."

Angie rolled her eyes. "Yes, Mom."

"I'm serious, Angie. You more than anyone know the risks of what can happen. Be smart."

"I will. I promise."

One of the bridesmaids stepped forward. "I'm not drinking tonight—I'll make sure she gets back safe with us."

Paige racked her brain for the girl's name. "April, right? The groom's sister?"

She nodded. "Yes. I promised the parents and grandparents I would be the responsible person and no one would get too drunk or arrested tonight."

"Okay. Do you mind exchanging numbers?"

"Not at all."

Paige sent April a text to the number she gave her and waited for her phone to ping.

"All set." April turned her phone so Paige could see the screen.

Angie hugged her. "Have fun!"

She rolled her eyes but couldn't stop the grin. Angie was too fun not to smile with. "You too, but safe fun. Hear me?"

Angie pointed at her and waggled her eyebrows. "You too."

Sliding through the bodies on the dance floor, she found Ash waiting for her on the edge of the crowd, watching her intently.

"Everything okay?" he asked.

"Yes. Ready?"

He nodded and took her hand, threading his fingers between hers again, leading her toward the entrance. Once outside, he inhaled deeply, as if he hadn't been able to catch his breath inside.

"Do you want to take a cab or walk?" He pointed at the cab parked outside the entrance.

She considered it for a moment. They were less than a quarter mile from the club, but she wasn't armed. "Let's take a cab."

He raised his hand to get the driver's attention, who lifted his in response and started the car. "After you."

The short ride was tense, but she didn't know if it was sexual tension or the nervous tension she felt from Ash. He helped her out of the cab in front of the hotel and took her hand again, leading her down the winding path to the villas.

He stopped in front of building twelve. "This is me. Do you still want to come up for a nightcap?"

"Yes. Why?"

He shrugged. "There's always a chance you'd change your mind once we got out of the club."

Paige stepped closer. He was such a contradiction. At times shy and hesitant, and at others confident and forward. "I'm definitely still interested in your…nightcap."

A slow smile spread over his lips. "That sounds really dirty when you say it like that."

She grinned and stood on her toes to wrap an arm around his neck, pulling his head down to kiss him.

Sliding his arms around her waist, he pulled her closer, pressing his erection against her. His groan turned into a deep, sexy growl.

A very loud retching sound, followed by splatter, separated them abruptly. They stared at each other before looking around, then up when they heard the sound again. A guy was hanging over the side of the second-floor balcony, puking into the bushes below.

"Shit." Ash rested his forehead against hers.

"You know him?"

"That would be my underage cousin who apparently decided to sneak into my room instead of going back to his." He lifted his head, disappointment all over his face.

"You need to take care of that?" She knew the answer and her disappointment might've been worse than his.

He sighed. "I do. His mom is really strict and will lose her mind if she finds him like this."

"Rain check on the nightcap?"

"Yes. Definitely." He pressed his mouth to hers, kissing her hard and deep, the way she'd expected him to in the club. She leaned forward for more only to be brought up short by the sounds of dry heaving.

"I'll walk you to your room first." Ash's voice was hoarse and strained.

She knew if she let him walk her to her villa, she could

convince him to forget about his cousin, but that wasn't the right thing to do.

"No need. I'm just a few buildings down." Stupid moral compass.

"Are you sure?" he asked.

"I can take care of myself. You need to take care of that." She pointed up.

"I'd rather be taking care of you." He kissed her once more—hard—then turned and bounded up the steps.

Contradiction. And now she was really fucking horny.

CHAPTER 5

"Wow! This is gorgeous!" April spread her arms out wide and threw her head back, soaking up the warm Caribbean sun. As the designated sober person, April was one of the few people not suffering a major hangover from the night before.

"Could you please stop shouting?" Suzie asked.

Ash shook his head, grabbed his snorkel gear, then zipped up his bag. They'd had to cancel the planned boat excursion because half the wedding party was too hungover to spend any amount of time on a boat. The only reason he'd been able to talk them into the beach was because he promised his sister she could sleep in the shade while the not-hungover people snorkeled. This way they were still doing a "group" activity, even if it was individually.

It had the added benefit of getting him in the water and out of the hotel, otherwise he'd be stuck listening to his dad complain about none of the "young people" going on the boat trip and spending "quality time" with the extended family.

"I want to live here." April walked up from the edge of the water to the shaded area they'd staked out.

"I'll happily leave you here if you don't be quiet," her brother said.

April cupped her hands around her mouth. "What? You want me to talk louder?" She shrieked and darted away from Conor when he sat up.

She didn't need to worry because he groaned and flopped back down, mumbling, "I hate you."

April laughed and grabbed her mask, snorkel, and fins. "Whatever, losers. I'm going to find Dory." She looked at Ash. "You coming?"

He nodded, distracted by a woman walking out of the water farther down the beach. "In a minute."

She followed his line of sight and grinned. "Have fun."

"Yeah." He waved absently and headed down the beach.

Bree, the woman he'd noticed, reached the pile of towels in the shade of a cluster of palm trees and lifted the corner of the towel. A hand reached up and pulled the corner back down, causing her to laugh. Apparently, his friends weren't the only ones who'd overindulged last night.

"Hey." He raised his hand as he approached.

"Hi," Bree said. "Ash, right?"

"Yeah. How are you guys feeling today?"

"I'm great!" she said with a grin. "Others…not so much."

The lump under the towels grumbled something.

"Paige?" He pointed at the lump.

Bree laughed. "No. Angie. She closed the bar down with your sister last night."

"Ah. Natalie and Conor are in pretty much the same condition. April and I had to force the rest of them out of the hotel today. Is Paige swimming out on the reef?" He scanned the water, where several snorkels were visible sticking out of the water.

"No, she and Denise swam around the point." Bree pointed down the beach toward a small outcropping of rock. "Paige said there's a cove with nothing but sand dollars on the ocean floor, but the only way to get there is boat or swim."

"You didn't want to go with them?" he asked.

"Too tired," she said. "I'm not used to all this water activity. I'm much more of a dry land kind of person."

He nodded absently, staring in the direction she said they'd swam.

"I'm sure they wouldn't mind if you joined them." Bree had a teasing smile on her face.

He grinned. "Thanks. I think I'll check out the sand dollars." He prepped his mask before sliding it over his head and adjusting the snorkel's mouthpiece. Wading into the water until he was hip deep, he dipped down and slid his feet into the fins. Flipping over onto his front, he took a few breaths to get used to breathing through a tube, then set off toward the cove.

It was always an adjustment, going from using his entire body to propel himself through the water to using only his legs. He still ended up using his arms out of sheer habit. Popping his head up every once in a while to make sure he wasn't heading out to sea, Ash made his way around the point, swimming without actively thinking about where he was going and why. Thinking about why he was heading toward Paige instead of waiting for her to return to the beach would lead to overthinking, and he'd chicken out and go back. Better to let the water and rhythm of swimming lull his mind into autopilot.

The edge of the coral reef under him revealed colorful schools of fish and other sea life. The reef tapered off to a white sandy seabed, littered with the occasional rock and dead coral formation. A large cove appeared around the point, and Ash spotted the two women.

One of them dove down and disappeared while the other continued to float on the surface of the water, belly down. Putting his face back in the water, he recognized Paige kneeling on the seabed, holding something in her hands.

She'd divided her dark hair into two braids that floated around her shoulders. She set down whatever she held and kicked off the floor, undulating her body upward in a way that made him think she spent a lot of time in the water.

"Hey!" Paige waved when she surfaced and Denise turned.

He didn't know if Paige had spotted him from under the water or after she'd surfaced, but he switched to a freestyle stroke to reach them faster.

"Hey." He pushed his goggles up to his forehead.

Paige did the same and wiped her eyes and nose. "This is a surprise. Are you stalking us?"

"Yes," he said. "Yes, I am. I sat outside your hotel room all morning, waiting for you to leave, and then followed you."

"If I'd known that, I would have just offered you a ride."

Ash grinned. It usually didn't go well when he tried to be funny. It felt good that Paige played along with the joke. "We were supposed to go on a boat tour this morning but everyone is too hungover. Natalie has already thrown up at least once—I wasn't about to put her on a boat."

Paige chuckled. "Angie keeps complaining the *sound* of the ocean is making her seasick."

"How did you know we were out here?" Denise still looked at him suspiciously.

"I ran into Bree on the beach when we arrived."

"Ah. Okay." She looked at Paige. "You good?"

"Yeah, go ahead."

"Remember to weigh down the body if you have to." Denise set her goggles over her eyes and turned in the direction of the beach, kicking at a steady pace.

"Weigh down what body?" he asked.

Paige grinned. "Yours, if you try anything."

She was smiling, and not a fake smile, so he assumed she was kidding. He'd never been good at picking up social cues. One of the reasons he did better one-on-one or with people he knew.

The banter between Paige and Denise reminded him of how he and Natalie talked to each other sometimes.

He grinned back. "So you're saying I should keep my hands to myself."

She shrugged. "I'm not saying that, but you should definitely not put them anywhere I tell you not to."

"Got it. Only put my hands where you tell me." Unfortunately, he didn't think that was an invitation to put his hands anywhere at the moment. "What were you looking at down there?"

"Sand dollars. This cove has a huge colony of them."

"Really?"

"Yeah, I discovered it the last time I was here."

He glanced around at the cove. Other than a small patch of sand surrounded by trees, it was enclosed on three sides with no apparent way in or out other than the way they'd come.

"How did you find it? Don't most people stick to the reef trail?"

She tilted her head. "I followed a sea turtle."

He grinned. "You followed a turtle and found a sand dollar colony?"

"Yeah."

He didn't know if the pink on her cheeks was from the sun or a blush. With her hair in two braids and no makeup, she looked completely different from the sultry woman he'd made out with the night before. He liked it. She'd been drop-dead gorgeous last night, but today she was heart-stoppingly beautiful.

"Can I see it?" he asked.

"Follow me." She lowered her goggles and executed a perfect duck dive, swimming straight down to the seabed and kneeling in the same way she had when he'd first spotted her. Bubbles floated up and she used her arms to keep herself down.

He settled next to her and looked down when she scooped up a purple, slightly rounded disk. She turned it over in her palm and grabbed his hand, holding his finger and brushing it over the underside.

It was…furry. He knew the white sand dollars that washed up on beaches were the skeletons, but he'd never seen a live one before.

It hit him—he was on the ocean floor in the middle of the Caribbean with a beautiful woman, petting a sand dollar, and he was completely in the moment. It was really fucking hard to smile around a snorkel mouthpiece, and holy hell, his lungs were on fire.

He pointed up and Paige nodded, returning the sand dollar where she found it. Before he even reached the surface, he took the mouthpiece out so he could suck in a lungful of air as soon as he breached. Damn, holding his breath for that long was completely different than breathing during laps.

Paige surfaced in front of him and took a deep breath.

"That was really cool," he said.

"I know. Do you mind taking a break for a few minutes?" She pointed at the small beach.

"Not at all." They slowly swam to the beach, letting the small waves push them up.

She pulled off her fins, waded through the surf, and sat down with her butt and legs mostly in the water. Removing her mask, she stacked it on top of her fins farther up the sand. He joined her and rested his elbows on his knees, staring out at the ocean. He could see people bobbing on the surface of the water around the coral reef, following the underwater ecological trail —the reason they'd picked this beach as an alternative to the boat trip.

"How many times have you been here?" he asked.

"This is the third time I've been to St. John."

"Do you scuba dive?"

"I can, but I prefer to snorkel and free dive. Why? Do you scuba?"

"No, just swim and occasionally snorkel. I can tell you're comfortable in the water."

She lay back and put one forearm over her eyes, resting her other hand over her stomach. "I love the ocean. I take every chance I can to be near it. In it. It's…calming. Some people do yoga. I float in the ocean. I can be surrounded by water and shut my brain off and let everything go."

Rolling on his side, he stretched out next to her, resting his head on his hand. "That's how I feel about swimming. I'm able to block out all the noise and shut off my mind."

The logo on her rash guard caught his attention. Without thinking, he took the hem of her shirt between his fingers and rubbed his thumb over the raised image. Moving the shirt exposed a small sliver of skin, and he remembered her warning. A small smile played on her lips, so he guessed he was safe from having his body weighed down and left for fish food.

"I admit I'm a little bit of a snob when it comes to the ocean though," she said.

Ash grinned. "How can you be a snob toward the ocean?"

"I don't like the east coast of the US. The sand is too hard and too brown. You can't see anything in the water. It's gross."

He chuckled. "Okay. Favorite beach?"

"Playa Conchal in Costa Rica."

"Why there?"

"The water's really clear, and it's a great snorkeling spot. Plus, I own a property within walking distance, so it's easy to get to."

"You own a property in Costa Rica?" he asked.

"Yeah. I use it as a vacation spot, but it's where I plan to retire." She turned her head and squinted up at him. "What about you? Why swimming?"

"I was a very active kid. My mom swears I as soon as I learned to walk, I ran or skipped everywhere. She put me in swimming as a way to get rid of some of my excess energy, and I took to it like—"

"A fish?" She grinned.

"Exactly. I practically lived at the pool during the summer. Lifeguarded in high school. Swam competitively in college and still swim every morning at the local YMCA."

"I'm not a lap swimmer," she said. "I'm very much a floater."

"And free diver. I thought I had good breath control, but I felt like my lungs were going to burst."

"I practice in the bathtub."

Now he had an image of her naked in the bath. At that moment, he realized he'd stopped rubbing the logo and was brushing his fingers back and forth on the soft skin of her belly.

"Paige?"

"Yeah?" Her voice sounded soft and a little sleepy.

A nervous flutter rolled through him. "Are you going to take a nap?"

She smiled. "Maybe."

Play it cool. Act like you know what you're doing. "Hmm. That's too bad."

"Why?"

"I'd really like to kiss you."

CHAPTER 6

The soft brush of his fingers, combined with the soothing sound of the waves and warm sand beneath her, had lulled Paige into an almost dreamlike state, but that woke her up. She lifted her arm slightly. She hadn't been able to tell what color his eyes were in the club last night, but now his light brown eyes, flecked with green, seemed to glow with the intensity of his stare.

Had they really only met yesterday? It felt...longer. She knew almost nothing about him, other than he was a programmer, had a sister, and liked the water. Not how old he was. Not where he was from or where he lived. A part of her wanted to know everything—to share everything.

Her cautious side warned her this was nothing more than a vacation fling and there was no use knowing more or getting attached. Any call or pull she felt was merely a projection of what she and Denise had talked about last night.

"Can I?" Ash asked.

"Yes."

Just because she didn't want to get attached didn't mean she couldn't appreciate everything else that came with a vacation fling. She grasped the back of his head as he leaned down.

He tasted like the sea. Like...home. She shoved that thought away quickly.

Taking his time, the same way he had the night before, he stroked his tongue along hers as if memorizing every inch of it. She wanted more. More than just physical. And it scared the ever-loving hell out of her. Instead, she asked for what she was familiar with.

She sucked on his tongue and pushed against him, rolling him onto his back, then threw a leg over his hips to straddle him.

He groaned and grabbed her thighs, dug his fingers into the soft flesh and nestled her into his erection. Thrusting up, he ground her against him, and it was her turn to groan as his thick shaft rubbed against her core.

There was nothing soft about his kiss now as he licked and sucked. His hands were everywhere at once, skimming and cupping her breasts, tweaking her nipples through the thin layers of fabric. His touch was soft and almost frantic, like he couldn't decide where he wanted his hands.

She couldn't decide where she wanted him to concentrate, either.

He finally settled on her ass and slid his hands under her bikini bottoms, gripping her cheeks, then sliding even farther, brushing against her cleft.

Paige gasped and arched her back, giving him more access.

Ash nipped at her jaw. "Can I put my hands here?" He circled her opening, featherlight and scorching hot.

Tendrils of desire shot through her from that small, simple touch and she shuddered. "Yes."

He dipped a finger into her. "What about here? Can I put my fingers here?"

"God, yes." She rocked back against his hand as he slowly slid two fingers in.

"You're so slick." He rolled her over on her back and slid a hand into the front of her bikini bottoms. "Lift your shirt?"

The intonation of his voice, asking for permission before touching her, was different. Empowering in a way she didn't expect. Lifting the hem, she contorted her upper body until she could pull it over her head. Her bikini top got caught in it, riding up over her breasts, but she didn't care.

"And here? Can I kiss here?" He licked between her breasts.

She grabbed handfuls of hair and held his head in place. "Yes." She felt his grin right before he latched onto one nipple. The electric bolts of desire shot through her from his mouth directly to her clit and she groaned.

He grunted and sucked hard. "So responsive," he murmured. Sliding his fingers deep inside, he twisted them and rubbed her clit with his thumb.

The orgasm came out of nowhere, hitting her hard. All she could do was dig her fingers into his hair and gasp as it rolled through her, tremors racking her body.

Ash lifted his head from her chest. "Beautiful," he whispered. He continued to rub and thrust, softer than before but with as much devastating force.

As the tension left her body, he withdrew his fingers and nudged her to her side, pulling her flush to him, her head tucked under his chin.

"That was some kiss," he said. "Very *From Here to Eternity*."

Their feet and lower legs were still in the water. Paige smiled against his throat. "I know the scene you're talking about, but I've never seen the movie."

"Really? We'll have to watch it sometime."

Her smile faded. There wouldn't be a sometime. There was this weekend and that was it. Possibly this moment was all they would get. She and her friends were going to dinner to celebrate her birthday that night, and tomorrow he'd be busy with the wedding. Sunday she went back to Charleston. That was it.

"I don't think this should count as the rain check," Ash said.

She mentally shook her head. Of course there wouldn't be more. There never was. That was the whole point of these vacation hookups.

"I agree. Especially since I haven't returned the favor yet." She trailed her fingers down the center of his abs, but he stopped her before she reached the waistband of his trunks.

She glanced up at him. "No?"

He cleared his throat and shook his head, keeping his eyes averted. "No."

Weird, but… "Okay." She flattened her palm on his stomach and rested her head back on his shoulder.

His finger tapped on the back of her hand. She wasn't sure what had him agitated, but there seemed to be a pattern to the tapping. She wished she knew Morse code.

He stopped abruptly. "You're not going to ask why?"

Was that why he was tapping? She lifted up on an elbow and gave him an amused look. "You said no. No means no."

"It's not that I don't want you to."

"Ash, you don't have to explain anything."

His brows pinched together. "You're not curious?"

"Well, yeah, but it's your decision."

"If you wrap your hands or lips around my dick, I'm going to want to fuck you, and we don't have any condoms."

She pulled her lips between her teeth and blinked at the way he blurted out his reasoning so forcefully. "Okay." She struggled not to laugh as she said it.

"I don't want you to think it has anything to do with you or that I don't like it. I do. A lot. But I'm a whole box of cookies kind of guy."

She couldn't stop her laughter at that. "A what?"

"You know how there are people who can buy a box of cookies and eat one at a time, and the box lasts for days?"

"Yeah…"

"That's not me. I eat the entire box of cookies in one sitting. I never buy cookies because I'll eat them all."

"So in your explanation, head is one cookie, and sex is the whole box?"

"Yes."

"But…what if head is one box of cookies, and sex is a separate box of cookies?"

His mouth opened and closed. "I have no response to that."

She fell back laughing, and he rolled over with her, tucking his head into her neck.

"I'm glad you find this amusing."

Something in his voice made her realize he thought she was laughing at him instead of the conversation. "I'm sorry. This is the strangest discussion I've ever had about sex—and I've had some strange ones. All I can picture is dick- and sperm-shaped cookies."

He rubbed his lips on her neck. "There's probably a market for them somewhere."

The lightness was back in his voice, which helped the tension release from her shoulders. "If I had any baking skills, I'd look into it."

"You can't cook?" He lifted his head but stayed leaning over her.

"I can cook. I can't bake."

A whistle pierced the air, and they both looked out into the cove.

"Denise." She pulled her bikini top down to cover her breasts.

"I guess we have to rejoin the real world," he said.

"Yeah." Paige pushed against his chest, and they sat up. Glancing around, she found her rash guard top and shook the sand out of it, then pulled it back on.

"You decent?" Denise called out.

"We're dressed." Paige smiled at her automatic response. It was something they'd always said when they were bunkmates in Iraq.

Denise got close enough to stand with the water at her waist and lifted her goggles. "People are grumbling for food, and we weren't sure how much longer you guys were going to be out here."

"What time is it?" Paige asked.

Ash looked at his watch. "About a quarter after one."

"Sorry." Paige stood and grabbed her fins and mask. "I didn't realize it was that late."

Denise shrugged. "No biggie. We're on island time."

Still. She'd gotten distracted from her friends. This wasn't one of her usual jaunts where she only had herself to worry about and could do whatever she wanted. They were there to celebrate her birthday, for fuck's sake.

Ash stopped her from walking into the water. "Are you okay?" he asked in a low voice.

Even though he was on the lower slope of the sand, she still had to look up to him. "I feel bad about ditching my friends. Coming to the reef was my idea."

"I'm sorry," he said.

She shook her head. "It's not your fault."

"If I hadn't followed you, you wouldn't have spent so much time out here."

"The only person responsible for my decisions is me."

He nodded, even though he didn't look satisfied with her explanation.

"I don't like being a shitty friend."

"Oh, for fuck's sake," Denise said. "You're not a shitty friend. Angie just woke up, Bree took a nap, and I've been reading. No one missed you."

Paige shot her a baleful look.

Denise lifted her hands up. "What?"

All right. She probably had a point. "We're coming."

"Well, hurry it up. We're hungry." She sank into the water, lowered her goggles, and swam back toward the resort.

"Is she always like that?" Ash asked.

"For as long as I've known her. Denise doesn't pull her punches. You ready?"

He hesitated for a moment, then said, "Yeah. Let's go back."

~

Back on the beach, their two groups had combined, and it was hard to miss the dirty looks the maid of honor sent her way as soon as Paige walked up. Not long after, Conor and his best man, Joe, arrived with bags of food.

"How much do I owe?" Paige accepted a plate of jerk chicken, some kind of fish, and rice and beans from Natalie.

"I raided your wallet for the pot," Angie said.

"Thanks," she said around a piece of fish. "This is so good. Where did you get it?"

"A stand about a mile up the road," Joe said.

"Mama T's?" she asked.

"Sounds right," Joe said. "All I know is I smelled it when we passed it on the way here, and it made my mouth water."

"This is roadside stand food?" Suzie asked.

"Yeah." Conor tore at a drumstick.

Suzie put her plate down on the blanket. "I can't eat this. Do you know what kind of gastrointestinal illnesses you can get from shady food places?"

"The kind that taste delicious," April said.

Paige smirked and looked down at her plate.

"Natalie, are you really going to risk getting the Hershey squirts the night before your wedding?"

Bree coughed, sending pieces of rice flying out of her mouth. Denise pounded on her back a few times.

"Sorry." Bree picked up her water bottle and unscrewed the top. "Wrong pipe."

Natalie looked at Suzie, then at her plate, and shrugged. "The wedding isn't until two. If I get the shits, it'll clean out my system, and I'll be super skinny for the wedding."

"I like her," Denise said.

Paige grinned. So did she.

"Hey, do you guys want to come to the rehearsal dinner tonight?" Natalie asked.

Bree and Denise looked at Paige since they had dinner plans to celebrate her birthday.

"We can't," Angie said before Paige could respond. "We're celebrating Paige's birthday tonight."

"It's your birthday?" Ash asked.

"Last week," she said.

"Happy birthday."

"Thanks."

"It must be a huge milestone if you're celebrating with a weekend in the Virgin Islands." Suzie's snark was so thick that Paige could have rolled it up and smoked it.

"It's a birthday, Suzie," April said. "Every year is a milestone."

"I travel every year for my birthday," Paige said.

"That's awesome," April said. "Where have you been?"

"Last year I went to Morocco. The year before was Japan. I try to do something different each year."

"Who do you go with?" Natalie asked.

"I usually go by myself. This is the first time in five or six years that I've traveled with friends."

Natalie smacked Conor on the leg. "We need to travel every year for our anniversary."

"Sure. As soon as we've paid off the wedding and our honeymoon."

"Promise?" she asked.

He kissed her sweetly. "Promise."

Fuck. There was that twinge again. And the weight of Ash's gaze on her made it twist even tighter.

CHAPTER 7

*A*sh tugged on the end of the tie and tightened the knot around his neck. Damn, he hated these nooses. He unbuttoned the top of his shirt and settled the tie over it so he didn't feel like he was going to choke at any minute.

Paige's gasp echoed in his mind. He couldn't stop thinking about her or their time on the beach. He usually wasn't one to initiate intimacy so soon in a relationship. Not that they were in a relationship. He didn't know what to call it, but it wasn't a relationship. Hell, he didn't even know her last name.

But there was something about her that stood out from every other woman he'd ever known. An air of mystery...of confidence and independence. Even he, who liked to spend more time alone than with other people, was impressed by the fact that she traveled around the world by herself because it wasn't something he would have ever had the guts to do. He found it intriguing, more than a little arousing, and he wanted to spend more time exploring it. Simultaneously he wondered what a guy like him could offer a woman like her.

From the corner of his eye, he caught Conor on his return pace. He reached the far side of the room, spun on his heel, gestured and muttered to himself, then walked back to the other end of the room.

Ash went to the side table and poured a shot from the bottle of whiskey Joe had brought with him. He held it out to Conor.

"Here, drink this. It'll calm you down."

Conor reached for the glass, then shook his head and shoved his hands in his pockets. "No, I want to be clearheaded during the ceremony."

Ash shrugged and downed the whiskey, savoring the warm burn. Not bad. He returned the glass to the table. "Are you worried you're going to screw up your vows?"

"That and something will go wrong. Natalie could change her mind at the last minute."

"Natalie isn't going to change her mind. She's stupid for you," Ash said.

"Things happen. You see it all the time on social media. A tornado rips through the area, or a flock of birds roosts in the eaves of the church and shits all over the wedding party, or the bride or groom finds out something really bad last-minute and calls it all off."

Ash froze. "Is there something you're worried about Natalie finding out?"

"No." He said it absently, then shook his head and looked at Ash. "No! Never. I love her, but she picked me. Me. Out of everyone she could have picked, she picked me. And Suzie never liked me. Ever. And she's been in a shit mood all weekend, so there's no telling what she's saying to Natalie right now. Probably trying to convince her to hijack a boat and make a run for it."

"Suzie doesn't like you because she had a thing for you and you asked Natalie out."

"Really? I didn't even meet her until after I'd started dating Natalie."

"Apparently, she had her eye on you before you asked Natalie out," Ash said.

"Huh. I had no idea."

"She's in a pissy mood because Ash is hooking up with Scuba Barbie," Joe said from his sprawled position on the loveseat.

"I thought you were passed out." Ash didn't try to argue Joe's point since he was probably right.

Joe sat up, digging his fingers into his eye sockets. "Just resting my eyes. What's up with that whole situation anyway? You guys bang yet?"

"What? That's not..." He wasn't sure how he wanted to finish that sentence.

"Not what it is?" Joe asked. "Of course it is. Dude, you're on a tropical island for a wedding. If I had a woman like that willing to let me get naked with her, I sure as hell wouldn't have been here three hours before the wedding to get ready. Pretty sure it's in the groomsman handbook."

Conor cocked his head. "You got here half an hour ago."

Joe stretched his arms over the back of the couch, his grin wolfish.

Ash studied him. Who was he having sex with? One of Paige's friends? Two of them were married, so maybe the younger one. He blinked and shook his head. What had they been talking about? He rewound the conversation in his head, stopping on the point he'd been about to make.

"Anyway," he said to Conor. "Natalie might be stupid for you, but she's not stupid. She fell in love with the perfect guy for her. I don't want to get all sentimental, but I'm glad I get to have you for my brother-in-law."

"That's...thanks, man. That means a lot."

Ash grinned. "You're welcome. Let's never talk about this again."

Conor smiled. "Deal."

The door to the room opened, and Conor's dad entered. "You boys ready?"

"You have the rings, right?" Conor asked Joe.

He patted the front pocket of his coat. "Right here."

"Okay. Yeah. I'm ready. Let's do this."

They left their room in the small building on the outskirts of the hotel property where the wedding was taking place, the blue Caribbean water serving as the backdrop.

Ash stopped in the hallway and clapped Conor on the shoulder. "I'll be right there. I'm going to wish Natalie good luck."

Conor's eyes widened.

Ash laughed. "It's all good."

Conor nodded and pushed through the doors that would take him to the gazebo.

Down the short hall, Ash knocked on the door to the bride's room.

April cracked the door and peered out, then swung it wide. "Oh, thank god ," she whispered. "Suzie is being unbearable and has Natalie freaking out."

"Of course she is. Where are our moms?"

"Halfway through a bottle of champagne, cackling to themselves about how many grandkids they're going to have and how they're going to split up the holidays. They've got it planned out through middle school. The only reason they stopped there is because they started talking about what sports the kids are going to do. *None* of which is helping Natalie calm down."

Ash grinned and shook his head. His mom's biggest disappointment in life was that he hadn't given her a bunch of grandkids yet. "Let me talk to Nat."

April stepped aside and gestured for him to enter. Natalie paced back and forth in much the same way Conor had, except she had to kick the back of her dress out of the way every time she turned.

She turned when the door clicked closed. "Oh my god . You're here to tell me he changed his mind. Shit." She put her hands on her forehead. "Shit. Shit. Shit."

"Natalie, he hasn't changed his mind. He's at the gazebo waiting for you."

She lowered her hands. "You promise?"

"I promise. I wanted to give you something before the ceremony." He pulled her to the far corner of the room and angled his back so no one could see them without standing over his shoulder.

"Remember when you were around fifteen and really into crystals?" he asked in a low voice.

She frowned and shook her head. "Yeah?"

Ash cleared his throat. "Well, I couldn't think of anything to get you for a wedding gift, but then I saw a link for gems and their meanings and I found this." It was an oversimplification—he'd spent days searching for the perfect stone with the perfect meaning.

He opened the small, black box to reveal a teardrop-shaped pendant on a thin gold chain. "I know it's too simple to wear today, but I thought you might want to carry it with you."

Natalie gasped. "Bash…it's beautiful. It looks like the ocean is trapped in it. What kind of stone is it?"

"It's Larimar. It's only found in the Caribbean and is supposed to help you speak from the heart. I was going to give it to you later, but I thought if you're as nervous as Conor, you might need it now."

She looked up. "He's nervous?"

Ash grinned. "He's afraid you're going to realize you can do better and change your mind."

"I could never do better."

"Let's not go that far."

She braced her hands on her hips. "Sebastian Mateo Moreno, you take that back!"

"I'm kidding. He worships you, and that's all I care about."

"I love him too."

"Good. Then can we get this done so we can go to the open bar? I'm already dreading all the socializing I have to do."

"Yes. Can you help me put this on?" She pulled the chain from the box.

He blinked. "You're going to wear it?"

"Of course." She turned her back to him and held the ends of the necklace on either side of her neck. "It's my something blue."

Finding it hard to swallow all of a sudden, he cleared his throat and tossed the empty box on the table next to them. He took the ends from her, clipping them together.

"I didn't think you were doing all that superstitious stuff."

"I'm not, but I can do something blue, and this necklace is perfect." She turned around. "Thanks for being a great big brother."

She threw her arms around his neck, and he hugged her tight. "Love you, Nat-Nat."

A throat cleared behind them. They released their hug and turned, finding the resort wedding coordinator behind them. "Everyone is waiting."

"Right." Ash kissed Nat on the cheek. "See you out there."

CHAPTER 8

The ceremony went off without a hitch, even with Suzie pouting on the other side of Natalie. Conor forgot his vows, said fuck it, literally, and spoke from the heart, which Ash thought sounded better than what he'd practiced anyway. Natalie bounced up and down when she said yes, eliciting chuckles from most of the guests. Then his little sister was married.

After taking five hundred and twenty-six photos, based on the number of shutter clicks he heard, Natalie and Conor went off with the coordinator to sign the official forms and have a quiet moment alone.

Ash leaned against the bar and checked his watch. They still had almost thirty minutes before the official start of the reception, which was going to last hours. Did that give him enough time to duck out and try to find Paige? They hadn't talked since they'd left the beach yesterday. He was scheduled to leave tomorrow afternoon, and he didn't want to depart without seeing her again. Maybe they could exchange numbers, figure out a way to see each other after this weekend? Really, he just wanted to see her again before he left. Things felt…unfinished.

"How was the ceremony?" a voice asked.

He spun to find Paige behind him, wearing a loose, floor-length dress that still managed to hug her curves in all the right places. It was strapless except for a necklace-looking thingy attached to the center of her cleavage that did all sorts of things for him.

He smiled slowly. "It was short."

"Those are the best."

"Are you crashing my sister's reception?"

"It's possible. Angie said your sister invited us when we were packing up to leave the beach yesterday, but who knows. We could just be here for the free bar."

"I was going to look for you later to see if there was a time for me to claim that rain check."

Paige got a teasing gleam in her eyes. "Are you busy right now?"

He glanced around, then at his watch. Was twenty minutes enough? Usually, the answer would be no. He got too wrapped up in his own mind too often. Overanalyzed what he was doing and how his partner responded, but he hadn't had that issue with Paige yesterday, so it stood to reason he wouldn't have that problem now. Right?

She placed a hand on his forearm. "It's okay. I was kidding about right now."

Grabbing her hand, he said, "Follow me."

He led her out of the tent, across the grass to the building they'd used to get ready for the wedding, praying it would be deserted. Turning the handle, he cracked the door and peered around the room before quickly pulling her in, then closed and locked the door behind them.

Framing her face with his hands, he kissed her gently, groaning and deepening the kiss when she wrapped her arms around his waist under his jacket, pressing herself against him.

Fuck, she undid him. His mind blanked but in a good way. The same way it did when he swam—all his focus was on Paige. On the tips of her fingers running down his back. On the weight of her breasts pushed against his chest. On the cool, minty taste of her tongue as it rubbed against his.

She pulled his shirt from his pants, and he sucked in his stomach when her fingers skimmed the skin above his waistband, sending goosebumps coursing over his skin. Her splayed hands ran up his stomach and chest. She pinched his nipples and nipped his bottom lip at the same time.

All the blood left his head in a rush and surged into his erection. His cock pressed painfully against the front of his pants. Shrugging out of his jacket, he yanked at the tie, thankful Natalie hadn't gone for full groomsman regalia because a vest would just be one more layer of clothing he had to get rid of.

Paige worked at the buttons of his shirt from the bottom while he started from the top. He groaned when her thumbs brushed his nipples again and pulled off the shirt, popping the buttons at the cuffs in his haste to remove it.

Her mouth replaced her hands, her breath hot against his skin.

"Oh...shit." He cradled the back of her head and nipped the tip of her ear. The vibrations from her moan spread over his skin, leaving the tiny hairs raised in its wake.

Fumbling with his belt, he finally wrenched it free and ripped the zipper down. Paige shoved his pants and boxers down to his thighs and took a moment to gaze at his erection when it sprang free.

Holy...he'd never worried so much about impressing a woman with his cock. Did she like it? Was it big enough? Wide enough? He'd never had any complaints, but he didn't think a woman would outright tell a guy his dick was wrong.

Her first and second fingers lightly traced the prominent vein down the center. When she reached the base, she wrapped her hand around and stroked up, then rubbed the drop of precum around the bulbous head.

His whole body shuddered at her slow, velvety touch,

completely at odds with the rushed and frantic feeling driving him. He grabbed fistfuls of her skirt and gathered it in his hands, tossing the hem up when he reached skin.

All skin.

She wasn't wearing underwear.

"Holy shit," he whispered.

Paige shifted and spread her legs. "You have my permission to touch me however you want."

He slammed his mouth on hers, driving his tongue into her mouth the way he wanted to drive his cock into her. Her folds were hot and slick as he slid a finger between them.

She moaned and stroked his cock faster.

He explored her pussy, spreading her arousal around and skimming her opening. god , she was going to feel so good when he sank into her. Or when she sank down on him.

Fuck, he just wanted to be inside her.

He shoved his other hand in his back pocket for his wallet...to find only his room key. Double fuck. Withdrawing his hands, he grasped her hips and pulled away from her grasp, resting his forehead against hers.

"We have to stop."

"What? Why?"

He swallowed hard. "I don't have a condom. Again. I left my wallet in the room safe since I wasn't going to need it."

"Oh. Is that all?" She cleared her throat and tilted his chin up.

He lifted his head and opened his eyes.

Paige reached into her cleavage and pulled out a thin foil packet.

He grinned. "What else do you have in there?"

"Why don't you find out?"

Sliding one hand back up her thigh, he pulled down one side of the top of her dress with the other. "Don't mind if I do."

He sucked her dusky rose nipple into his mouth and rubbed the top of her clit at the same time.

She moaned and pressed against his hand. "Finger fuck me."

He groaned and followed her command, sliding two fingers into her. She gasped and stroked his cock in time to the pace he set. His orgasm was coming fast, the tingle behind his balls almost incessant.

Withdrawing his fingers, he grabbed her hand and led her to the loveseat, pushing her to sit. Kneeling between her spread thighs, he flipped up her dress and pulled her closer to the edge of the cushion. Easing her legs over his shoulder, he licked up her slit, barely flicking the tip of her clit. He could lose himself in her musky scent.

Paige grabbed handfuls of his hair and held his head close, rolling her hips in silent demand.

He pressed the flat of his tongue against her clit and drew a circle.

"Fuck. Yes. More. Rub my clit faster. Right there."

She told him exactly what she wanted, and it turned him the fuck on. His balls grew heavy and achy. He wanted to make her come with his mouth. As with anything, once he found a pattern, he could perfect it.

"Oh! god ! Right there! Don't. Fucking. Stop." Her hips jerked so hard it almost forced his head away until he found the rhythm she set.

Her thighs clenched around his head, and she froze, digging her heels into his back as she came with a shout, shoving her pussy against his face. When she finally relaxed, he pulled away and wiped his mouth, looking at her.

She held the condom up for him, a challenge in her eyes. Instead of satiating her, the way it had yesterday, this orgasm had only fired her up.

He took the condom and tore off the end. He loved a challenge. Loved figuring out how things worked. Why should a woman's orgasm be any different? A unique piece of code waiting to be unlocked. He rolled the condom on and rubbed his shaft through her slick folds before lining up with her entrance.

Pausing, he looked at her, waiting for permission.

"Hard. Fast." Her words sent a shudder coursing through his body.

"Your wish, my command." He slid into her in one smooth stroke. Holding still, buried deep, he shuddered as her smooth inner muscles gripped him and held him in her thrall.

Paige arched her back and squeezed around him.

"Fuck." His voice was harsh and guttural. He slid out and back in. Not hard, but forcefully.

"More," she said.

He grabbed her hips and withdrew, pulling her on him as he thrust forward again.

"Ah! Yes!" She squeezed her breast.

He pulled down the other side of her dress, sucking her nipple into his mouth, scraping his teeth against the sensitive flesh.

She shifted under him, and he felt her bracketing his cock with her fingers as he drove in and out. Leaning back, he watched as she alternated between rubbing her clit and sliding her fingers on either side of his dick.

It was the most erotic thing he'd ever seen.

"So fucking hot." His balls tightened, and he knew he only had seconds. Pulling Paige farther off the edge of the cushion, he shortened his strokes.

Her fingers rubbed furiously, and her legs tightened around his waist, limiting his range of motion.

It didn't matter—he was at the point where he needed to bury himself deep and explode. He gritted his teeth and grunted, picking up speed. He wanted to get her there first. Leaning forward, he licked her nipple, then sucked it hard.

Paige curled under him and pressed her mouth against his neck, screaming into his skin as she came. She clenched around him like a vise, and that was it.

His balls drew up, and he exploded, thrusting his hips without any finesse or rhythm, just trying to draw out the glorious feeling of relief and endorphins rushing through his blood.

All too soon, he was drained. Dropping his head between her breasts, he wrapped his arms around her waist and tried to catch his breath.

Her hands rubbed up and down his back. "You give really good nightcap."

His shoulders shook as he laughed. "Your rain check was phenomenal." He lifted his head and moved a strand of hair away from the side of her face. "Do you have plans for tonight? I'd like to schedule another one."

"I think I can squeeze you in somewhere."

Ash groaned when she flexed around his softening dick because it was no longer softening.

"I don't suppose you have another condom in that magical cleavage of yours?"

"No, I only brought the one."

He slid out and pulled the condom off. "Then we need to table this discussion for later."

Paige glanced down at his growing erection and grinned. "Happy to."

CHAPTER 9

Paige slid into the cloth-covered chair at a table toward the back of the room.

"Hey," Bree said. "Where have you been?"

"Exploring."

Angie leaned away from Paige and studied her with narrowed eyes. "Exploring what, exactly?"

She lifted a shoulder. "This and that."

"Oh my god! You got laid!"

Bree laughed and Denise grinned.

"Could you shout that a little louder?" Paige asked. "I don't think the bride's grandmother heard you."

Angie folded her arms on the table and leaned forward. "I can't believe you got laid during the reception."

"Coat closet?" Denise asked.

"Room where the groom was getting ready."

"Nice."

"Pool-Boy?" Bree asked.

Paige grinned. "He has a name, you know."

Bree smirked. "I know, but it's more fun to call him Pool-Boy. Goes along with the whole cougar vibe."

"Well, you're grinning like the cat that ate the canary, so I'm guessing it was good," Angie said.

Paige grinned wider and popped a mini quiche in her mouth. How could they still have standard US wedding reception food at a Caribbean resort?

Angie rested her chin on a fist and frowned. "Lucky."

"It's a wedding, Ange. Every unattached guy here is expecting to take advantage of a woman they think is sad and lonely because they haven't found the man of their dreams," Paige said.

Angie lifted her head and stared at her. "Wow, that's cynical."

Paige pointed a quiche at her. "But is it wrong?"

"No," Denise said at the same time Bree said, "Yes."

Denise looked at Bree. "You still quote Disney movies."

"Damn right I do."

"I hope you're having a boy, and he's the most rough-and-tumble boy in the history of boys," Denise said.

"Doesn't matter," Bree said. "I'll dress him up in Disney prince costumes until he's ripping them off his body and running scared."

"What if he decides he likes princesses instead?" Angie asked.

"Then I'll get him all the princess dresses he wants. No rule that says he can't have both."

There was that fucking twinge again. That was what she'd expected her life to be, once upon a time. Oh well, there was no going back and rewriting the past. She was who she was and she would never apologize for it or regret the choices she'd made.

"Angie, there's a guy at the bar staring over here." Bree tilted her head a little in the direction of the bar. "He's good-looking. You should go get a drink."

Angie and Paige turn around to see the guy leaning against the bar, looking their way. He raised his glass toward them. Paige waved.

"I am feeling a little thirsty." Angie stood and walked away. The guy straightened and smiled when she approached.

Paige turned back around. "Poor guy."

"Why?" Denise asked.

"Angie has a thing for our armorer."

Denise blinked twice. "You have an armorer? As in, a person to manage an armory?"

"Is it unrequited?" Bree asked.

Paige grinned at the disparate questions. "It's not, but they're dancing around each other. Our pilot keeps sleeping with the receptionists, and they keep quitting. Graham is to the point where he's ready to fire him, so I think Angie and Jeremy are avoiding admitting they're into each other. Yes, we have an armorer and an armory. You should come visit sometime."

"An armorer and a pilot," Denise said. "I guess things are going well for TLC."

"They are. I want a dedicated female team, so I'm working on hiring more women. I also need to sit down with Graham next week to discuss hiring more staff. I'm at the point where I'm task-saturated, and it's starting to interfere with my social life."

Denise threw her head back and laughed. "If you had told me the first time we met that you'd be talking about having an armory and a pilot and forming a female tactics team, I would have laughed."

"You are laughing."

"Good point."

"But I would have laughed too," Paige said. "This was the last thing I ever expected to be doing."

"I think it's great," Bree said. "You're obviously good at your job. I heard about the contract in Guatemala. That was fantastic!"

"That was more luck than anything. One of our guys happened to be in the right place at the right time, and it worked out to TLC's benefit."

"It still cracks me up your company is called TLC," Denise said.

Paige grinned. "Me too. It took Graham a while to figure out why I laughed every time he said it. I keep trying to come up with innuendo tag lines like, *when things get hard, you need TLC.*"

Denise and Bree laughed.

Angie returned to the table, draining the drink in her hand before setting it down hard. "That was a bust."

"What happened?" Paige asked.

"Asshole's here with his girlfriend. And of course, now I look like a bitch because I was talking to him. Like I knew."

They all looked at the couple arguing by the bar. The woman slapped the man and stormed away, the guy following.

"Should we worry about that?" Bree asked.

"If he puts his hands on her, then yes," Denise said.

The guy pulled on the woman's elbow, stopping her and cajoling until she let him kiss her.

Paige's mouth twisted, and she turned back around. "Looks like that's a thing with them."

"I've never understood why people need that kind of drama in their lives to make things interesting," Denise said.

"It's hard to tell who's manipulating who in that scenario," Bree added.

Tapping on a microphone drew everyone's attention, and a hush fell over the reception.

Ash stood in front of the wedding party, looking like he'd rather face a pack of ravenous hyenas than be in the middle of the dance floor with all eyes on him. He hadn't put his tie back on when they'd gotten dressed, and the sight of his open collar made Paige smile.

"Hi." Shrill feedback from the microphone made everyone wince. He pulled it away from his mouth. "Sorry...sorry. Test. Okay. Right. Story time. Thirty-two years ago, my parents brought Natalie home from the hospital. Even though I was only three, I vividly remember seeing that little pink hat on her head and telling them to take her back and get a boy."

The guests laughed, and Natalie stuck her tongue out at Ash.

Angie nudged Paige and whispered, "He's thirty-five. Not nearly as young as we thought."

She was as surprised as her friends since she and Ash hadn't gotten around to talking about their ages…or anything else of a personal nature.

"At least now I only feel like I'm raiding the pre-K room and not the cradle."

"Please," Denise said. "That doesn't even qualify you for cougar status."

"Shh," Paige said.

"I knew things were getting serious for Natalie and Conor when she brought him home for Thanksgiving," Ash said. "They came in the door, and I remember thinking he looked a little green around the edges."

Conor dropped his head in his hands while Natalie laughed and rubbed his back.

"I was right because as soon as he shook my dad's hand, he threw up on his shoes."

Several people gasped, and more than a few laughed, including Ash's dad.

"Turns out, he wasn't just nervous about meeting the folks—he had a stomach bug and was sick all weekend. To make matters worse, Natalie came down with it the next day and, despite being absolutely miserable, Conor took care of her. He got her soup and crackers. Held her hair back when she was puking. Sometimes, puking into his own bucket while holding her hair back. And I knew then, no matter what, he'd take care of my baby sister. To Conor and Natalie: may there be more hand-holding than hair-holding."

"Aww…that's so sweet." Bree clasped her hands under her chin, staring at the dance floor as Natalie and Conor stepped forward for their first dance.

Denise chuckled and shook her head. Paige agreed with Bree.

It was sweet, heartfelt, and obvious that he'd put some thought into it.

"Are you going to meet his parents?" Angie asked.

Paige stared at her wide-eyed. "No."

"Why not?" Angie asked.

"Sweetie, that's not how hookups work. I'm going to actively avoid meeting his parents."

"But you've met his sister," Angie said.

"We partied with his sister. That's completely different than meeting his parents. I didn't even know how old he was until five minutes ago."

The DJ switched to a fast, bass-pumping song, and Paige caught Denise's wince.

"Are you okay?" she asked.

"It's getting a little loud for me," Denise said. "Normally it wouldn't be an issue, but with the club the other night…"

"And you don't have Sprocket with you," Paige said.

"Who's Sprocket?" Angie asked.

"Her service dog," Bree explained.

"We can go," Angie said.

Denise waved her hand. "No. You guys stay here. I'll go to the hotel beach and find a quiet spot."

"I'd rather find a quiet spot on the beach with my friends than stay at a wedding reception for people I just met," Paige said.

"Can we go back to the beach we were at yesterday?" Angie hunched her shoulders forward and dipped her chin. "I didn't get a chance to see the reef."

Paige laughed. "I'm good with that, if everyone else is."

"Works for me," Denise said.

"What about Pool-Boy?" Bree asked.

Paige glanced toward the dance floor and spotted Ash dancing with an older woman, smiling affectionately down at her. It was a sweet picture, and that stupid twinge told her it was definitely time to leave.

"I'll let him know to find me later." She stood, then pushed her chair back under the table, waiting for the others to do the same and gather their things. Bree's attention moved over Paige's shoulder, and she turned before she felt the touch on her arm.

Ash stood behind her. "Hey, you're not leaving, are you?"

"I'll catch up with you guys in a few minutes." Paige waited for Denise, Bree, and Angie to say their good-byes and leave. "We're going to go to the beach for a while since Angie didn't get to do any swimming yesterday."

"Without saying good-bye?"

The hurt was clear in his eyes, and she gave him a soft smile. "You didn't give me a chance. I was going to tell you to call our room when you're finished here."

"What room number?"

"Twenty-two, one-oh-three."

He looked at his watch. "Nat and Conor are supposed to leave in about an hour."

"Give me about three hours. I'm not sure how long we'll be at the beach, but we didn't really eat, so we'll probably get hungry before too long."

His eyes pinched, and he ran a hand through his hair. "Okay. I'll see you in a few hours?"

Paige squeezed his upper arm and smiled. "Have fun with your family. I'll see you later."

~

Paige inhaled deeply and soaked up the late afternoon sun. The sand was warm under her towel, and the sun wasn't blazing hot or blinding. This was her favorite part of the day.

"You're not going to try to see him again after this weekend, are you?"

Paige turned her head and squinted at Denise. "No."

"Even though you've been looking at him like he's the last box of Thin Mints on the last day of cookie sales?"

She grinned, remembering her conversation with Ash. "That doesn't work for me—I'm a Samoas girl."

"Fine. Like he's the last cookie in the last box of Samoas," Denise said.

"Even though," she said.

"Huh. Why?"

Paige sat up and leaned against her upper legs, scooping sand over her feet. "Because this is fun and easy. Anything more than this is complicated and difficult."

"It doesn't have to be."

She looked over her shoulder. "It's always complicated and difficult."

Denise sat up as well. "Not always. Sometimes it's only as complicated and difficult as we make it."

Paige stared out at the water, the vastness beyond the reef. "I won't ever get so deep into a guy that I lose my sense of self. It took me too long to figure out who I really was."

Denise frowned. "Is this about me and Preston?"

"What?" It took Paige a moment to connect the dots to the guy Denise had been involved with at Abu Ghraib. The one she found out had killed a boy during an interrogation. The guy Denise had almost killed before Graham stopped her. "Oh. No, this is about me and PJ."

"Who's PJ?"

Paige dropped her chin to her knees. "Remember I told you I volunteered to go to Iraq, and you thought I was nuts, because who the hell does that?"

"Yeah."

"I volunteered to go to Iraq to get out of Charleston because the guy I thought I was in love with proposed to a girl I thought was my friend. Neither of them told me they were dating, much less that it was that serious."

"Oh. Why didn't you ever tell me? We were bunkmates for almost a year."

"I was…embarrassed. Ashamed. I believed all his bullshit. Not only that, I asked for more, knowing it was bullshit. I lost myself. I liked what and who he liked. I disliked whatever he disliked. I waited around for him to call. I was…honestly, I was pathetic. And the only way I knew to break away from whatever toxic, manipulative, destructive hold he had over me was to leave and go as far away as I could. Iraq was the farthest place I could think of that I could get to quickly."

"That's why you were so adamant about me not getting involved with Preston," Denise said.

"I could see it happening. Although I don't think you ever lost yourself. I think he was just really good at bullshitting and gaslighting you."

"Yeah. It was easy to see in hindsight." Denise rested her chin on her knees and scooped sand over her toes. "I never thanked you for being the one to tell me about Ali."

A disbelieving laugh escaped Paige. That had been one of the worst moments of her life. Of hers and Denise's.

"Are you kidding? I've been trying to figure out a way to apologize for being the one to tell you for the last seventeen years."

Denise faced Paige, resting her temple on her knees. "We're kind of fucked up. You know that, right?"

Paige grinned. "Yeah, but I can live with that."

Denise grinned back. "Me, too."

CHAPTER 10

$\mathcal{A}$sh leaned against the bar and accepted the glass of whiskey from the bartender. An hour after Paige and her friends had left, the reception was in full swing, with Natalie and Conor leading a rousing rendition of "YMCA." Even their Nonna was out on the dance floor.

He drummed his finger against the wood of the bar and tapped his foot. He liked music and he even liked dancing, but usually not in public or near large groups of people. The other night had been an exception, one that had been completely about getting close to Paige.

A hand slid up the center of his back, and he turned, a wide smile ready for...

The smile died. "Hey, Suzie."

She slipped her hand around his upper arm, squeezing his bicep. "Hi, Sebastian." Her voice was breathy, her blue eyes glassy.

"No one calls me Sebastian except my mom and Nonna. I've told you that before." He grabbed his glass and took a sip, trying to dislodge her hand, but it moved with him as if it were glued in place.

"Right. Sorry. Aaassshhhh." She could have been trying for sultry, but it came out slurred. "You haven't danced with me."

She affected an exaggerated pout that he supposed other men found attractive, but he thought it just made her look like a child who'd been told they couldn't have another cookie.

"I haven't danced with anyone," he said.

"You danced with your mom. And your nanner. Nonner." She wobbled and tightened her grip on his arm to steady herself.

Ash frowned. "How much have you had to drink?"

Suzie slid her other hand across her chest and leaned against him. "Enough that I'll let you do any freaky thing to me you want." She emphasized the *t*.

He barely kept his lip from curling in disgust. If she was going for sexy and trying to turn him on, she'd failed miserably.

"I'll pass." Extricating himself proved difficult. She latched onto him like the stray kitten he'd found one time, digging in her fingers instead of needle-sharp claws.

"Come on, Ash. You know you want me."

He sighed heavily. "No, Suzie. I really don't."

"Why? Because of that woman? She's old. How could you pick her over me?" She gestured down her body.

Obviously, she hadn't looked in a mirror recently. Her eye makeup was smeared, and one of her fake lashes had detached at the corner and flopped like a small caterpillar clinging to her eyelid every time she tried to bat her eyes at him. Half of her complicated hairstyle had come undone and stuck up in a teased mess.

To put it in Natalie-speak, she looked like a hot mess. None of which he said to her. "Well, for one, she didn't have to get smashed to have sex with me."

"You already fucked her?"

Ash scanned the crowd to see who heard Suzie shout the question. A few people glanced their way, but that was still too many. He hated being the center of attention. Thankfully, Natalie was one of the people who had looked over, and he motioned for her to come nearer.

She excused herself from the small group she was talking to and joined them, a worried smile plastered on her face. "Hey. What's going on?"

"Sebastian won't have sex with me."

Ash didn't know if she was accusing him or complaining or both. "She's had a little bit too much to drink."

"I'm fine." Her assurances were ruined when she wobbled in her heels, and he had to catch her.

"Yeah…let's get you somewhere you can lie down," Natalie said. "You'll feel better after a nap."

"I don't want a nap. I want to be fucked."

"Jesus." Ash rubbed the center of his forehead.

"Maybe after your nap. Come on—I'll take you," Natalie said.

"No," he said. "You shouldn't have to leave your reception to take her back to her room. I'll take her."

"*I'll* take her." April joined them and wrapped an arm around Suzie's waist. "I'll put her on the couch in the room where we got ready. There's a bathroom if she has to puke, and it's close so we can check on her."

"Are you sure?" Natalie asked.

"Of course. It'll save me from my aunt hounding me about when I'm going to get married."

"Thank you," Natalie said.

"Thanks." Ash watched April lead Suzie away from the reception tent. She was good people.

"Come dance with me," Natalie said.

"Nat—"

"It's my wedding, and you have to do what I say," she said.

He heaved a sigh and drained his whiskey, then crooked his arm to lead his sister to the dance floor and into a foxtrot.

She looked at their feet and grinned. "You remember."

"Kind of hard to forget. That was the worst summer of my life."

"Cotillion wasn't that bad," she said.

"For you, it wasn't bad. For me, having to sit still, clap exactly nine times, and wear a tie and jacket when all I wanted to do was jump in the pool, was absolute hell. You probably don't remember the fights I had with mom every morning as she dragged me out the door."

"Poor thing." She patted his shoulder. "Being forced to be civilized and cultured."

"Exactly. I was twelve. Twelve-year-old boys aren't supposed to be civilized and cultured. They're supposed to be barefoot and dirty."

"In other words, we should dump all twelve-year-old boys on an island, *Lord of the Flies*-style every summer."

"Maybe not quite that drastic. Just from sunup to sundown."

She laughed up at him. "So…Suzie couldn't convince you to fuck her?"

He shuddered. "Ugh. No. Sloppy drunk is not attractive."

"And it doesn't have anything to do with an attractive birthday girl you recently met?" she asked with a teasing glint in her eye.

"Definitely," he said.

"Are you going to try to see her after this weekend?"

His smile faded. "I don't think that's what she wants."

Natalie cocked her head. "Why do you say that?"

"The fact that I don't know her last name, where she's from, or anything personal about her other than she loves the ocean."

And her breath hitched when she gasped as she came. Not the best of thoughts to be having while he was dancing with his sister.

"Then ask her those things," Natalie said. "Ask her if she wants to see you again."

Sweat broke out between his shoulder blades and trickled down his back at even the idea of asking Paige if he could see her again. What if she said no? Fuck, what if she said yes? Then he'd have to maintain a normal coherent conversation about regular life, and what the hell did they even have in common other than their love of the water?

"Stop," Natalie said. "You're overthinking it."

"Pretty sure I'm thinking about it the right amount."

"I like her," she said. "And I know *you* like her."

Ash gave her a baleful look.

"Even if I hadn't seen you sneaking into the ready room with her before the reception, I'd know because you're comfortable with her. You've been so relaxed this weekend, and I don't think you've thought about work once since you met her. Have you?"

Huh. He hadn't. Except for the few minutes at the bar before Suzie joined him, but that was because he'd been antsy to see Paige. He pressed his lips together and stared down at Natalie. Could he open himself to the possibility that Paige would laugh in his face if he suggested they see each other again?

Although she probably wouldn't laugh. She'd say something polite and reassuring while still getting her point across.

"All I'm saying is you should consider it," Natalie said.

"I'll consider it."

"Good. Now, I'm going to break my own rule and talk about work."

He gasped. "Language, Natalie Angelica. There are impressionable ears here." She smacked him on the upper arm, and he grinned at her. "Don't hurt your hand."

"Shut up before I give you a purple nurple."

He laughed and pressed a hand over his chest. "Okay. Work. What about it?"

"I didn't have a chance to finish the financial review before we left to come here, but I should have it done Monday or Tuesday after we get back from our honeymoon."

Ash shook his head. "I'm not worried about it, Nat. I especially don't want you working on it during your honeymoon. Jeez.

Conor will kill me, because when it comes to numbers, you're almost as bad as I am about tuning the world out."

"No one is as bad as you," she said.

"I know for a fact there are people worse than me." The song faded, and he turned Natalie under his arm, then spun her out as the song ended.

Their mom rushed up to them, arms spread wide. "Oh! I knew those cotillion lessons would pay off one day! You two looked so beautiful dancing together." She wrapped her arms around them before smooshing kisses on their cheeks.

Natalie smirked at him over their mom's head, and he rolled his eyes.

"It's time for cake!" His mom was more excited than usual, and he wondered how many glasses of champagne she'd had.

Natalie grabbed his wrist. "You promise you'll ask her?"

Ash blinked, then remembered their conversation about Paige. "I promise I'll think about asking."

She pointed her finger at him as their mom dragged her away. "You better ask."

He tilted his chin, acknowledging her order without really responding to it. He said he'd think about it and he would. It would probably go something along the lines of the time he'd asked Erica Barns to junior prom. After she'd stopped laughing, she'd told him he was really sweet but she was too far out of his league to go to prom with.

There. He'd thought about it. Then he buried the thought through the cake cutting, the garter toss, which he successfully dodged, and the bouquet toss, which ended with several women on the ground wrestling for the heavy clump of flowers, much to the chagrin of several men.

He didn't think about it again until he got back to his hotel room and looked at his watch. It had been less than three hours, but he dialed Paige's room anyway, his heart pounding in his chest.

"Hello?"

Shit. He fumbled the phone and almost dropped it. He hadn't expected an answer yet. "Is…may I speak to Paige?"

"Hi, Ash. It's Paige."

He could hear the smile in her voice. "Hi. I wasn't expecting anyone to answer yet."

"But you called anyway?"

"I was hopeful," he said.

"Bree and Angie were starving, so we came back so they could change and have dinner."

"Did you…have you eaten?"

"No. We just got back from the beach. We're going to clean up and order room service."

"Oh. Okay." What else should he say?

"I could stop by after we eat," she said. There was a slight hesitation, as if she wasn't sure he'd agree to that plan. Was she as nervous about seeing him again as he was about seeing her?

"That sounds good," he said.

"Great. What room are you in?"

"Two-oh-one. Building twelve."

"See you in a little while."

CHAPTER 11

CHARLESTON - MONDAY MORNING

*P*aige sipped on the extra-large latte with a double shot of espresso and clicked on the email icon on her computer. Their connecting flight from Miami to Charleston had been canceled, and rather than wait fourteen hours for the next flight, she and Angie had rented a car and driven back. Even splitting the drive, she hadn't gotten a lot of sleep—she'd never been a good car sleeper.

She sighed and stretched her neck. There were almost three hundred emails to sort through. Why hadn't she taken today off too?

Angie knocked on her open door. "Are we doing a staff meeting this morning?"

Paige shook her head. "No. I'll reschedule it for tomorrow. I need to catch up on emails first. "

Angie's whole body sagged. "Oh, thank god . I do not have the energy to do that this morning. I'm going to make a really strong pot of coffee. You need some?"

Paige raised her cup. "I'm good for now."

"Cool. I'll see you later."

She groaned. She was never going to stay awake sitting down.

Kicking off her heels, she raised her standing desk and pulled up a rock playlist on her phone. As the first drumbeats of Disturbed's "Down With The Sickness" filled her office, she cracked her knuckles and let the heavy bass fuel her with false energy.

A few hours and dozens of emails later, she knocked on Graham's door. "Got a few minutes to go over some things?"

He looked up from his computer and swiveled in his chair to face her. "Sure. How was your trip?"

Paige closed the door behind her and sat in one of the leather seats facing his desk. "It was good. It was nice catching up with Denise and Bree. You know, when we aren't worried about biker gang wars and skirting the law."

A couple years ago, they'd helped Denise with a situation involving a member of a biker gang and Denise's kidnapped niece and nephew. Denise had called Graham as a last resort, and Paige had gone with him to take care of things. It had been a difficult situation for everyone, but it had led to her and Denise reconnecting.

His eyebrows rose at her reference. "Did you guys talk about that?"

She shook her head. "No. We kept it completely personal."

"How are they?"

"They're good. Really good. Denise was more relaxed than I think she's been since I met her, and Bree is pregnant."

Graham grinned. "Good for her. How far along is she?"

"Not very. She took the pregnancy test the first day." Paige sighed and smiled softly.

"You good?" He could read her better than anyone else.

She propped her elbow on the high arm of the chair and rested her chin in her palm. "Yeah. It just got me thinking about things."

"What kind of things?"

"You know. The way life takes turns you don't expect. It's just..."

She hadn't discussed her restlessness with Graham. They were close—close enough that more than a few people assumed they were romantically involved. They weren't, nor had they ever been. But neither did they constantly share deep emotions with each other.

"Just?" he prompted.

She shook her head. "This wasn't the direction I envisioned my life taking."

He froze, two thin lines forming between his brows. "Do I need to worry about you quitting on me?"

"What? No, of course not. I love my job. I love my life. It's just different than I expected it to be when I was twenty-four, twenty-five. Not a bad different. Just…different."

She shrugged.

"Anyway," she continued. "I have several emails from potential clients that want corporate or personal security services—which, as I've made known more than once, I think we need to grow. I know we started off with the goal of being more tactically focused, and that made sense ten years ago, but we need to move away from that being our primary objective."

Graham leaned back in his chair and crossed his arms. They'd been having the same discussion for the last couple of years, and he always pushed back. He'd spent most of his time in the Army in Special Operations and he loved it. After seeing contractors who had less training and experience than he had, raking in million-dollar government contracts during the height of the wars in Iraq and Afghanistan, he'd started his own company when his time in the Army was finished.

He'd offered Paige a job, it became a partnership, and she'd never looked back.

"Tactical operations are expensive," she argued, "time-consuming, and we have to lowball to compete with the bigger contractors who aren't worried about cutting corners and doing shady shit. I'm not saying go away from it completely, but it shouldn't be our primary focus. The security contract in Guatemala has been lucrative for our accounts and our reputation, but it also took a big chunk out of our available funds initially, as did the rescue operation in Crimea."

His lips thinned, and Paige knew he was thinking about the fiscal impact of those two operations.

"We didn't want to take money from the families of the people we rescued, which I agree with, but we took a hit for it financially. The upside of that is with all the press we've gotten, we have a lot of interest in our services, but we need to make sure we're tailoring them in a way that makes sense and not spreading ourselves too thin."

She sat forward in her chair. "We need to focus our mission. The big contracts in Iraq and Afghanistan are a thing of the past. I know you don't like it, but you know I'm right."

They sat in silence for several minutes. The flow of this conversation was familiar—he wouldn't say anything because he didn't have a strong argument against what she said. He was just resistant to change. She let him stew for a few minutes, then threw the final punch.

"It's time for you to be gone less. I don't mind running TLC, but when was the last time you spent more than a few days with Sierra?"

His arms bunched before he forced himself to relax. He intentionally released the tension from his face, then his shoulders dropped, and finally his fingers softened. It was fascinating to watch. And more reaction than she'd ever gotten from him in the past.

"That's a low blow, Paige."

"I know. Which is why I made it. You have a daughter you hardly ever see and it's not because of how things are with her mother. You only have a few more years where she's still little enough to worship her father. After that, she's off to college and living her own life, and you'll have nothing but aches and pains to keep you company."

"I already have those."

Paige smirked. She might actually have him this time. He rubbed a hand over his bald head and leaned forward, scooting closer to his desk. The fabric of his shirt strained as it stretched across his wide shoulders.

"All right. As many times as you've talked at me about this, I'm assuming you have a plan."

She scoffed. "Of course I have a plan, but it means hiring more people. An administrative assistant and human resources person to take some of the day-to-day off my hands, preferably people Turner isn't going to sleep with."

Graham grunted in agreement.

"We also need a financial officer. My three business accounting classes aren't going to cut it for much longer, and it will be less expensive than farming out the services piecemeal. We need someone who can handle the contracts and the payroll. I also want to start a cybersecurity arm and put Angie in charge of it."

"Does she want to do that?" he asked.

"Maybe not, in which case she doesn't have to, but I'd still like her help to establish it."

He clasped his hands together. "I trust you to do what's best for TLC, even if you have to drag me along, kicking and screaming the whole way."

Paige smiled. "Good, because I set up interviews for a financial officer before I went on vacation. The first one is this afternoon."

That made him laugh. "Of course you did."

She flipped open her large planner. "Let's go over the schedule for this week. I moved the staff meeting to tomorrow. There was no way Angie or I were prepared for it this morning. I have several meetings set up this week for potential clients. I think you need to sit in on a few of them—I'll send you a calendar invite with all the information."

She scanned down her list of notes, making sure she hadn't

missed anything. "Oh. I have a note about Tinker being on a last-minute personal security detail. What's that about?"

"Oh, an actor filming in Yemassee has a stalker, and we were recommended for local security."

"See? Personal security." If Graham was the type of person to roll his eyes, he would have. "How serious is the stalker?"

"I don't know. It's all online. Some woman went whacked-out superfan. She thinks he's a fictional character from some romance novel and is convinced he's her one and only. Some of her social media is beyond creepy though. Angie has screenshots and IP information to run down today."

"Okay. I'll check in with her and see if she needs any help or if there's something we should pass on to Tinker. Which actor?"

Graham turned to his computer, clicked his mouse, and scrolled. "Henry Cavill?"

Paige blinked. "Did you say Henry Cavill?"

"Yeah. You know who he is? I'd never heard of him."

"How have you never—? Never mind. You're telling me you got a call to guard Henry Cavill's body and you didn't immediately call me?"

"You were on vacation. I had strict instructions that if I called you this time, you'd quit."

She pressed her lips together and inhaled sharply. "New rule: any calls to guard Henry Cavill's body get directed to me."

Graham's shoulders shook, and he wiped a hand over his mouth. "You know it's personal security, not guarding his body, right?"

"Not the way I'd do it." She slammed her planner shut and stormed out of his office.

Henry fucking Cavill. What the hell? Uninvited, the image of another dark-haired man flashed in her memory. Goosebumps rose on her arms as she remembered her fingers threaded through his thick locks.

The toe of her shoe stubbed the carpet, and she stumbled,

catching herself on the doorframe of her office. Shit. Tossing her planner on the desk, she dropped into her chair, covering her face with her hands.

This was going to be one of those lifelong regrets, she knew it. One huge fucking what if, followed closely by what the fuck were you thinking? And she had no way to fix it.

Her desk phone rang and she picked up the handset. "The Leonidas Corporation. Paige speaking."

"Hey, darlin'." Graham Senior's low Southern drawl rolled over her, smoothing her frayed edges. "There's a gentleman here for an interview with you."

"Thank you. Would you mind walking him back?"

"'Course not. We'll be there in a bit."

"Thanks, Senior."

She took a deep breath and flattened her hands on her desk. Right. Work. Financial officer interviews. Pulling up her calendar, she found the name of the first applicant and opened his resume.

~

*P*aige pretended to glance over the resume while surreptitiously watching the woman sitting across the desk from her. Light brown hair coiled close to her head. Flawless, Instagram-worthy makeup, and impossibly long eyelashes that curled at the ends. She couldn't tell if they were natural or extensions—and if they were extensions, Paige wanted to know where she got them. Only the surreptitious picking at her cuticles gave away her nervousness.

"Samara, your resume is very impressive, but I notice you don't have any references for your previous employer."

"Um." She cleared her throat and elongated her neck. "I was fired."

Paige set down the resume. "What was the reason?"

She looked down at her hands and licked her lips, swallowing hard.

"Samara, we'll conduct a background investigation if we offer you the position, which will include calling the HR department of your last employer."

Other than nodding, she didn't respond.

Paige sighed. It sucked, because Samara was her first choice for the position based solely on her resume. She hadn't gotten a good feeling from the other three candidates, all men who appeared more interested in whether they'd get to go on missions and shoot guns than the numbers they'd be required to crunch. Samara was the only woman applicant and by far the strongest, to the point that Paige had wondered why she'd even applied for the position.

Bracing her hands on her desk to stand, Paige said, "Thank you for coming, but I—"

"I'm transgender."

Paige lowered back into her chair. Of all the reasons for termination she'd expected, that hadn't been one she'd considered.

"One of the partners found out, and he had me fired."

"He fired you for being transgender? That's illegal."

Samara snatched a tissue from the box on the desk and dabbed at the corner of her eyes. "Officially, they fired me for lying on official documents because I put female instead of male."

"And you didn't challenge it?"

"How? Being transgender *and* Black in South Carolina? He threatened to have my license revoked if I fought it. And I certainly didn't want to work there after that."

Rage made it impossible for Paige to speak, and she vibrated with repressed anger. She hated bullies.

Samara sighed and picked up her tote. "Thank you for your time."

What just happened?

"Samara, wait. Please sit down." Paige took a breath, searched for the calm beyond the fury.

"I'm sorry if I gave the wrong impression, but I'm at a loss. I've never dealt with this situation before. I don't...I don't want to say the wrong thing and I don't have the words to express how disgusted I am with the way you were treated. Not professional words anyway. Instead, let me ask you—why do you want this job? You have a background in forensic accounting and you were the CFO of two of the last three companies you worked for. You are immensely overqualified for the position."

Samara sat stiffly with her bag in her lap. "I saw the piece on your security contract for the archeological excavation in Guatemala."

"Okay."

"I don't think you negotiated enough for what you're doing. You'll break even, but just barely."

Paige leaned back and crossed her legs. It was very likely they'd end up with very little profit, but she wanted to hear Samara's reasoning.

"How do you figure?"

"Assuming you're paying salary, bonuses, insurance, travel, sustenance, plus whatever materials, uniforms, and basic services you're providing, based on the figures in the article, you're going to be slightly ahead when it's time to renegotiate the contract, and at that point, there will be other companies ready to pounce and underbid you."

"You figured out all that from three sentences in a five-paragraph article?"

"I'm very good at my job."

Paige smiled. "I'm impressed. You're the only applicant that took the time to actually look at what we're doing. But that doesn't explain why you want to work here."

Samara inhaled deeply. "During one of the video interviews, a reporter asked you if being a woman working in a male-dominated field hindered you in any way, and you asked him—"

"If being an idiot working in an intellectually-dominated field hindered him. Not my best PR moment." Paige shook her head. That sound bite was what made her add a PR person to the list of additional people she wanted to hire.

"But you didn't hesitate. You didn't laugh it off or brush it aside. You didn't take his shit, and more than anything, I want to work for a woman that doesn't take anyone's shit."

Jesus, that was a lot of pressure. "I'm flattered, thank you. You're right, I don't take anyone's shit, but I can't promise this will always be a safe space for you. There's a zero-tolerance policy for harassment, and I mean zero, but the guys who work here are all ex-military, and they can be rude and crass and talk out their asses more often than not. I'm also worried that with your background and experience, you'll be bored working on payroll and contracts."

Samara shook her head. "I like routine, so working on payroll and contracts won't bore me. I don't care about language or off-color jokes. I just want to be accepted for who I am." She paused and licked her lips. "Would I have to tell anyone I'm transgender? I am a woman and I don't want to be labeled as anything else."

"Other than me and Angie, who will run your background check, you decide who knows. That's your personal business, and you can share or not."

A knock on the door drew Paige's attention. "Come in."

Angie pushed the door open, and her small dog rushed between her legs, stopping at Samara to bark for pets.

"Sorry, I didn't realize you were still interviewing," Angie said. "I can come back."

"That's okay. We're almost finished. What's up?"

"Graham asked me to look at that stalker's online persona."

"Okay?"

"She's a romance author. I can't tell how much she really

believes and how much she…" Angie pursed her lips and wiggled her head side to side. "Embellishes for her fans."

"So you think it's all an act and there's no real threat?" Paige asked.

"I'm not sure. I could use your eyes on it though to make sure I'm not reading it wrong."

"Okay. Let me finish up here and I'll take a look."

"Cool." She looked at Samara. "Cute shoes, by the way. Come on, Princess."

The dog trotted out of the office, following Angie.

Samara smiled, staring after the dog. "I would really like to work here."

Paige returned her smile. "How about a ninety-day trial period for you to determine whether you'll be comfortable here, and that this is a good fit for you and TLC?"

"I accept."

Paige grinned. "Great. Let me grab some paperwork, and we'll get started. Then I'll give you a tour of the building."

Samara returned her smile. "Perfect."

CHAPTER 12

$\mathcal{A}$sh absently tapped the pencil on the desk, his gaze darting back and forth across the computer screen while he read through the code. He almost had it figured out. He just needed the tail of the worm to close the door behind itself when it left—like a lover sneaking out at dawn.

Shoving the pencil between his teeth, he tapped on the keyboard, editing the script.

"Bash."

He jolted and spat out the pencil, shoving away from the desk. The chair slid off the edge of the plastic mat and came to an abrupt stop when it hit the carpet. It toppled over and sent Ash rolling to the floor.

Jumping up with a shout, he crouched, fists raised, and faced the intruder.

"Slow down, Chuck Norris, before you pull something."

Ash sagged and stood upright. "Holy shit, Natalie. Warn a guy next time." He righted the chair and pushed it back under the desk. "What are you doing here?"

"Your cell phone is off."

"I'm working and didn't want to be distracted."

She walked out of the office. "Patrick keeps calling?"

"Yes." He sighed and followed her into the living/dining room combination, then stopped and stared at her. "What's wrong? You're supposed to be on your honeymoon. Why are you back early?"

She turned and gave him a weird look. "Bash, it's been a week. We got back two days ago."

He rubbed his eyes. "Shit. Seriously? What day is it?"

"Tuesday night. You forgot to set your alarms, didn't you?"

"No." In the open kitchen, he picked up an empty glass from the counter, looked in it, sniffed it, shrugged, and filled it up from the water dispenser on the fridge. "I set one to remind me to eat."

"That was the only one?"

"I didn't need any others." He chugged the entire glass of water and refilled it.

"Bash." Her voice was pure exasperated admonishment.

"What?" He'd zoned out. Who cared? It wasn't like he had a physical job to show up to.

"So you've been holed up in here for the last eight days? Never mind, I can smell the answer." Natalie sighed. "At least you've eaten."

He looked at the counter and dining room table, piled with to-go containers and remnants of the meals he'd ordered. "Yes. That I have remembered to do."

"Thank goodness for food delivery," she said.

Ash ran his hands through his hair and rubbed his fingers together. Gross. He needed a shower. "I'm almost finished with the code. I'm tweaking a few things to make sure it's perfect before we start testing it. I want to be able to run a complete program, not a ninety percent solution."

"That's why I'm here. Why don't you shower, because you stink, and I'll clean off the table?"

"No." For fuck's sake, he was a grown-ass man. He didn't need his sister coming in and cleaning up after him or mothering him. "I'll do it."

"Well then, do it and shower." She curled up in the armchair and stared at her phone.

He frowned at her. She'd never had any intention of cleaning up after him. She just wanted to goad him into doing it. Not sure if he was impressed or annoyed, he toed open the lid of the trash can, only to find it full. Pulling the bag out, he tied it off and got a new bag from under the sink, quickly filling it with a week's worth of food containers.

Damn. It wasn't unusual for him to zone out for a day or two, but a week was kind of long. Getting lost in the code had been the easiest way not to think about Paige. Even then, he'd find his fingers hovering over the keyboard with his mind wandering to that last night they'd spent together.

It was the first time he could remember getting distracted by something when he was hyperfocused. It usually took something like an alarm or someone physically getting his attention—such as Natalie scaring the crap out of him—to draw him out of his zone.

He took the bags to the outside trashcan. After a quick shower, he found his sister at the dining room table with a stack of papers.

"I'm sorry it took me longer than I thought it would to review the financials, but I wanted to make sure I wasn't mistaken before I brought this up."

He sat next to her. "Brought what up?"

"There's money unaccounted for," she said.

"Could it be a calculation error? Maybe you forgot to carry the one."

She slowly straightened her spine and gave him the dirtiest look ever. If she could have killed him with her glare alone, he'd be a dead man.

Ash held up his hands. "Sorry. Sorry. I won't question your math skills."

"Besides," she bit out, "carrying the one incorrectly wouldn't account for more than $150,000 missing."

"What?" He grabbed the paper from Natalie.

She pointed to the figure in red parentheses. One hundred fifty thousand, three hundred twelve dollars. And seventeen cents.

He flipped through the stacks of papers like he had any clue what he was looking for. "How is it missing? Where did it go?"

"I don't know. I'm a regular CPA, not a forensic accountant. You're in the seed funding stage of growing M.A.G. so there aren't a lot of controls in place to track the money that comes in and what goes out."

She pointed at the pages he held. "For the first three to four months, the bookkeeping was really clear, and it was really easy to see where and who the funds came from, and what the expenditures were." She paused.

"But?" Ash prompted.

Natalie sighed. "About nine months ago, it became less clear. Random deposits into the business account without any indication of where the money came from. There are a lot of conversion notes but no corresponding deposits. There are also a lot of debits that I can't attribute to anything. I can tell you how much money came in from investors and point out where there are payments without invoices or receipts, but I can't account for all the money between what was supposed to come in, what the accounts show came in, and what you actually have. I can only work with what I've got."

He didn't understand half of what she'd said, but he knew that tone. "What aren't you telling me?"

"I had to pull teeth to get this information, Bash. I had to threaten Patrick that I would advise you not to go forward with Series A funding if he didn't give me everything, and I still don't think I have everything I should. And he didn't even send it to me—Alexis did."

"Alexis?"

"Yeah. She said Patrick told her to send it to me."

"Do you think he took the money?"

She shrugged and shook her head. "I don't know. I don't want to think he'd screw you over like that, especially when he has as much on the line with this company as you do, but…" She spread her hands. "He was very resistant to your suggestion that I take over the financial preparations for the next phase of funding."

He buried his head in his hands. "Fuck. Should I confront him?"

"I think you should let him know there's money unaccounted for and see how he reacts before you accuse him of anything."

Ash nodded. "Then what? No matter how he reacts, we need to find out where the money went, right?"

She gathered the papers up and tapped them together. "I already took the liberty of contacting a company to look into it. They have an accountant on staff with a background in forensic accounting who can do a deep dive, as well as a cybersecurity tech who can find out if the systems were compromised in any way."

He gave Natalie his own dirty look. "The systems were not compromised. I tested them myself."

"It's not going to hurt to have someone take an unbiased look at them. Without you looking over their shoulder. Especially to show that you didn't have any role in this."

Fuck. He hadn't even thought of that. Knowing it was best for the company and the launch didn't make it any more palatable though. They needed to show current investors they did their due diligence to find the money.

"All right," he conceded. "I'll call them tomorrow."

"Already done. You and I have an appointment on Thursday afternoon in Charleston."

"South Carolina? That's two hours from here. There wasn't anyone local?"

She inserted the stack of papers into the pocket of a black folder. "They came highly recommended."

"What's the name of the company?"

"The Leonidas Corporation."

Ash frowned. "Why does that sound familiar?"

"Maybe it's the name Leonidas." She shrugged.

"Oh, from the Battle of Thermopylae. Probably."

"I was thinking the movie *The 300*, but sure. Old history stuff."

He rolled his eyes. "Whatever, junior. Don't you have a husband to get home to?"

"He's working tonight."

"I thought the whole reason for him to start his own practice was so he didn't have to work nights and weekends."

"It was, but he still volunteers at the trauma center. They had a serious case and asked him to come in."

"So you decided to come hang out with me so you wouldn't worry?"

"Something like that. Plus, it's Tuesday, there's nothing on TV, and you have no social life, so I knew you'd be home."

Something tickled Ash's memory. "It's Tuesday?"

"Yes."

"What's the date?"

"The twelfth," she said.

He pushed up and grabbed his phone from the charger in the kitchen, tapping his thumb against the edge while he waited for it to turn on. Three reminders immediately popped up, one after the other. "Shit! I do have something to do. I'm supposed to be at a networking thing with Patrick. Fuck."

He tossed his phone to Natalie. "Can you order me a rideshare?"

Rushing into the bedroom, he pulled on slacks and a button-down shirt. Thank god Nat had shown up when she did and made him take a shower. Wetting his hands in the bathroom sink, he ran them through his hair, trying to get it to lay flat. It might be time for a haircut.

Pulling a black blazer off the hanger, he grabbed his shoes and rushed out to the living room.

"Three minutes." Natalie handed him his phone. "No tie?"

He looked down and ran a hand over the front of his shirt. "No. I'm gonna pull a George Clooney."

She threw her head back and laughed. "You know the only reason you can pull that off is because you're half Italian, right?"

"Yes, which is why I use it to my advantage." He shoved his feet in his shoes and kissed her on the cheek. "Lock up when you leave."

"Have fun!"

"Yeah. I'll get right on that."

~

*A*sh thanked his rideshare driver and unfolded from of the low sedan, buttoning his jacket after he closed the door. In the foyer of the River Street Inn, he spotted a sign for the networking event and followed the arrow pointing to one of the restaurants. Stopping in the doorway, he scanned the crowd and found Patrick across the room, talking to two other men.

He hated networking. It was worse than a wedding reception. At least at the reception, he'd known some of the people, even if he didn't have a lot to offer to the conversation. Here, he knew no one.

Patrick schmoozed and romanced investors into giving them lots of money. He referred to them as the "fool" portion of the friends, family, and fools of initial startup investing. Ash designed programs and wrote code. It didn't require interacting with people. Fools or otherwise.

Patrick spotted him and raised a hand, murmuring something to the people he spoke with, then heading toward Ash.

"You forgot a tie," he said as a greeting.

"I didn't forget it. I don't see the point in putting a noose around my neck. I already feel like I'm choking."

"Look, I wouldn't ask you to come to these things if it wasn't important. Investors want to talk to the person who knows the specifics of the programming. I can only reference *Wreck-It Ralph* so many times before they think I'm talking about a video game and lose interest. Just stay on topic and don't get too…techy."

"Yeah, sure." The expectations of strangers with money were overwhelming. Once again, he was reminded why he hated large groups and meeting new people. Except…he'd been completely comfortable with Paige. Maybe because he'd zeroed in on her right away and hadn't had time to say the wrong thing or start talking about his work.

"Ash—you with me?"

He gave himself a mental shake. "Yeah."

"Try not to zone out while you're talking to investors, okay?"

"Yeah. I got it." He stopped Patrick from walking off. "Before we start making the rounds, Nat found a discrepancy in the financials."

"I'm sure she just has her numbers wrong. This is why I wanted to hire a professional."

Ash bristled at the insinuation even though he'd said almost the same thing. "Natalie is a professional, and we're hiring another company to take a look because $150,000 missing is more than getting numbers wrong."

That shook his flawless façade. "Wait. What?"

"There's one hundred and fifty thousand, three hundred and change missing. You didn't know anything about it?"

"What the fuck?" Patrick glanced around at the people looking at them. He smiled and adjusted his tie, always worried about appearances. "Of course not," he said in a lower voice.

"Nat and I have an appointment in Charleston on Thursday."

"Why Charleston?"

"The company Nat found came highly recommended," Ash said.

Patrick adjusted his shoulders back and stretched his neck. "I'll go with you. Have Natalie send me the information."

"Sure."

"Do you need to set yourself a reminder?"

Ash glared at his business partner. "No. I'll remember this one."

CHAPTER 13

"**B**ut why do I have to do it?" Paige knew she sounded whiny, but she didn't want to do the tactics training.

Honestly, she hated tactics training. It was one of those ugly necessities of being one of the few women in a security company that performed tactical operations—she had to actually train to do the job.

"Because Tinker is still in Yemassee until we confirm the stalker isn't actually stalking, and we need an even number of people," Graham said.

Her eyes widened, and she smiled. "Well, that's perfect! I'll go to Yemassee and take over Henry Cavill's body, and Tink can come back here and do the tactics training."

Graham laughed at her. Laughed! "Sorry, Mayhem. You need to be here to cover all the new corporate accounts we're taking on."

Her and her big ideas. "Then someone else can sit out the training. Voilà! Even number."

Samara's wide eyes flitted between them as they argued. She looked like she wasn't sure what to make of the entire discussion.

"Four-man teams."

Paige curled one side of her upper lip and glared at Graham. "I hate you."

"I know. That's what makes it so much fun. Now, what's the appointment for this afternoon?"

Paige pursed her lips but turned to back to the matter at hand. "Angie scheduled this one. It's a small start-up—M.A.G. Cyber Security."

"What does M.A.G. stand for?" Graham asked.

She flipped through the notes and shook her head. "It doesn't say." Angie needed to learn about the five W's.

"Why are we meeting them?" Graham asked.

She read directly from Angie's notes. "They're a start-up and want to move forward with the next stage of investor funding, but during a financial review, the CPA discovered over $150,000 unaccounted for."

Samara let out a low whistle. "That's a lot of money to suddenly find missing. Especially for a start-up."

"That was my thought as well," Paige said.

"One of the partners?" Graham asked.

"Or the CPA." Paige looked at Samara. "If we decide to take this account, what will you need access to?"

"Their business accounts and any and all records. Permission to look at their personal accounts would be helpful."

Paige nodded. "Do you have an example of any agreements they'll need to sign to give us permission to access that information?"

"I do," she said.

"What time is the meeting?" Graham asked.

Paige checked her watch. "In about forty minutes."

"Do you need me there for it?" he asked.

"No. I just wanted to make sure you were aware it was happening and why."

Graham stood. "Okay. Let me know if you need anything from me."

"Will do. Samara, let's get those forms together so we have them ready."

~

*A*sh held the outer door for Natalie and followed her through the second set of doors into a small foyer. An older man with close-cut gray hair and a thick gray mustache sat behind the curved desk, staring at his phone.

Ash checked his watch again. Patrick should have been here by now. He'd texted Ash that he was leaving Savannah right after he and Natalie had left, so he should have been right behind them, but it was thirteen minutes before their meeting, and Patrick hadn't arrived.

The man behind the desk looked up. "How can I help you folks?"

Natalie stepped forward. "Hi. We're with M.A.G. Security. We have a two o'clock appointment."

He pushed up from his chair and held out his hand. "Aiden Graham. Senior."

Ash shook with him. "Sebastian Moreno. This is my sister, Natalie Mills."

"Nice to meet you folks. If you'll follow me, I'll lead you back to the conference room."

"There should be another gentleman joining us, but I think he's running a few minutes late," Ash said.

"Would you like to wait for him?" Graham Senior asked.

"I'd hate for you to make two trips," Natalie said.

"No problem. I don't move around a lot otherwise."

"You don't mind?" Ash asked.

"Not at all."

"Thank you," Natalie said. "We appreciate that."

"Like I said—no problem. We're gonna head down this way."

They followed him down a short hall to an open office area. A few of the desks were occupied by men who looked like they'd be more comfortable in a gym rather than sitting behind a desk. A woman with dark hair piled on top of her head sat in the far back corner in front of a bank of monitors. She looked familiar, but Ash had a hard time placing her. It also could have been how distracted he was by her computer setup.

They turned left down a short corridor and left again into a small conference room.

He had no problem placing the woman at the end of the table even with her head down, looking at a tablet.

"Paige, your two o'clock is here. Sebastian Moreno and Natalie Mills," Graham Senior said.

She looked up, the pleasant, friendly smile fading as her eyes widened and her mouth hung open slightly. Ash clenched his teeth to keep from doing the same.

Those full, dark pink lips had been wrapped around his cock less than two weeks ago. The cock that immediately throbbed against the zipper of his pants at the memory.

"Ash. Natalie. What are you—? How—?"

"Oh good. You made it," a voice behind them said.

Ash turned to find the dark-haired woman standing in the doorway. She and Natalie hugged and it clicked—Angie.

"Thank you for fitting us in on such short notice," Natalie said.

"Of course. Thanks for thinking of us. It would have been a lot easier for you to go to a local company," Angie said.

"You spoke so passionately about your job—you were the first person I thought of."

"I'm just happy we're in a position to help," Angie said. "Maybe. Depending on what the problem is."

If he had to guess, his sister and Paige's friend had no problems talking about their personal lives. He smelled a setup.

A tall, slender woman stopped in the doorway behind Angie. "I was passing through the foyer and the other partner arrived, so I walked him back with me."

Patrick pushed through the three women. In his three-piece suit, he looked like a stereotypical elitist businessman. All he was missing was the pocket watch chain and monocle to look like a slicked-back version of the Monopoly banker. Alexis followed behind him in a form-fitting dress more appropriate for drinks at an elegant downtown restaurant than an office meeting. What was she doing here?

"Bash," Natalie said under her breath.

He shifted. "Paige, let me introduce you to my partner, Patrick Greene, and his wife. Alexis. Patrick, Alexis, this is—"

"Paige? Holy shit." Patrick rushed around the conference table and scooped Paige into a bear hug, lifting her off her feet.

Her arms came up, but more to ward him off than embrace him. Her eyes shuttered, and her face went devoid of emotion. In the few days they'd been together, her dark amber eyes always had a twinkle in them. Now...nothing.

Patrick set her down and held her at arm's length. "Wow. You look great. I almost didn't recognize you."

"Patrick," Alexis's voice held a warning, and her pinched mouth and eyes, squinty around the corners, gave away her annoyance.

"Oh. Right. Paige, you remember Alexis, right?"

Alexis went in for a fake air kiss. Paige went through the motions of moving her head, but nothing else.

Usually oblivious to subtle social cues, even Ash picked up on Paige's discomfort. Hell, she might as well have been wearing a bright neon sign that read, *What the fuck?*

"Would you—?" Paige cleared her throat. "Please excuse me for a minute. Angie? Come with me, please."

Her sedate pace out of the conference room belied the tremor he'd heard in her voice. He watched the sway of her hips, hugged in a fitted, knee-length skirt. When he looked away, he found Patrick's head canted, taking in the same view. Alexis didn't try to hide her indignation, her arms crossed and a look of pure fury on her face.

"I take it you guys know Paige," Ash said.

Patrick started, having been caught staring, and a slow smirk formed. "Yeah. We were stationed here in Charleston together—way back. She went to Iraq, and we lost contact."

Huh. A wave of jealousy crashed over Ash. It was irrational because he had no claim to Paige, but there was something in Patrick's voice he didn't like. A hint of smugness that usually indicated Patrick was patronizing him about something. He clenched his jaw and exchanged looks with Natalie.

She seemed as surprised by the latest turn of events as he was. "Sorry," she mouthed.

"Well, um…I'm Samara." She clasped her hands in front of her. "I'm the accountant who will be helping with this case. Can I get anyone some water or some coffee?"

CHAPTER 14

Paige closed the door to her office gently behind Angie and set her hands on her hips. "You and Natalie decided to play matchmaker."

Angie wrung her hands together and grimaced. "Yes and no."

"Explain the yes and the no."

"Well, I mentioned to Natalie that we lived in Charleston, and I did IT and worked for a security company. We exchanged numbers in St. John, and she texted me, asking what kind of security we did, and I explained we do a little of this and that."

She waved her hands in front of her. "I didn't mention any of the secret stuff we do. Natalie called earlier this week and explained the issue with Ash's company. You've been talking about expanding our portfolio, and we talked about doing some cyber stuff, and I thought it was kismet. I tried to talk to you about it, but you told me if I thought it was a good opportunity that you trusted me and to schedule the appointment, so I did."

"I'm guessing that's the no part. What's the yes part?"

Angie shrugged. "We both figured if you two had a chance to see each other, then you might hit it off again, and are you going to fire me?"

Paige pressed a thumb to the soft spot at her temple and rubbed. "No, I'm not going to fire you."

"Really? Because you look really angry and flustered, and you don't ever get flustered or angry, except for that one time when Addison was kidnapped, and you called me in here with you, so I figured it was to fire me."

What a clusterfuck. Paige collapsed in one of the seats in front of her desk and Angie took the other one, curling her legs under her. "I'm not angry. Shocked and, yes, flustered. I needed someone to freak out with, and Samara is too new for the boss to have a meltdown. But from now on, when you make an appointment, you need to provide the five *w*'s."

"The what?"

Paige ticked them off with her fingers. "Who. What. When. Where. Why."

"Oh. Okay, I can do that."

She nodded and rubbed her finger across the center of her bottom lip, staring blankly at her desk.

PJ fucking Greene. And Lexi. Jesus. If she were superstitious, she'd think her conversation with Denise on the beach had conjured him from thin air.

"So...are you having a freak-out because of Ash?" Angie asked.

"No. Yes, him too, but mostly no." She dropped her hand and looked at Angie. "Did either you or Natalie think of the fact that if we take this case, he's a client and there can be no personal relationship?"

Angie's lips parted. "Oh. No."

Paige blinked and nodded shortly.

"Is it the other partner?" she asked. "You looked really shocked to see him."

"That's an understatement. We were stationed together, here in Charleston actually, more than fifteen years ago."

"But it's more than that..."

"Yeah. It's more than that." So much more.

A knock derailed her train of thought. The door opened, and Graham popped his head around the edge. "Everything okay? Samara said you were upset about something."

"Yeah, come in," Paige said. "Ange, can you let them know I'll be right there? Ask if they want water or coffee or…something."

"Of course." She unfolded from the seat and traded places with Graham, closing the door behind her.

Graham stretched his legs out and crossed them at the ankles. "Has someone been kidnapped again?"

That teased a smile from her. "I wish. That would be easier. I might have a serious conflict of interest with this client."

"What kind of conflict?"

"I've fucked both the partners." No use sugarcoating it.

Graham blinked twice. "At the same time?"

She smirked and shook her head. "No. Several years apart. One of the partners is my former military supervisor, who I fraternized with for almost two years before I deployed to Iraq for the first time. Where I met you." She waved a hand at him. "The other partner I slept with about two weeks ago while I was on vacation."

To his credit, he didn't react to her explanation. "You know what the odds of that happening are, don't you? Two of your former…whatever you want to call them…being business partners, showing up here and hiring TLC?"

The situation did feel more than a little ridiculous. Seriously… what was the likelihood of something like that happening? "I'm buying a lottery ticket and booking my next vacation to Las Vegas kind of odds."

He grinned. "And taking me with you. If you don't want the case, pass it off to someone else."

"Who? Are you going to take it?"

He inched away from her slightly and frowned.

"That's what I thought."

"Then don't take it." He shrugged.

"I have to."

"No, you don't, Paige. The glory of working for ourselves is that we don't have to do anything we don't want to."

She perked up. "So I don't have to do the training this afternoon?"

"Except that. You still have to do that."

She twisted her mouth. "Liar. In any event, so long as the case is as straightforward as it appeared on paper, we'll accept it. I just wanted you to know about the potential conflict."

"Are you going to fuck either of them again?"

She opened and closed her mouth. She couldn't come right out and say no. Given the opportunity to fuck Ash again, she doubted she'd say no.

"You're hesitating," Graham said.

"I don't sleep with clients," she said.

"That didn't answer my question." He raised one eyebrow in that smug, taunting way she hated. Before, when he was Major Graham and not just Graham, he'd used it to intimidate those under his command. Now…

"Quit doing that—you're not the Rock."

He lifted it even higher.

"Jerk."

Grinning, he asked, "You good?"

She gave him a half smile. "Yeah." With a deep breath, Paige stood and smoothed down her skirt. "Let's get this shit done."

In the conference room, everyone was milling around the end of the table, and it looked like PJ and Ash were arguing. Someone had brought in bottles of water and a few cups of coffee.

"Sorry about that." She pasted on her professional smile. "If everyone will take a seat, we can get started."

Ash caught her eye as she walked around the table and mouthed, "Are you okay?"

Nodding tightly, she sat in the chair closest to the back wall. Even though the table was round, she considered it the head of the table. After her abrupt departure, she needed to conduct this meeting from a position of authority, and being seated at the head gave that to her. Or at least the illusion of it. Samara sat in the seat on her left and Angie took the one on her right.

She flipped open the legal-sized folder in front of her. "We have the basic information you provided when Natalie scheduled the meeting, but why don't you tell us specifically what you're looking for us to do."

Ash looked at Natalie. "Do you want to start since you found the money missing?"

"Sure. I was asked to conduct a general audit of M.A.G.'s financials several weeks before my wedding in preparation for the next stage of funding," Natalie explained. "When a company is in the start-up stage, the funding is called seed funding, and the investment is usually from friends, family, and investors who really believe in the mission of the company. The next step is Series A funding, when the company tries to pull in high-level investors in exchange for shares in the company. Series A investors usually want to see proof of concept on the company product or service before they invest. It's also usual to show Series A investors the financial status of the start-up to assure them they aren't going to be swindled out of their money."

Paige looked up from her notes and glanced at Samara. She nodded in confirmation.

"Isn't there still a possibility that investors will lose money?" Angie asked.

"Yes," Natalie replied. "But that risk is part of investing in a new company. Investors want at least the assurance that they are investing in a company in good faith. The financial records provide that."

"Who handles the day-to-day financials?" Paige asked.

"Patrick," Natalie said.

It took a moment for her to remember Patrick was PJ's first name.

"Actually, Alexis handles the financials." Patrick shifted in his seat, smoothing down his tie.

Paige caught the look Lexi flashed Patrick before slipping on a small, fake smile.

"What?" Ash's gaze darted between Patrick and Alexis.

"You weren't aware Lexi controls the money?" Paige asked.

"I don't go by Lexi anymore."

Paige looked down at her notes. "Of course not," she muttered.

Next to her, Angie coughed and reached for a bottle of water.

"And I wouldn't say I control the money," Alexis continued. "Patrick controls the money. I simply keep track of it."

"Not very well," Natalie said.

Don't laugh. Don't laugh. Don't laugh. Hoo boy, she was going to need a drink tonight.

"I'm doing the best I can." Alexis enunciated the words, her anger barely controlled. She jerked her hand away when Patrick placed his hand on hers.

Paige cleared her throat. "All right, let's get back on track. Natalie, when did you discover the money was missing?"

"The numbers weren't adding up from the very beginning. I finished my preliminary review the week before the wedding, but I honestly got sidetracked by all the preparations and decided not to look at it again until we got back from our honeymoon. I finished up the review on Sunday night and double-checked everything on Monday. I called Angie to set up the appointment and told Bash about it Tuesday night."

"Bash is…?" Paige asked.

Ash raised his hand. "Me. Short for Sebastian. Only my family calls me that—everyone else calls me Ash."

She nodded. Jesus, she needed to get everyone's legal names. "So you told Ash about it *after* you made the appointment to come here?" Paige glanced at Natalie.

Natalie nodded. "Yes. I wanted someone to look at it as soon as possible."

"I'm assuming a hold has been placed on all associated business accounts until this is resolved," Samara said.

Ash looked at Natalie, who shook her head. "I don't have access to the accounts, so I couldn't do anything."

"I'll take care of it this evening," Patrick said. "Tomorrow if the banks are closed by the time we leave here."

"Who has access to the accounts?" Paige asked.

"I can technically access the accounts," Ash said.

"What do you mean by 'technically'?" Paige asked.

"My name is on the account and theoretically I can access the money, but I never have. I'm not even sure if I have a login to the online accounts."

She looked at PJ—Patrick—and was sidetracked from her original thought to wonder what had ever attracted her to him. Yes, he was good-looking in a blond-haired, blue-eyed, All-American quarterback-next-door kind of way, but there was a softness to him she didn't remember. With his tailored suit and precise haircut, he was trying too hard to project an image of prestige and class that just didn't come across. He looked like someone who should command attention but instead seemed like a poor imitation. Maybe after spending years working with people who had nothing to prove, other than how well they could blow things up, she was no longer impressed with the illusion of confidence.

"You're the only one with access to the corporate accounts?" she asked.

"And Alexis. She has my login information," he said.

Ash's hand smacked the table. "What?"

Natalie sighed, loudly, and rested her forehead in her palm.

"What is Lex—Alexis's role in the company?" Paige asked.

"She doesn't have one," Ash said at the same time Patrick said, "She's my administrative assistant."

"Since when?" Ash asked.

"She's always helped out," Patrick said.

Paige lifted her hand from the table when Ash started to say something. Best not to let them go down a rabbit hole just yet. "Then she's on the payroll of the company? And Natalie, you're on the payroll as well?"

Patrick shifted in his chair again. "She's not on the payroll, per se—my income is her income."

Paige scribbled in her notes: *Not paying Lex*.

"I'm contracted by M.A.G. to prepare their financials for the launch of the program," Natalie said.

"What is the legal status of M.A.G. Security?" Samara asked. "Are you an LLC, a partnership?"

"Right now, we're a limited partnership," Patrick said. "We wanted to protect our individual assets in the event the company didn't prove viable."

"Can you tell us more about the company? What services or product will you provide?" Paige asked.

"Here we go," Patrick said.

Ash glared at him, then gave his undivided attention to Paige. "I wrote a security program that finds and fixes weaknesses in existing cyber infrastructure and programs. There's wide application for it in the financial and government industries."

"How does it find the weaknesses?" Angie asked.

"You've seen the movie *Wreck-It Ralph*, right?" Ash asked.

Angie nodded.

"The code basically acts as Ralph and Fix-It Felix all rolled into one. It smashes against the existing program until it finds a weakness or hole and then comes behind itself and fixes the code, closing up the gap."

Even without an IT background, Paige understood the far-reaching implications of a program designed to do what Ash said his did. "And what are your plans for the company? Will you license the program or will you hire yourselves out as a service contractor?"

"We're going to sell the program, not license it," Patrick said.

Ash frowned. "Since when?"

"It makes more sense to sell it."

"No, it doesn't," Natalie said. "You make more money licensing the software to different companies than selling it outright. You can only sell it once. You can license it thousands of times. Why do you think you have to subscribe to Adobe instead of buying programs?"

"We'll discuss it later," Patrick said through clenched teeth.

Paige flipped her pen over her fingers. Tension sat heavy between these four people, but she wasn't willing to address it right then and there. If they decided to hire TLC, she'd sit down with Natalie and Ash alone…and Patrick, although she was looking forward to that even less than being alone with Ash.

She glanced at Ash through her lashes. His dark suit jacket fit perfectly across his broad shoulders, and his open collar displayed a light dusting of dark hair she knew was crisp and springy when she ran her fingers through it. Desire swirled and pooled between her legs, and she pressed her thighs together.

Damn it. This was not the time or the place.

"All right. In order to move forward, we'll need permission to pull the financials of your business and personal accounts, including Natalie and Alexis. We'll also need to schedule interviews with everyone who has a role in the company—official or unofficial."

"All my accounts are joint," Alexis said.

"Then it won't matter." Paige pulled papers from under her notes. "These give us permission to access your accounts. These give us access to your business files, both electronic and physical—both partners will need to sign these. This is the contract hiring us to perform the investigation, which includes the fee schedule. And this is a nondisclosure agreement guaranteeing none of the employees of The Leonidas Corporation will divulge any proprietary information belonging to M.A.G. Security, unless said information violates federal or state law."

She handed the documents to Ash.

"Feel free to take them with you. Have your lawyers look over them and discuss whether you want to hire us."

"Can you give us a few minutes to discuss this privately?" Ash asked. The strain in his words made his voice low and gravelly.

"Of course. My office is around the corner to the left if you need anything else."

*A*sh waited several moments after Paige closed the door behind her, tapping his finger on the table, before looking at Patrick.

"What the hell? When were you planning to tell me you were trying to sell the program outright instead of licensing it? I never agreed to that."

"We agreed I would take care of the business aspect while you took care of the program design," he said.

"We agreed you would get investors for the business and start-up, not that you would make unilateral decisions without consulting me."

"I didn't think you wanted to deal with the licensing or contracting when it would mean having to provide updates."

"Updates and patches are easy once the program is written. This was not your decision to make."

Patrick held up his hands as though Ash needed placating. "Okay. Okay. We'll license."

"I don't think you should give them access to the accounts," Alexis said.

Ash wasn't sure why he should give a shit what she thought.

Before he could say as much, Natalie said, "Regardless of who you hire, they'll need access to the accounts and files. They need to find out what happened to the money."

"Are you sure it's even missing?" Alexis asked. "And what does it matter where it went? Sell the program, or license it, or whatever, then make the money back."

Natalie stiffened. "I'm not even sure why you're here since you're neither a partner nor an employee, but that's fraud." She looked at Ash. "I have a legal and ethical responsibility to report this to the IRS. It doesn't have to be *this* company, but you need to hire someone to look into this."

"What do we know about The Leonidas Corporation anyway?" Patrick asked.

"Seriously. Paige wasn't exactly the epitome of trustworthiness when we knew her." Alexis crossed her arms and looked toward the door.

Her disparagement of Paige angered Ash more than her contempt for Natalie. Before he could form a coherent and extremely personal retort, Natalie jumped in.

"And how long ago was that? The Leonidas Corporation has a multimillion-dollar security contract with the government of Guatemala for a major archeological site, and they rescued two military service members from a human trafficking ring a few months ago."

Even Ash had heard about that.

"That was them?" Patrick sounded impressed despite himself. Alexis looked like her usual snotty self.

Natalie nodded. "Yes. They've done other government contracts as well. Samara, the accountant who will do most of the investigation, worked for a high-profile company as a forensic accountant before moving to Leonidas. I promise I did my due diligence and looked into them."

Ash squeezed her hand. "I trust you." He turned to Patrick. "Either you sign today or you have another company lined up within twenty-four hours. Or I'll have to assume you and Alexis had something to do with the missing money."

Alexis gasped and Patrick scowled. "I'm out just as much, if not more, than you, Sebastian. You forget—I'm the face of this company. You'd still be buried in the IT department if it weren't for me."

Ash leaned forward. "And you'd still be selling life insurance if it weren't for me. This company doesn't exist without me and my code, and you know it. So sign the damn papers."

He refused to break eye contact. Refused to back down because he had a suspicion he was being taken for a fool. People thought since he got lost in code and wasn't the most social person that he was malleable and easily manipulated. Just because he liked ones and zeros more than drinks and schmoozing didn't mean he was an idiot.

Patrick snatched the papers and sifted through them.

Alexi looked at him warily. "Patrick—"

"Shut up."

She sucked in air through her teeth and glared at him but didn't say anything.

Patrick signed at the bottom of each page, then threw them and the pen across the table. "We're leaving."

Shoving his chair back so hard it hit the wall behind him, he grabbed Alexis's hand and dragged her up, leading her out of the room.

Ash sighed as the door shut behind them and looked at Natalie. "I have to ask one more time—are you sure it's not an accounting error?"

"Not on my part. I ran the numbers several times. It's possible Patrick didn't give me all the correct information, but it's not because I didn't carry the one."

Ash managed to work up a small smile at her attempt to lighten the mood. "I don't want to believe Patrick would do something like this."

"I know," she said softly. "But Alexis had access to the money, so even if he didn't do it, he handed her the means."

"Fuck." He rubbed his hands over his face and through his hair. "How did shit get so messed up? I just wanted to go into business for myself and make some money with my code instead of making someone else money."

"I know. If it makes any difference, I'm proud of you for standing up for yourself, big brother."

"Thanks."

"Want me to go get Paige?"

He dragged the papers toward him. "Sure."

Nat rubbed his back before leaving, much quieter than Patrick and Alexis had. He sifted through the documents, scanning the pages to make sure there wasn't language buried that gave TLC the right to buy an island in his name. He reached the section outlining their fee and whistled.

He should probably do some research to see if a ten-thousand-dollar retainer was industry standard, but he couldn't work up the energy at the moment. Given how much they stood to lose if it all went ass up, it seemed reasonable, especially since it included the systems audit as well.

He signed next to Patrick's signatures and stacked the pages, tapping them on the table to get them even. Glancing at the door, he decided to take the agreement to Paige instead of waiting for her to come to him.

That was a conundrum. Seeing her had been a shock—a pleasant one, but still a shock. He'd never been in this situation before and wasn't sure how he was supposed to act with her. Did they pretend it never happened? Did they treat each other as friends who'd seen each other naked, even though he knew that her skin tasted like a piña colada—a hint of coconut and salt? Could they see each other naked again? Hiring TLC might put a kink in that potential.

He glanced down at the papers in his hand. Hmm…maybe he should have considered that before signing.

At the end of the hall, he glanced around the large space and found Natalie sitting with Angie in her cubicle.

Angie noticed him approaching and smiled. "Hey. Paige is changing. They're doing tactics training this afternoon and they were short a person so she got dragged into it at the last minute."

"What's tactics training?" he asked.

"Well. Basically, they go out and shoot each other."

Natalie sat up in her chair. "What?"

Angie laughed. "Not really. They use Simunition—simulation rounds. It's kind of like paintball. Do you want to stay and watch? I usually make popcorn."

Ash looked at Natalie, who shrugged, but she had a shit-eating grin on her face. He shifted his gaze to Angie, then back to Natalie, and glared. Had they played matchmaker with him and Paige? Had there been more to this meeting than a simple coincidence and convenience?

Fuck. Was the money even missing?

No. Natalie wouldn't have made up that kind of story just to set him up with a woman. She would have found a way to do it, if this hadn't presented itself—she just took advantage of the situation.

Before he could grill them on what they were trying to accomplish, the door behind them opened and Paige walked out. She wore camouflage pants, a tan shirt that showcased every curve and had sleeves the same pattern as the pants, and her hair was pulled back in a low ponytail.

Damn, she looked sexy and badass as hell. He shifted his weight to ease the pressure against the front of his pants since he couldn't shove his hand in there and adjust his burgeoning erection.

"Hey." She looked down at herself and rocked back on the heels of her boots. "Sorry, we have training this afternoon."

"No need to apologize, Angie told us. Our appointment probably went longer than you expected." He held out the papers. "All signed."

She took them and glanced through them. "All right. I'll scan these tomorrow and send you a copy for your records. Samara will go through the information on hand and let you know what else she needs from you. We'll make arrangements to do a site visit first thing next week, if that works for you."

"Okay. I'll inform Patrick. We use a company called Work Space that rents out offices in downtown Savannah. I'll send you and Samara the address." He tried to maintain the same professionalism she was.

"PJ and Lexi left already?"

It felt odd that she used nicknames he'd never known them by. "Yes."

Her shoulders relaxed. "Well, we'll see you next week then."

He glanced at Natalie and Angie stepped forward. "Actually...I invited them to watch the training. Is that okay?"

Paige's eyes widened, and her lips formed a small *o*. "Uh. Sure. I guess. Just keep everyone in the tower."

Angie jumped up and down and clapped. "Yay!"

"Samara said she might want to watch as well," Paige said. "Can you grab her on your way out?"

"Of course."

"Thanks. I need to go down to the team room." She pulled her office door closed and strode toward the front of the building.

CHAPTER 16

*P*aige inhaled and softly blew out the breath between pursed lips. Her stomach flipped like she was on a rollercoaster instead of riding the elevator down to the basement.

She didn't enjoy doing the tactics training, but she'd never been nervous before. Of course, no one she'd had sex with had ever watched her before either. The problem was, she was good at the tactical stuff and not just "for a woman." She kept up with the men of Leonidas—she had to as one of their bosses and, until recently, as the only woman on the team. Being good at it didn't mean she enjoyed it. Didn't mean she got a thrill out of it. The thrill had worn off years ago, which was one of the reasons she wanted to focus more on the corporate aspect of the business.

Selfish? Maybe. But she'd done her time, she had her t-shirts, and she was ready to pass that particular duty off to someone younger and more eager to storm the castle. At this point in her life, she wanted to take it down from the inside.

But until that happened, she sucked it up and did the training.

Joining everyone else in the equipment room, she grabbed her vest and helmet from her locker. "We have guests watching with

Angie and Samara today, so be on your best behavior. Who has the bag?"

Graham pulled a Crown Royal sack from the back of one of the storage cabinets and gave it a shake, ensuring the poker chips were mixed well. One at a time, they reached in and grabbed a chip, dividing into red and blue teams. Paige ended up on a team with Harrison, Jayne, and Devon against Graham, Turner, Jordan, and Addison.

It was nice having another woman on the team—even if they were on opposing sides this time around. Dani only did the combatives and the occasional personal security detail, and Angie didn't do any of the training.

"Heads is towers, tails is no towers." Graham flipped a quarter in the air and caught it, slapping it onto the back of his other hand. The reveal of heads was met with a mixture of groans and excited *yeses*.

She was definitely in the groans category.

"Make your bets and put 'em in the bag," Harrison said. Everyone grabbed an envelope from the stack on the back table, wrote their name and who they thought would be the last person standing on it, and put twenty dollars inside before shoving them in the bag.

Jayne, their armorer, issued everyone their weapons and seven magazines of simulation rounds, then offered to run the betting bag up to Angie in the tower to hold onto. Trudging out to the small village they'd built on the back side of the property, where it butted up to the Ashley River, Paige tried to ignore the itch between her shoulders that indicated she was being watched.

She knew she was being watched. Angie usually watched them train, but this was different. This had weight and pressure. Like fingers tracing down her nape, making the fine hairs stand on end. Rubbing her neck to get rid of the sensation, she climbed to the top of one of the towers, making a concerted effort not to look behind her.

Harrison and Devon had carried the ropes and harnesses up to the top. Finding hers, she stepped into it and pulled it over her butt and hips, cinching it into place, wiggling and squatting to get it comfortable. Not that there was anything comfortable about having a two-inch canvas strap wrapped around her thighs.

"Don't forget to check each other's gear," she called. "Harrison, do you mind?"

"No problem." He tugged at her harness and gave her a thumbs-up, then she returned the favor.

"Well, fuck," Devon said.

"What?" she asked.

"Graham's doing an Aussie crawl."

She looked over her shoulder at the other tower where Graham was standing on the ledge of the tower, facing forward, a hand on one hip, holding the rope in the other.

"Remind me to up his company life insurance policy when we're done," she said.

Jayne appeared at the top of the stairs and looked at Paige. "Graham said he'll throw an extra two hundred in the pot if you do it Aussie-style."

"It sounds dirty when you say it like that," Harrison said.

"Of course he did." She flipped Graham off. At slightly more than a hundred and ten yards, he had no problem seeing it and threw his head back, laughing. "Fucker."

"You gonna do it?" Devon asked.

She looked at her team, their expectation evident. It wasn't about the money—they wanted to see if she would accept the challenge since they knew she was there grudgingly. "Fuck. You better make sure we win."

"Huzzah!" Devon raised a fist in the air.

"White people are crazy," Harrison said.

"Yeah, yeah. Help me with my harness," she said.

He helped her reconfigure the harness for a front-facing descent down the wall.

Standing on the edge of the platform, she stared down at the ground.

"You ever do this before?" Harrison asked from beside her.

"A couple of times. But I hate it." She looked up and flipped off Graham again.

~

*A*sh settled into the camp chair on the open top of the two-story structure. Angie and Paige had called it the observation tower, but it was decked out with a large canvas shade, a huge grill, a picnic table, and several chairs.

On the edge of the course—or battleground, whatever it was—they had a clear view of both towers on either end of the field that had a dozen or so buildings arranged like a little village between them.

"Oh, shit," Angie said.

"What?"

"Paige is going face-first." Surprise and awe lit her voice.

"Is that normal?" Samara asked.

"In general or for Paige?" Angie asked.

"Both," Samara said.

"Sometimes and definitely no. I've only ever seen her do it once before."

"Then why is she doing it now?" Ash asked.

"Well, she just flipped Graham off, and he's laughing, so he probably challenged her to do it, and Paige doesn't balk at a challenge."

Hmm. He'd have to remember that. He wasn't really sure why he needed to, but he wanted to know every fascinating aspect of this complicated woman.

A man he assumed was Graham raised his arm over his head. A few seconds later, Paige did the same.

Angie picked up a can from beside her chair. "You might want to cover your ears." She raised her hand and blared the air horn.

Graham arced over the side of the wall and raced down. Paige leaned forward and slowly arced out at the edge of the wall, then hesitated.

"I don't think she's—oh, nope. There she goes," Angie said.

Once Paige started moving, she didn't stop until her feet were under her on the ground.

"Do you ever do this?" Natalie asked.

"Me?" Angie pointed at herself. "No. I just like to watch. It's like live-action *GI Joe*."

"How long have you worked here?" Nat asked.

"Almost five years."

"Is everyone a veteran?" Ash asked.

Angie tilted her head. "Most of us are. Dani—she teaches combatives and hand-to-hand fighting techniques—and I are the only exceptions." She leaned around Natalie. "Samara, were you ever in?"

She shook her head, her tight curls bouncing. "No. This is the closest I've been to anything having to do with the military."

Angie nodded and leaned back in her seat, munching on popcorn.

"How did you end up working for TLC?" Natalie asked.

"Dani's my best friend. Her brother works for them. He's on a job out of town, which is why Paige is filling in. Dani started doing a few personal security jobs for them—special events and stuff like that. Not stuff like this." She pointed her popcorn at the team. "They needed a full-time IT person, and she recommended me. Oh. Turner's dead. Good. He deserves it."

"What?" Natalie craned her neck to see the field.

"Fake dead, not real dead," Angie said.

"How can you tell?" Samara asked.

"He laid down. If you get shot, you have to lay down where you are and play dead."

Ash watched the two teams maneuver through the course. He'd lost sight of Paige while Angie was talking.

He understood her self-confidence now. How could she not be confident? She was a real-life Black Widow. A chameleon who could go from sultry to beach babe to businesswoman to warrior in the space of hours.

"How do you know who wins?" Samara asked

"There's a flag at the base of each tower." Angie pointed out the different flags on the edge of each wall.

"It's literally capture the flag?" Natalie asked.

"Exactly. Ope, looks like Graham's team is going to win."

Ash looked at the end of the field where Paige and her team had started. Two crouching men approached the tower. One of the men flinched, kicked out a leg, and spun around to look behind him, a hand on his ass. He threw his arms up, then lay down on the ground. The other man dove behind a short stack of wood and hunched down, scanning the way they'd come.

All was quiet for several minutes. Even Angie had paused mid-chew and seemed to hold her breath, leaning forward in anticipation of what happened next. In the silence, Ash heard two short pops, and the man behind the wood stood up and pointed his rifle.

Ash couldn't hear what he was saying, but Paige emerged from the doorway of a building, hands up. She flinched and looked down, then back up.

"Ha! Graham just shot her again," Angie said.

"Why hasn't she laid down yet?" Samara asked.

"If I had to guess, she's distracting him."

"Are they…?" Natalie pointed back and forth between the two.

"Together?" Angie asked. "No. They're really close, but I don't think they've ever been romantically involved. They're more like brother and sister."

Natalie nudged Ash's foot with hers. So kind of her to look out for him.

Graham jerked and grabbed his ass, the same way the other man had, and spun around. Paige threw her head back, her laughter carrying to them in the tower.

"Who?" Angie pushed up on the arms of her chair, craning her neck.

A man emerged from the scaffolding of the tower and fired at Graham once more.

Angie fell back in her chair, laughing. The last man standing jogged across the field, jumping over a prone body as that person tried to grab at his feet. He grabbed the flag from the other tower and lifted it over his head.

Paige blew kisses at Graham as if she'd just won the Miss America pageant, then lifted her gun at him when he rushed her.

She was beautiful, smart, and badass. In a word, magnificent.

The air horn surprised him, breaking his reverie.

He looked back at the small village and Paige, high-fiving her teammates.

She was completely out of his league.

CHAPTER 17

*P*aige hopped down from Big Blue, her beat-up pickup, thankful she'd worn her rain boots when she landed in almost two inches of water. She'd parked in the front parking lot, where the oil leak she hadn't had a chance to get fixed wouldn't mar Graham's pristine garage floor and cause him to have a coronary. The storms that had rolled through the night before flooded a lot of the Low Country, and she didn't want to risk driving through low water in her Fiat Spider convertible, which was why she kept the truck.

Shoving her skirt back down her hips, she opened the back of the extended cab and grabbed her office wardrobe for the week. She clicked the fob over her shoulder to lock the truck and headed to the front of the building.

Hearing her name called, she turned and found Ash walking in her direction from a few spaces away. She hadn't noticed anyone else pull into the parking lot.

"Hey. Do we have a meeting this morning?" Had Angie scheduled something without telling her?

He fell in step with her. "No. I told Angie I'd show her my

141

program today. I also wanted to be here in case Samara had any immediate questions."

"She could have sent you an email or called you."

"I know, but I want to make sure this is handled quickly, with as much transparency as possible." He touched her elbow, drawing her to a halt. "I also wanted the chance to speak to you in person. Privately."

His low voice sent shivers racing down her spine. Under normal circumstances, she would absolutely want to continue their…connection, but now he was a client. It was never smart to get involved with people when the power dynamic was out of balance. Co-workers, employees…clients. But that wasn't a conversation to have in front of the building.

"Of course," she said. "Let's go in. I'll get you set up with Angie and Samara, and then we can talk."

"After you."

She was conscious of his eyes on her as he held the door open and followed her through the foyer.

"Morning, Senior," she said.

"Morning, Mayhem."

She shook her head at him, resigned to the fact he'd become their semi-permanent receptionist. It worked and she knew he liked being useful, even if it was mainly to greet their visitors and screen phone calls.

"Mayhem?" Ash asked.

Paige sighed. It had been too much to hope he wouldn't notice that. "It's my call sign."

"You picked Mayhem as your call sign?"

They reached her office, and she flipped on the light, hanging her clothes on the hook behind the door. "You don't pick call signs, they pick you. Or they're picked for you. Angie is probably in the break room guarding her coffee pot. Let me change shoes, and I'll walk you down there."

"Cute boots."

"Thanks." She kicked off the paisley patterned boots and slipped into her heels, making her almost as tall as Ash.

His gaze traveled from her feet, up her legs, paused briefly in the vicinity of her chest, and settled on her face. His brown eyes blazed with fierce desire, and he licked the corner of his lips as if catching the last sweet taste of a decadent dessert. Or as if he anticipated tasting her.

Her skin prickled with awareness. "We should discuss this now."

Ash blinked, almost like he was trying to break a trance, and stepped closer. It could be her imagination, but she'd swear she could feel the heat radiating off his body. Once again, he wore a crisp white shirt with the collar open. His strong pulse beat steadily at the base of his throat, and it took everything she had to not lick it. Fuck, she needed to slam the brakes on her train of thought.

"Agreed," he said.

"What?"

"We should discuss this. I'm not going to pretend I'm not insanely attracted to you or that I haven't replayed that weekend in my mind more than a few times, but I think we should keep it professional while your company is investigating mine."

Her brows pinched together. That was almost exactly what she'd been about to say, although she was going to keep the first part to herself, so why did hearing it piss her off?

"Of course."

His gaze dropped to her mouth. "Good. So we're in agreement."

He licked his lips again.

"Perfectly," she whispered. They weren't touching. Or speaking. And yet she had no doubt what he was thinking because she would guarantee she was thinking almost the exact same thing.

Ash stepped closer, the barest distance separating them. So close she could feel his soft exhalations on her lips. Her nipples puckered, remembering that same breath fanning across them after he'd licked them. Sucked them.

"I think…" he said.

"Yes?" she asked softly.

He took a small step back and inhaled sharply. "I think we should find Angie."

Paige swayed as she straightened away from him. "Right. Coffee." She smoothed her palms down her skirt, surreptitiously drying them.

He stepped aside, clearing a path to the door. She'd never been so self-conscious of a man walking behind her. Normally, she'd add a little extra sway to her step, but after that intense moment in her office, she concentrated on walking as straight as possible without her knees buckling.

They found Angie in the kitchenette, as Paige suspected. She stood in front of the coffee pot, arms crossed, glaring at Jayne, who didn't even like coffee. He just messed with it to get a rise out of Angie.

"Why Mayhem?" Ash asked.

"What?"

"Why is your call sign Mayhem?"

Shit.

Jayne laughed. "Where'd he hear that?"

Paige twisted her mouth. "Senior, on the way in."

Angie raised her hand and waved it around. "I know this one! Because on one TDY she started three different bar fights in three different bars on three different nights and almost started a war with a local biker gang."

"Her full call sign is Mistress of Mayhem, but we shorten it," Jayne said.

"Three?" Ash asked.

"I take exception to being touched."

Ash held his hands up. "I know the rules."

She glared at him and tried to ignore the sexy grin he sported. "Ange, Ash said he was going to show you his program today."

"Yes, please." She clasped her hands together under her chin and batted her eyelids, her eyes sparkling like an anime character's.

Jayne crossed his arms and glared at Angie, who was oblivious to his obvious displeasure at her response.

"Great!" Paige said. "I'll leave him with you. Can you check with Samara and ask what time she'd like to sit down with him?"

"Sure."

"All right. I'll be in my office." She spun on the balls of her feet and left the break room—without her much-needed coffee. Dammit.

~

*P*aige threw her pen on the desk and scraped her hair away from her face, clasping her hands behind her neck and resting her elbows on her desk. Even with the door closed, she could hear Ash and Angie occasionally laughing over something.

What the hell could they be laughing about? And why hadn't she demanded Angie's space be enclosed when they'd done the renovations?

She couldn't concentrate. She'd answered the same email twice in the space of an hour, then read through fourteen applications for the HR position and didn't remember a damn thing about any of the candidates, even though she'd made notes on each one.

Ash showing up that morning had thrown her for a loop and knocked her plan to use the weekend to psych herself up to see him sideways. Then he'd thrown her for another loop when *he* told *her* they should keep it strictly professional.

Their chuckles filtered through the door again.

Paige gritted her teeth. Of course they would be laughing—

they were closer in age, they shared a tech background, Angie was beautiful and fun. Hell, even their names were alliterative.

Fuck.

She was jealous.

She didn't do jealous. If a guy wasn't interested, she shrugged it off and moved on to a guy who was. She didn't get wrapped up in a guy or who he was paying attention to. She hadn't since…PJ.

That was a whole other issue.

Fucking PJ and Lexi. Or Patrick and Alexis apparently, because those names were oh-so grown up. Okay, so she'd always thought PJ was a douchey name for a grown man. It was the name of a frat guy, and it had absolutely suited him. If she'd been a betting person back then, she'd have given their marriage two years, maybe three, tops.

It wasn't that she was still hung up on him, but…it stung her pride a little to see them still together. It had taken her a long time, and most of her year in Iraq, to realize exactly how shallow and self-centered Patrick was.

And how naïve and blind she had been. Iraq had opened her eyes in so many ways, and she couldn't imagine being that same silly, ignorant girl.

Which was one reason she never gave another man power over her emotions. Her relationships were short, sweet, and to the point. Maybe not sweet in a romantic sense, but sweet in the sensual, sweaty, sexy assignation sense.

There she went with the alliterations again.

She heard another laugh and gave up. Pushing away from her desk, she stormed to her office door and yanked it open. Angie's area took up the far side of the open workspace, directly across from Paige's office.

Their heads were close together. Ash reached forward and pointed at something on one of Angie's many screens while she typed on the keyboard. He'd taken off his suit jacket, and his shirt pulled tight across his shoulders.

Paige had dug her nails into those shoulders and wrapped her legs high and tight around his waist as he drove into her with a single-mindedness she'd never experienced. She'd had good sex before, but sex with Ash had been *good*. Really good. Go-back-for-fourths good. Which she'd been tempted to do instead of sneaking out of his hotel room at the crack of dawn.

"Paige? You all right?"

She jumped, not realizing Samara had approached from the hall. "Yes. Of course."

"You sure? You look like you want to punch something. Or someone."

Shit. She needed to get control of her emotions. And her face. She pasted on a smile. "Yes. Have you had a chance to sit down with Mr. Moreno yet?"

"No. He and Angie have been hunkered over her station all morning."

Paige nodded. "Let's go see if they're at a stopping point. We try to cut out early on Fridays, and I'm sure he needs to get back to Savannah sometime this evening."

They walked over to Angie's desk. When she'd come on board with TLC, she'd requested computers and monitors with very precise specifications—none of which Paige understood, but she'd assumed they were top-of-the-line based on their cost.

"Angie?"

She turned and grinned. "Paige! Oh my god , you have to see this code. It's brilliant. I ran it against our servers which, as you know, are tight because I keep them that way, and this code still found a couple of holes. The application possibilities for this program are seriously endless. Never mind banks and government agencies, anything that keeps and stores personal information or passwords. I mean, just home computers alone. And…I'm boring you."

Paige shook her head and offered a bemused smile. "Not at all. I'm glad you're so excited about it. Are you guys at a good stopping point? Ash still needs to sit down with Samara for an interview and go over the financials. And it's Friday, so I don't want to keep anyone here longer than necessary."

Angie jumped in her seat and clapped. "Oh! It's game night!"

"That too," she said.

Angie turned to Ash. "Thank you for showing me this. It's seriously awesome, and you're going to make so much money with it."

A dark stain rose high on his cheeks. Was he blushing? Because Angie complimented his program?

"Thanks," he said. "Now we just need to market it accordingly and get the investors excited about it."

"I don't think you're going to have any problem with that. I'm going to do a quick scan of your business's host server while you're with Samara."

He shook his head. "You won't find any weaknesses."

"I'm going to look for any malware embedded in the supporting infrastructure. One downside to your program is it only looks for flaws in the defense of the primary code—it doesn't look for excess code that doesn't belong there."

Ash rubbed his chin. "I wrote the code on the assumption that anyone using this software would already be using antivirus software."

"Which is completely dependent on the IT department of the company making sure patches are up-to-date and automatically pushed. Since your website resides on someone else's servers, there's no guarantee they're doing it, so your peripherals are only as secure as the parent server."

"Yeah, that was one of the issues I had with outsourcing our office space and web hosting—being dependent on someone else's servers—but at the time, we didn't have the capital for me to build the servers the way I wanted to. It's one of those things I plan on taking care of once we get through the next stage of funding. When we have the influx of funds, we'll be able to lease our own office space, and I'll build the servers personally."

"Where do you keep the program now?" Paige asked. "On your office servers?"

He shook his head. "No. It's on my personal server at home."

"Does anyone have access to it?"

"No, I'm the only one."

"What about physically?" she asked.

"Just me."

Paige nodded. "Okay. I'll leave you with Samara for now."

He stood and looked at Samara. "I guess I'm in your hands now."

That tiny surge of jealousy flashed through Paige again. The only hands she wanted on Ash were hers.

$\mathcal{A}$sh left Samara's office as the actualization of exactly how fucked he was set in. How could he have been so clueless about what was going on with the company? He'd blindly trusted Patrick when he said he had it handled and they were in a good place.

They were not in a good place. The finances were all over the map. There were multiple expenditures with no receipts or invoices explaining what they were for. He rubbed his hands over his face. Even without the money missing, they weren't in a good place. They were close to being overdrawn, and Patrick had taken out a corporate credit card without telling him.

No wonder he wanted to sell the program outright. It was the only way to recoup and cover their losses quickly. According to the information Samara had shown him, they'd received over half a million dollars from their early investors. Now they had barely enough liquidity to see them through the next three months. That explained why Patrick constantly pushed him to finish the program. There was no telling what Patrick had promised the initial investors. Hopefully there were contracts on file in their office. There should be if the investors were legitimate. Looking at things now, there was always the possibility they weren't.

Angie's workstation was vacant and looked to be shut down. Paige's office was dark. Were he and Samara the last ones in the building? He turned to go ask her but heard a shout from the hallway.

"Oh, come on!"

He turned into a large conference room at the top of the hall. Angie and four guys he recognized from the day before were playing a first-person shooter game on one of the largest TVs he'd ever seen.

"Sorry, Jayne," Angie said.

"No, you're not."

She laughed and shook her head. "No, I'm not."

Jayne tossed his controller on the table. "I'm getting a beer." He spotted Ash. "Hey. Can I help you?"

"Hey, sorry. I was looking for Paige. Is she still around?"

"Pause!" Angie turned her chair enough to look over her shoulder. "Hey, Ash. She went to work out. She should be back up soon. You want to hang out and play?"

Ash looked around the table of guys who looked like they should be gracing the cover of a *Soldier of Fortune* magazine, then at the game on the screen. "If it's okay with everyone else."

"The more the merrier," one of the men said.

"You want a beer?" Jayne slapped him on the shoulder as he passed.

"Yeah, thanks."

"Cool. You can take my spot."

~

"What the fuck, man? How'd you know that was there?" the scary, bearded, tattooed guy with the incongruous name of Tinker asked. He'd strolled in a few minutes after Ash started playing, said, "'Sup, I'm Tinker," and grabbed a controller.

"I told you I'd played before," Ash said.

"You said you'd played before, not that you knew all the cheats," Harrison said. "This is some epic shady white boy shit right there."

"You're right. I probably should have mentioned I was a beta for this game," Ash said.

"What's a beta?" Turner asked.

"Someone who tests the game before it goes public. We make sure there are no glitches, run through the game, try to figure out all the cheats, that sort of thing."

"Mmm-hmm. Shady white boy shit." Harrison side-eyed him while taking a sip of his beer.

Ash grinned. Yeah, maybe. But this was the most fun he'd had in a while. He hadn't seriously played video games in a couple of years. This might have been the last game he'd played. It was nice to talk and shoot the shit with people over video games. It had always been easier to deal with people virtually than in person, although he hadn't had any problem interacting with this group.

Maybe it was the fact they were playing a game. Or maybe it was Angie's invitation, but they had welcomed him without any judgment. It was…fuck, it was nice. Natalie wanted him to get out more, and after the fun this evening, he might consider it. Possibly. Eventually.

"So you guys do this in real life and then come in and play first-person shooter games. You don't get enough of it out in the real world?" he asked.

"Spend a lot of downtime between missions," Tinker said. "Got to do something."

"You can only jack off so many times a day," Turner said. Ash had learned he was the company's pilot. They had a pilot. One who was not shy about sharing his sexual exploits.

Harrison lowered his controller and glared at Turner. "Seriously, dude? Why's everything got to be about sex with you?"

Turner looked at him, his eyebrows raised. "You're telling me you didn't jack off on deployment?"

Harrison twisted his mouth and turned his attention back to the game.

"That's what I thought," Turner said.

"Doesn't mean you need to share how often you spank your monkey."

"Could you all stop talking about your masturbatory practices?" Angie asked.

"What?" Turner asked. "Like you don't flick your nub?"

Angie glared at him, then turned back to the game. "Of course not," she said primly. "My vibrator does it for me."

"Oh!" Loud laughter filled the room.

This kind of banter was new to him. Especially with Angie in the room. Ash couldn't imagine talking like that around his sister. Actually, he didn't know anyone he'd trade barbs like that with.

Turner leaned forward. "Details or it didn't happen."

Across the conference table, Angie leaned in the opposite direction and wrinkled her nose. "Eww. No."

"Come on, share."

"I wouldn't piss off the person who has virtual control over your life, Sleazy," Jayne said.

Turner sat back in his chair. "Ange knows I'm joking."

"Why Sleazy?" He'd found out earlier that Tinker's name was actually Christian, and they called him Tinker because he was a mechanic and built custom motorcycles.

"Because he's a manwhore," Angie said.

"Aww, don't be jealous, Ange. All you have to do is ask."

Angie looked at him with her head tilted as if she was trying to figure something out, then a sly grin spread over her face.

Turner's eyes widened. "What? Why is she looking at me like that?"

Angie turned back to the screen, still smirking.

"Might want to change the password on your bank accounts," Tinker said.

Angie scoffed. "Like that would make a difference."

An uncomfortable silence filled the room until Tinker guffawed. "Shit, man, you'd think you'd know better than to piss off a woman."

"Every woman I leave has a smile on her face."

"That's because you don't stick around long enough to piss them off," Jayne said.

"Exactly."

Harrison looked across the table at Ash. "Ignore them. They fight like this at least once a week." His phone pinged and he looked at the screen. "I'm out. My girl's making dinner, so I got to grab something to eat."

Angie looked over her shoulder. "Why are you grabbing something to eat if your girlfriend is making dinner?"

"Because she can't cook, and I don't like to starve. Ash, great meeting you." He slapped him on the back on his way to the door. "Later, white dudes. Angie."

He left with a chorus of good-byes following him, and Ash checked his watch. "I should hit the road as well. I have to drive back to Savannah tonight."

Angie spun her chair around. "No! You should stick around and go to Finn's with us."

"What's Finn's?"

"Finnigan's Pub," Tinker said. "It's an Irish bar off Market Street. Mostly a local spot."

"They've got a great Irish band that plays on Fridays." She looked at the doorway. "Paige! Tell Ash he should come to Finn's with us."

Ash looked over his shoulder. Paige stood in the doorway wearing skinny jeans and a tight green V-neck t-shirt that, under most circumstances, would be conservative, but it molded to her, emphasizing the dip of her waist and curve of her hips. Her hair curled around her face in waves, still damp from the shower she must have taken.

"You should come to Finn's with us?"

Did she phrase it as a question because she was confused by Angie's prompt or because she didn't really want him to go?

"I can't go to an Irish bar and not drink and I have to drive back to Savannah."

"You can crash at my place," Tinker said. "I live a few blocks from the bar."

Ash blinked, trying to hide his surprise at the offer—and his pleasure. "Thanks, I appreciate the offer, but I need to be up early tomorrow. Another time."

"Yeah, man. Offer stands. Anytime."

Ash set his controller on the table and shook hands with everyone. Angie jumped up and hugged him, surprising him again, and making him promise next time he'd go to the bar with them.

He wasn't sure there would be a next time which was…disappointing. He couldn't remember the last time a group of people he wasn't related to accepted him so freely or easily. But he didn't foresee a need for him to make another trip to Charleston. Next week they'd be in Savannah. Hopefully they'd be able to figure out where the money was and then they'd be finished.

He stopped in the doorway in front of Paige. "See you on Monday at nine?"

She nodded and he caught a whiff of her perfume, some light, warm scent. It sent languid tendrils of arousal coursing down his body like soft fingers trailing across his skin. He definitely needed to get out of there.

"Bye." He turned down the hall and was halfway through the open workspace when she called to him. He turned, hope unfurling in his belly.

"I need to lock the door behind you," she said.

"Right." The small bud curled back up on itself.

He pushed on the horizontal bar, but she placed her hand on it, stopping him from opening it.

"If you're leaving because of what you said earlier about keeping things professional, you don't need to. Angie and Samara are the only ones who will be involved in the investigation, and I know they can keep things professional." She lifted a shoulder. "Well, as much as Angie keeps anything professional."

"That's not why I'm going."

She squinted. "You really have something early tomorrow?"

"Not until the afternoon."

The space between her brows twitched. "Then you should come to Finn's."

"Will you be there?"

"Yes. I usually go for a few hours."

"Then I can't go," he said.

She shook her head. "I don't understand."

He stepped closer. "Because I really want to kiss you right now. And if I go to a bar with you, I'll convince myself it's a good idea. And if I kiss you, I'm going to want to fuck you. And that wouldn't be professional."

Her gaze dropped to his mouth while he spoke, and the tip of her tongue peeked out to wet the center of her upper lip.

It was all he could do not to shove her against the door and suck it into his mouth. "Have a good night, Paige."

She swallowed hard. "You too."

He pushed through the doors and strode across the dark parking lot before he could change his mind.

CHAPTER 19

Paige walked into the bright, airy entry of Work Space, a shared coworking office in Savannah. The white-washed, exposed ducts and conduits gave the space an edgy, urban feel that said, *we're not like other offices. We're cool. We're hip. We know the four-one-one.*

"Hi! Welcome to Work Space. How can I help you?" the man behind the reception counter asked.

"Hi." She looked at the name tag on his shirt. "Kurt. I'm meeting Patrick Mills and Sebastian Moreno of M.A.G. Security."

Other than a slight twitch at the corner of his eye, his face was perfectly blank. He blinked and said nothing.

Paige raised her eyebrows slightly and stayed silent, waiting. Most people tried to fill up silence, especially when they had something to hide. For some reason, Kurt had something to hide so she waited.

"Uh...who?" he asked.

"Patrick Mills. Sebastian Moreno. M.A.G. Security."

"Right." He shuffled through some papers on the desk. "Right. They mentioned something about that. Right. Ah! Can I have you sign in here, please?"

He set a pen on the clipboard that was already on top of the chest-high counter.

"Sure. There are two other people who will be joining us shortly." She filled out her name, leaving the contact information blank.

He pushed the clipboard closer. "We need your phone number and email."

"I don't want to be added to any email lists," she said.

"Oh. This is just for accountability purposes. In case there's any kind of emergency. You know." He shrugged one shoulder.

She cocked her head. "No. How would you use this information in the event of an emergency?"

"Well, I suppose we would call to make sure you were okay."

She raised her eyebrows and pressed her lips together.

Kurt swallowed and took the clipboard from the counter. "I'm sure this will be fine."

The door behind her opened and she turned, dragging her gaze away from Kurt. Samara and Angie entered, followed closely by Ash.

Paige froze and held her breath for a heartbeat. Why was her reaction to the first sight of him so visceral? What little sleep she'd managed over the weekend, after his parting shot on Friday, had been filled with erotic dreams of the two of them. More than once, she'd considered throwing her rules out the window and calling him to let him know he needed to find another company, because there was no way she would be able to stay professional except...her damn professionalism wouldn't let her. They needed to wrap this up quickly.

"Morning," she said.

"Hey." His voice was low and she didn't know if he meant it to be intimate, but it was.

Angie held two large tumblers. "Ange, how many coffees do you need?"

Angie looked down at the cups. "I wasn't sure what kind of setup they'd have here, so I came prepared."

Paige smiled and nodded. "Morning, Samara."

"Morning." She looked between the three of them. "Should we get started?"

"Yeah. Follow me." Ash pointed past the reception counter and led the way.

Paige took up the rear and looked back over her shoulder. Kurt's thumbs flew across his phone screen.

Picking up her pace to catch up with Angie, she leaned closer to whisper, "Look into the guy at the counter when you have a chance. His first name is Kurt."

"Frat boy name. Bound to be douchey," Angie said.

"That and he started acting weird when I said I was here to meet Ash and Patrick," Paige said.

"On it."

Ash unlocked a door about halfway down the corridor.

"Is the door always locked?" Paige looked around the small office. Two modular desks took up most of the space, and a small round table sat in the other half of the room.

"As far as I know, if no one is here, it's locked," he said. "I'm honestly not here that often. Patrick uses the space to meet potential investors and hold meetings. I show up whenever someone wants to meet the program designer."

"Why rent a permanent space when you hardly ever use it instead of renting an office as needed?" Samara asked.

"I asked the same thing. Patrick said it would be better to have the space and not need it than need the space and get stuck with something that didn't convey the 'message' we're trying to send."

"What message is that?" Angie asked.

He shrugged. "Damned if I know."

"What do you do the rest of the time? When you aren't here or working on the program?" Paige asked for purely professional reasons having only to do with the investigation.

"Three days a week, I volunteer at a local middle school, teaching an after-school program. The rest of the time, I work from home."

"And you can afford to do that?" Samara asked.

He grabbed the back of his neck. "I had about a year's worth of income saved up before I stopped working full-time. Both Patrick and I take a small salary from the initial investment. I still do freelance programming and I've designed a few apps, so I get a little bit of income from that. And I rent out the upstairs apartment of my house, which covers almost my entire mortgage."

He gave them a sheepish smile. "And I don't have a social life, so the only thing I ever spend money on is food delivery."

"What about your partner and his wife?" Samara asked.

"They have a much more active social life," he said.

Angie grinned.

"What do they do for income?" Samara asked.

"Aside from what we pay ourselves, I have no idea."

Paige sat in one of the chairs around the table. "How did you guys meet?" She couldn't imagine they ran in the same social circles. Mostly because Ash wasn't artificial enough to know the type of people Patrick and Alexis probably made friends with.

Ash settled in the chair facing her, crossing one leg over the other knee. "We worked at the same brokerage company for about two years. I was in the IT department, and one day I was fixing his computer for the umpteenth time, complaining that the company wouldn't let me push the fixes I wanted to make the systems more effective. I told him about the program I was working on, and he made an offhand comment that I should go into business for myself.

"I didn't think too much of it, but a couple of weeks later, he approached me and said he couldn't get my idea out of his head. He said he had a buddy who was a tech investor and asked if I'd be interested in going into business with him. I looked over his proposal and agreed to do it on the condition the company be split sixty/forty."

Paige rubbed the spot between her eyebrows. "You agreed to go into business with a guy you barely knew with an investment from someone you didn't know at all?"

"Of course not. I insisted on meeting his friend."

Paige nodded. At least he'd done that much.

"Then I hacked both of them," he said.

Samara coughed and dribbled coffee back into her cup. Angie threw her head back and laughed.

"You…what?" Paige asked.

"Personal and work emails, social media, finances." Ash shrugged. "I hacked their lives."

There were probably felonies involved in that. "And?" she asked warily.

"Forsyth, the investor, was clean. He had some rather risky investments, but since we were one of those risky investments, I wasn't going to complain."

"And P—Patrick? What about him?"

"His debt-to-income ratio wasn't the greatest, but pretty average for a white male in his late thirties."

"What about his wife?" Samara asked.

"Alexis's name was on all his accounts, so I didn't bother looking into her. And, at the time, I didn't realize she would be as involved in the company as she has been."

"I'll look into her today," Samara said.

Paige nodded. "What about business files? Are there hard copies? Are they all digital?"

A dark blush spread across his cheeks. "I don't know. I realize now I was an idiot to trust that Patrick had everything handled. Especially after going over the financials with Samara last week. In my defense, his business plan was solid, and he was more than forthcoming with information in the beginning. It was stupid to get complacent."

"Not stupid!" Angie said.

"Trusting," Paige said.

One side of his mouth twisted up. "Isn't that the same thing?"

"No. Trusting means you expect people to be honest and to do the right thing because that's what you would do," Paige said.

"Po-tae-toe, po-tah-toe."

Paige tried for a reassuring smile, but wasn't sure she managed to pull it off, judging by his continued frown. More than anyone, she knew how easy it was to trust Patrick. To be pulled in by his charismatic charm and snake-oil-salesman bullshit. She couldn't fault Ash for falling for it the same way she had. She only hoped he learned his lesson faster than she had.

He braced his hands on his knees and pushed up. "Anyway, any hard copy files should be here in the two-drawer filing cabinet. One of the side benefits of renting this space—we used it as our business address and received our mail here. Everything else should be saved to the cloud."

"I'll download what's available," Angie said.

"I'm going to set up in the main room, but let me know if you need anything and I'll try to help," he offered.

"What time are they supposed to be here?" Samara asked. "I still need to sit down with the both of them."

"I told them you'd be here at nine," Ash said.

Paige checked her watch. Nine thirty. "Let's go through what files we have on hand."

"Sure." Angie walked around the desk and pulled open a drawer. "This is a mess."

Paige walked over to the desk. Hanging files overstuffed with papers filled the drawer from front to back. Angie closed it and pulled open the top drawer, revealing a stack of more documents.

Paige stared down at the disordered filing system. "Angie, can I have one of your coffees?"

$\sim$

They spent the morning sorting through the papers in the cabinet, stacking them into different categories for Angie to scan later. With only a short break for lunch, they were all tapped out by early afternoon.

Paige was ready to call it a day when Ash entered the office, a worn leather satchel across his shoulders.

"Hey," he said. "How's it going?"

"Okay," Angie said. "Although I wasn't able to find a lot on the cloud for the past twelve to fifteen months. The record-keeping was great for the first four months and then tapered off until there was almost nothing. The only files that were saved consistently were the bills for the rent on this office and receipts for expenditures, and I think those were saved directly after being scanned."

"Patrick complained about what a pain it was to scan and save all receipts he was claiming," Ash said. "So I had him download an app that saved any receipts he scanned directly to our cloud. All he had to do was point his camera at it."

"At least he was consistent with that," Angie said. "There were receipts as recent as a week ago."

"Are you guys going to be much longer?"

"Please god , no," Angie said.

Paige smiled. "I think we can call it a day. There's not much left to go through, and we can do that tomorrow."

"Got a hot date?" Angie asked.

Ash ducked his head as a dark red blush crept up his neck.

Paige froze. Was it a date? Yes, they'd said they would keep it professional, but that was only three days ago.

"Not unless you call a dozen twelve- to fourteen-year-olds a date," he said.

The tension eased out of Paige's shoulders. "Is this the after-school program you volunteer with?"

He nodded. "I teach coding at one of the underprivileged schools."

"That's really cool," Samara said.

He ran his hand up and down the strap of his bag and stared at something in the middle distance. "Would any of you be willing to come with me?"

"Why?" Angie asked.

"There aren't a lot of girls in the group, and the few that are keep talking about dropping out. I've already lost two in the last month. It's really discouraging because they don't see any women doing the work they could do. I thought if they could see one of you…" He shrugged.

"They would see a positive female role model," Samara said.

"Yeah."

"I'll go," Samara said. "I don't know anything about coding, but I can talk about math."

"I'm definitely in," Angie said. "I didn't have the most legal start to computer programming, so I am a great role model."

"Maybe leave that part out," Ash said.

She turned to Paige. "You coming? I mean, if anyone's a positive female role model, it's you."

Samara's expression was expectant, and Paige thought back to her words during their first meeting. "Sure. I don't know how much I have to offer since I know absolutely nothing about coding."

"You're the COO of a security company—I'm sure you can find something to talk about. They'd probably get a kick out of learning you boss a bunch of guys around. Or you can talk about your time in the Air Force and your time in Iraq," Angie said.

She'd probably leave that part out. She didn't talk to too many people about her time in Iraq. It didn't make for the politest dinner conversation.

sh told them the name of the school so they could pull up the directions on their map app. They parked their cars in the teacher's lot and helped Ash unload several plastic bins full of laptops from the trunk of his car. Paige calculated the cost of the equipment. Even if they were basic laptops, it was at least four thousand dollars' worth of computers in the trunk of his car. After signing in at the front office and getting visitor passes, they followed him to the classroom.

It was depressing. The walls were a bare, institutional gray, the desks chipped and dented, and there was a gouge across the whiteboard at the front of the class. She couldn't imagine having to come to a place like this and then trying to actually learn something.

"Yo, Mr. A." Each kid who walked through the doors gave Ash a high five or a fist bump before going to a desk. "Who're the hotties?"

Paige couldn't help but laugh when the gangly boy, who'd obviously grown faster than his brain could control his appendages, asked the question.

"These are colleagues of mine, Daniel. Be respectful."

A dark blush stained the boy's cheeks. "Sorry, Mr. A."

As Ash waited for the kids to take their seats and for the conversations to quiet down, Paige counted just three girls.

"As you can see," Ash announced, "we have guests today. I asked them to come to speak to you about women in STEM."

"You're all scientists?" a dark-haired girl in the back asked.

"I'm a computer programmer," Angie said.

"This is Angie," Ash said. "Like she said, she's a computer programmer, like me. This is Samara."

She raised her hand and waved.

"She's a forensic accountant," he continued.

"What's a forensic accountant?" a thin boy in the back asked.

"That's like when you get murdered with numbers," another boy said.

His comment elicited some laughter.

"Well, you're not too far off," Samara said. "In much the same way a forensic scientist looks at clues to figure out who committed a crime, I look at numbers to figure out who's stealing money."

"That's so cool," another girl said.

"What do you do?" the third girl asked.

"I'm the Chief Operations Officer of a private security firm," Paige answered.

A hand went up. "What's that mean?"

"It means she's our boss," Samara said.

"And she runs our company, which, other than the five of us who are women, is all men," Angie said.

Two of the girls looked at each other, eyebrows raised like they were impressed.

"Who has questions?" Ash asked.

Every single hand in the room went up.

❧

"I promise, if you email me, I will respond. I don't give my business card out to just anyone," Paige said.

She'd ended up talking about her time in the Air Force but kept it to her vanilla assignments. While all the kids had been interested in what the three of them did, it was the girls who had the most questions. She'd never considered herself a mentor, but the girls were bright, inquisitive, and intelligent. They'd asked smart questions, and she could tell they were all driven. Some ideas were forming that she wanted to talk over with Samara and Angie.

"Thanks, Ms. Paige." The girl looked down at the card in her hands.

"You're welcome, Aliyah."

"Will you come back on Wednesday?" Maria asked.

"I'm not sure what our schedule looks like for the rest of the week, but we'll try," Paige said.

None of the kids wanted to leave, but Ash eventually shooed them all out with promises to try to bring Angie, Samara, and Paige back later in the week.

"Wow," Samara said once all the kids were gone. "You do this three times a week?"

"Yeah," Ash said. "Outside of programming, it's one of the few things I really enjoy doing. I mean, I'm still doing programming, but I'm teaching it to other people."

"I'm kind of hungry," Angie said. "Do you guys want to grab dinner before we head back to the hotel?"

"I could eat," Samara said.

Paige shrugged. "Sure." She hadn't given much thought to what to do for dinner.

"There's a great local seafood place close to the river you guys should try," Ash said.

"That sounds great," Angie said. "You're coming, right?"

"Oh. Uh." He glanced at Paige.

She glared at Angie, who returned a blank stare and polite half-smile. It would be rude not to invite him at this point, but she didn't trust Angie's motives. "You should come."

"If you're sure," he said.

"I'm sure."

~

*P*aige glanced at the time on her phone. Angie and Samara should have joined them by now—they'd pulled out of the school parking lot right behind her.

"They aren't coming, are they?" Ash asked.

"I think we've been set up." As if on cue, her phone dinged, and she looked at the screen. "With no surprise to anyone, something came up and they can't join us."

He stood. "We don't have to stay."

"It's fine. We're here and now I'm craving seafood."

"If you're sure..."

She wasn't, but walking out of the restaurant just because Angie and Samara bailed smacked of cowardice. "I'm sure. Let's eat."

They asked for a table for two and were seated quickly on the outdoor patio with views of the river.

Paige snuck glances of Ash over the top of the menu. A lock of hair had fallen over his forehead, giving him an even more boyish look.

Focus, Davis. Food, not sex.

The menu was similar to several restaurants in Charleston, so choosing her meal took no time at all.

"Hi, I'm Kayleigh. Can I start you folks off with a drink?" The server smiled expectantly.

They both ordered water and boil pots—shrimp for him and crab for her.

"Why did you wrinkle your nose when she mentioned peel-and-eat shrimp as an appetizer?" Ash asked.

Paige laced her fingers together on the table. "Do you know what happens to cooked shrimp when it sits in water? It turns to paste."

"I'm guessing you found that out the hard way?"

"Yes. When I was around fourteen, my parents took me to some fancy event that had a chilled seafood buffet. They came back with a plate of shrimp. I peeled one and put it in my mouth and it squished."

Even the memory made her want to gag. "My mom saw the look on my face and grabbed a bunch of cocktail napkins and held them under my mouth and said, 'Spit it out!'" She cupped her hands together to reenact her mom's actions. "I haven't eaten cold shrimp since."

"I don't like raw oysters," he said. "It's like eating a loogie someone hocked in your mouth."

She scrunched up her nose again and laughed. "I'm with you there. What about fried oysters?"

"Those are okay."

Kayleigh returned with their waters. "Here you go."

"Thanks," Ash said.

Paige raised her glass. "Here's to fried oysters and hot shrimp."

Ash clinked his glass against hers. "Hear, hear."

He set his glass down. "Thank you again for coming this afternoon."

"You're welcome. I wasn't sure what to expect, but I had fun."

She had enjoyed their time at the school. More than anything, she'd enjoyed watching him interact with the kids. He'd been in his element with them, relaxed and relatable but also clearly in charge. He'd joked easily but put them back on task when he needed to. It was a completely different side of him than she'd seen before.

"How long have you been volunteering at the school?"

"About two years. It started as an outreach program with the company I worked for. One of those *we give back to the community* kind of things to make the company look good and give them a tax write-off. It was only supposed to be a few weeks, but I really enjoyed it. And the kids enjoyed it, so I worked with the school to be able to continue the program even after the company's sponsorship ended."

"I think that's great," she said. "I used to tutor kids as part of a volunteer program when I was in the Air Force, mostly English. Some math, but I wasn't much use to them beyond college algebra."

"How long were you in the Air Force?"

"Twelve years." She braced for the usual questions.

"Wow. Did you like it?"

Paige cocked her head. That wasn't one of the usual questions. "For the most part, I did. I think it was probably like most jobs—there are some good things and some bad things."

"What were the good things?"

He continued to surprise her. Most people went right to the macabre. "I got to travel. I made some really good friends, like Denise and Bree. I got to do things I never would have done if I hadn't joined."

"Well, even if it was the worst job in the world, some good came from it."

She smiled. That was sweet. And yeah, even with all the shit she went through and experienced, she came out stronger.

CHAPTER 21

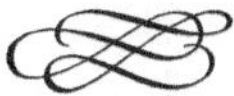

Paige rubbed the heels of her hands across her brow and yawned, side-eyeing the last pile of papers. They'd spent all morning scanning the paperwork they'd sorted the day before. Angie had set up in one of the daily office spaces to continue her deep dive into M.A.G.'s files. And the lives of Patrick, Alexis, and Ash. She'd been avoiding Paige all day after ditching her at dinner last night. Ash hadn't been in yet either, but she didn't think he was avoiding her.

Dinner had been nice. They'd talked about the different places they'd lived and funny things that had happened to them growing up. It had been comfortable, and they'd lingered long after the last plate had been cleared away. She couldn't remember the last time she'd been on a date—and realistically, that was what last night turned out to be, even without a goodnight kiss—and felt no pressure from the guy.

Samara's phone rang and she looked at the screen before answering. "Hey." She glanced at Paige. "Hang on." Stepping out of the office, she said, "I can't. I'm at work."

Paige tried to respect Samara's privacy, but it was hard not to overhear the conversation.

"This is only my second week at work. I'm in Savannah. It would be bad enough for me to ask to leave early, but I'd have to leave now to make it there in time. What about Mom? Patty? Shit."

Pushing away from the table, Paige leaned around the office door. "Samara? Go take care of whatever you need to."

Samara turned, tears in her eyes. Paige waved her back into the small office and closed the door.

Resting the phone against her chest, Samara said, "I'm sorry. My sister's childcare fell through, and she needs someone to pick up my niece and nephew from their after-school care. My brother-in-law usually does it, but he picked up extra shifts at work and—"

Paige grabbed her by the shoulders. "It's fine. Go. One afternoon isn't going to make or break this."

"The thing is…it would be all week, and we're supposed to be here at least through Wednesday."

"Can you go through the financials from the TLC office?" Paige asked.

She nodded. "Yes."

"Then you don't need to be here. We can set up the teleconference to coordinate and go over the info."

"Are you sure?"

"Yes. Family first."

"Thank you. Thank you." She threw her arms around Paige and hugged her tightly.

Paige squeaked in surprise at the strength of the hug before Samara released her.

"Sorry. I need to…." Samara pointed at her purse.

"Yup."

Samara grabbed her purse and travel mug, then rushed out the door.

Paige returned to her seat, rolled her neck, and heaved a sigh. That stack of papers wasn't going to sort itself.

The door clicked and she looked up.

"Hello, Paige."

Patrick stood against the shut door.

"Patrick." She leaned back in her chair and made a show of looking at her watch. "Weren't you supposed to be here yesterday?"

"I had to take care of some things." He stepped forward, crossing the small space between them.

"Hmm. Well, we managed to find the files, which was all we needed you for this morning. I would have had you sit down with our CFO, but she had to take care of some family business."

"I wanted to see you." He sat in the chair next to hers and scooted even closer. "Alone."

"Why?" She tilted her head and scanned his face. What she really searched for was an inkling of what she had once felt for him. Those words used to send a thrill through her. Used to convince her that he cared as deeply for her as she did for him. Except when he'd said "alone" back then, he'd meant he didn't want anyone to see them together.

She'd bet a shiny nickel that he meant the same now.

He laughed. A low rumble she'd once loved. Now she heard the artifice. The forced cadence.

"Same old Paige."

That didn't merit a response. She was nowhere near the same person she was the last time she'd seen him.

"What do you want, Patrick? If it doesn't have anything to do with TLC's investigation into the missing money, there's really no reason for us to talk."

"Have dinner with me."

Very clearly, she said, "If you and Alexis want to discuss the investigation over dinner, sure. Let me know what time works for you both."

He grabbed her hand and clasped it between his. "I've missed you, Paige. You don't know what it was like, worrying about you all these years. You left without saying good-bye. I didn't even know you'd deployed to Iraq until Carrie mentioned it to Lexi."

"Alexis." She pulled her hand back, but his grip tightened.

"I didn't know what happened to you. I didn't know if you were dead or alive. All this time there's been a hole in my heart. One you left."

She tugged harder, finally freeing herself. "A hole I'm sure your *wife* was only too willing to shovel dirt into."

"She's cheating on me. Has been from the beginning. She only married me for the prestige of marrying an officer."

And you married her to have a trophy wife. "That's not my concern—I'm not a marriage counselor."

He fell to his knees in front of her.

Paige reared back and held her hands up. What the hell?

"It's you, Paige. It's always been you. Seeing you now...after all these years..." His gaze roamed her body from chin to knee, hovering the longest over her chest. "I know it now more than ever. It was always supposed to be you."

She pushed her chair away from him and stood.

"Look, Patrick, I don't know what you're on or what you've been drinking, but this is inappropriate. Even ignoring the fact that you're married, I am investigating how more than $150,000 went missing from your company."

He stood, reaching forward to pull her into his embrace. "None of that matters. All that matters is how I feel. How we feel. I know you still have feelings for me."

Nauseated was a feeling.

Before she could break his hold and drive her knee up into his babymaker, he jerked away from her, yanked from behind, and she braced her hand on the table to keep from falling.

Ash punched him in the face, knocking Patrick against the desk behind him.

Paige stared at Ash. He stood, feet braced apart, fists clenched at his sides, his chest heaving. Surprised by his actions—she would not have guessed physical confrontation would be his first reaction—she was also really, really turned on. She spent too much time around dominant men not to find overt displays of possessive maleness attractive. Especially when those displays were exhibited by men who didn't normally display possessive tendencies.

He turned and glared at her, no small amount of disgust in his eyes, before stepping over Patrick's leg and storming out of the office.

Wait. What? What the hell was he disgusted with her for?

"He broke my nose."

Paige looked at Patrick, still leaning against the desk but now looking at the blood on his hand. "Good. You deserved it. Put your hands on me again, and I'll break more than your nose."

Angie appeared in the doorway and looked at Patrick, then Paige. "What…happened?"

"Mr. Greene learned the hard way not to put his hands on a woman without her permission," Paige said.

"Did you—?"

She shook her head. "Ash. Is he out there?"

"No. He left."

"Son of— Do me a favor? Gather up all the paperwork—we'll finish going through it tomorrow." She snagged her tote from the edge of the desk and rushed past Angie, jogging to the front of the building as fast as she could in her heels and her tight, knee-length skirt. Pushing through the front door, she scanned the parking lot for Ash or a car leaving.

"Damn it."

She growled low in her throat and reentered the building. If he thought he was going to defend her honor and then blame her for it and storm off, he had another think coming.

Angie sat in front of her laptop in the main coworking space. Paige had no desire to check on Patrick in the office.

"Angie, please tell me you have Ash's home address," she said.

"I do… What are you going to do?"

"I'm going to calmly lose my shit, call him an asshole, and probably hit him."

"Oh. Okay." Angie pulled out her phone and typed on it. "I texted it to you."

Her phone pinged in her purse. "Thanks."

"Use protection." Angie's singsong advice was low but still loud enough for Paige to hear as she stalked away.

She flipped her off over her shoulder.

"Hostile work environment!"

"We shoot people—of course it's hostile." Her response drew more than a few wide-eyed looks…and Angie's laughter as Paige pushed open the door and exited the building.

~

*A*sh tossed the beer cap in the garbage can and took the bottle into the living room, collapsing onto the couch and kicking his feet up on the ottoman. He should get a dog. A dog that would climb up on the couch and rest his head in his lap and stare up at him with soulful brown eyes while Ash wallowed in his self-pity.

The picture of Patrick and Paige wouldn't get out of his mind, no matter how hard he tried to remove it. He'd gone from red-hot rage, to anger, to disappointment, to…this miserable feeling eating at his gut.

It made sense that Paige was more interested in Patrick than him. Patrick was everything Ash wasn't. Outgoing, he never had trouble knowing what to say, he never met a person who didn't immediately like him—especially women.

He had his suspicions that Patrick and Alexis weren't faithful to each other, but it wasn't his business, so he stayed out of it. But Paige…that surprised him. He wouldn't have thought she'd go for a married man, but maybe it was because of their past.

Maybe she still had a thing for Patrick and was taking her chance.

The front door opened and slammed closed. Shit. Had Angie or Paige called Natalie?

"I don't want to hear it."

Paige appeared in the archway of the living room. "Too fucking bad."

He jerked his feet off the ottoman and sat up straight. "What are you doing here?"

"Really? You punch your business partner, look at *me* like I did something wrong, and don't think I'm going to follow you when you storm off?"

He stood and set his beer on the end table. "Look, I know I shouldn't have punched him—"

"I don't give a shit that you punched him. You saved me from breaking a nail. What I care about is you looking at me with disgust."

"I didn't—"

"You did." She tossed her bag on the chair. "What the fuck, Ash?"

"I didn't— I didn't like seeing you with him. Especially after we agreed to keep it professional." Fuck. "Especially after dinner last night." He turned his back to her, unable to look at her while she rejected him.

Something soft hit him in the back of the head. "What the—?" He spun around and looked down, finding one of the decorative pillows Natalie insisted he needed at his feet. "Did you just throw that at me?"

"You're lucky I didn't find something harder to throw to knock some fucking sense into you!" She snagged a paperback from the table next to the chair and threw it at him, missing his head by inches only because he dodged.

Rushing forward before she could find something else to launch in his direction, he wrapped his arms around her, trapping hers by her side. Having seen her rush face-first down a wall, he should have known that was a bad idea. She twisted her arms, then her body, and he was flat on his back with Paige's knees on his shoulders before he knew what had happened.

She hovered over him, her hair framing her face in loose waves, her eyes blazing with gold fire.

"Fuck, you're beautiful."

That may have been the wrong thing to say. She screamed through clenched teeth. Shifting her weight, she punched him in the pocket of his shoulder. He knew it was the wrong thing to say when she tried to stand.

It might take him a few times, but he eventually learned his lesson. He wasn't done learning this one, so he switched their positions, tackling her to her back and trapping her legs between his. Grabbing her wrists, he rested his upper body weight on his elbows, then tucked his face into her neck.

"You smell good too."

She turned her head away. "Let me up."

The quiet sadness worried him more than her anger. Lifting his head, he searched her face—the side he could see, anyway.

"No," he said.

She jerked her head back to glare at him. "Let me up."

"Tell me why you're here."

"I'm here because you're an asshole." She jerked on her hands.

No doubt she'd make him get off her if she wanted to, which meant she didn't really want to hurt him.

"Because I punched Patrick?"

"No."

A clearer picture of what might have actually happened was forming, but he needed the specifics. It wouldn't be the first time he'd misjudged a situation, and yeah…it made him an asshole.

"Because of how I looked at you after I punched him."

"Yes. Now get off me."

He dropped his head to her neck again and pressed his lips to her jawline. "I'm sorry, Paige. I saw you together and I assumed the worst. It made me… I reacted. Poorly."

"It made you what?"

Figured she wouldn't let that go. "It made me angry. Jealous." He took a shallow breath. "Hurt."

"I didn't want him to touch me. He'd just grabbed me when you pulled him away. I didn't have a chance to knee him in the balls."

He smiled against her neck. "I'm sorry."

All the tension left her body. "I think you should hire another company."

He jerked his head up. "What? Why?"

"Because I don't lose control of my emotions like this. Because it's unprofessional and because…I don't want to keep things professional with you." The anger was gone from her eyes, but they still shone golden.

"Paige."

"Fire me," she whispered.

"No."

"Then I quit."

His lips twitched. "No."

He lowered his mouth to hers, hovering, barely touching, waiting to see if she would pull away or demand he fire her again or punch him.

She did none of those things, so he pressed his lips more firmly against hers. She opened her mouth with a sigh, her tongue sliding against his as she angled her head. He released her hands and cradled the side of her face.

Her legs shifted restlessly under him and she groaned.

"What's wrong?" he asked.

"I can't move my legs in this stupid skirt."

He rolled to the side and slid his hand under the hem, inching the skirt up her thigh. "I love this skirt. I love all your skirts. The way they hug your ass and show off your legs. Your skirts are perfect."

"Not when I want to wrap my legs around your hips, they're not."

He grinned. "No, I suppose not."

"Ash?"

"Yes?"

"Do you have a bed?"

He looked up from watching his hand slide up her thigh and hip. "I do."

"Is it comfortable?"

"Yes."

"Hmm. Can we move there? Because the floor is killing my back."

"Let's go." Smoothing her skirt down, he stood and pulled her up. He tucked a loose strand of hair behind her ear and leaned down to kiss her. What was supposed to be a quick brush of the lips deepened. It was soft. And hot. Their tongues sensuously tangled together.

Paige took a step away and he followed.

She backed toward the hall, and he turned her in the direction of his bedroom, making sure she didn't hit the wall. Kissing and touching the whole way, they slipped buttons through holes, slid down zippers, and kicked off shoes, leaving a trail of clothing as they went.

By the time they reached his bedroom, he'd unhooked the clasp of her bra and slid it down her arms, skimming his fingers over her soft skin. Stopping at the foot of his bed, he tongued her stiff nipple, then sucked it into his mouth.

Her fingers fisted in his hair, and she moaned, the ends of her hair tickling his fingers as her head fell back.

He grabbed the back of her thighs and picked her up, climbing onto the bed and walking up on his knees until he could lay her on the pillows.

"Take these off." She eased the waistband of his boxers down his hips.

Ash rolled to his back to kick them off, and Paige took advantage, straddling his hips, grinding her hot, wet pussy along his shaft.

"Fuck," he whispered. He splayed his hand over her hips, up her sides, and back around to cup her breasts. He couldn't get enough of her. He wanted to memorize every dip and curve, every mole and freckle.

She rested her hands on his chest and rolled her hips. "You have condoms, right?"

"Nightstand." He tilted his head to the right. "Top drawer."

She leaned forward and yanked open the drawer, coming back with a foil square.

"You should check the expiration date," he said.

She stilled and glanced at him before tilting the foil toward the light. She grinned. "We're good."

"Thank god ."

Sliding down his thighs, she tore open the packet and rolled the condom on. Then she rose onto her knees, hovering over him while he held his dick up, poised at her entrance.

She sucked her lower lip in her mouth as she slid slowly down. Her tight channel enveloped him, and his fingers flexed on her hips in an effort not to slam her down.

Finally, after deliciously torturous seconds, she was seated fully. She stared at him through lowered eyelashes, making it impossible to tell what she was thinking.

This moment felt different than the times they'd fucked in St. John. It felt…important. Momentous. It was more than sex, and he needed to see her eyes.

Sitting up, he slid his arms under hers, pressing them chest to chest, and grasped the sides of her face.

She wrapped one arm around his shoulders and rested the

palm of her other hand on the side of his face, running her thumb back and forth over his cheek.

Kissing along her jaw and down her neck, he rolled his hips up. Her soft sigh feathered across his ear.

They set a slow, easy pace. Retreating and surging in unison. Kissing and licking. Nipping between whispering dirty words to each other. When his orgasm gathered strength and he knew he was close, he took her hand and moved it between them, placing her fingers on her clit.

Instead of getting herself there, she grabbed his thumb and rubbed it back and forth, using him to get herself off. As soon as he felt the first ripples of her orgasm, he lost hold of his own. He fell back on the bed and dug his heels into the mattress, driving his hips up while Paige ground down.

As the last waves of pleasure faded, he sat up again and wrapped his arms around her. Paige held him tightly and buried her face in his neck.

He'd been right. It was momentous. And he was completely screwed.

CHAPTER 22

"I still think you should hire a different company."

Paige felt, more than saw, Ash look at her. She'd been lazily tracing circles over his stomach while they cuddled after the most mind-blowing sex she'd had in a very long time. And despite the warnings she'd given herself, it had been more than sex.

They'd made love.

She wouldn't say she was in love with Ash, but if she wasn't careful, she'd get there. She could already feel herself sliding down that slippery, slimy slope, and she didn't know what was worse—that she was sliding or that she didn't want to stop.

"What would you do if you found out I was somehow involved with the missing money?" he asked.

"I'd notify your business partner and the police, and have Samara file whatever report she needed to with the IRS."

"So you wouldn't try to hide it or cover it up because we're sleeping together?"

She frowned. "Of course not."

He shifted under her. "That's why I'm not worried about hiring someone else."

She slid her head back to look at him. "There's more to it than that. If Patrick or Alexis are involved, they can claim I tried to cover up your involvement based on favoritism, even if I didn't."

"Then they won't find out we're together."

"Kind of hard to hide that after you punched Patrick and I tore out after you," she said.

"You tore out after me?"

Amusement tinged his voice. Which did not amuse her. "I was angry."

"I realized that when I took a pillow to the back of the head and almost took a book to the face."

He flinched when she poked him between the ribs. Going on the offensive, he rolled her over, trapping her arms against his chest and kissing the hollow of her throat.

"Will you tell me about you and Patrick?" he asked.

Paige stared up at the ceiling. "There isn't that much to tell."

"Will you tell me anyway?"

Did she really want to tell the guy she was currently naked with about the guy she used to get naked with? Not really, but he probably deserved to know. She took a deep breath.

"Sure."

He lifted his head. "Really?"

"Yes. But not while you're looking at me."

"Why can't I look at you?"

"It's kind of like when someone goes to confession. I don't want to see you judging me."

"Are you Catholic?"

"Pfft. No. But I understand admitting your sins to a void."

He lay back down and even covered his eyes with his other hand. "Okay. I'm not looking. Or judging."

"Like I said, there isn't much to tell. He was my OIC—"

"What's that?"

Oh yeah. He'd never been in the military. "Officer in Charge. He was my boss. There was a group of us that always went out and partied together. Him, Lexi, me, and a few other people. He shared a house downtown with a few other guys we hung out with. One night I drank more than I intended to and was going to crash on their couch. One of his roommates was making out with a girl he'd brought home from the bar, and things were getting… uncomfortable since they wouldn't take it upstairs. Patrick said I could crash in his room until they were done. One thing led to another, and we ended up having sex."

She checked to make sure Ash's eyes were still covered.

"Then things kept leading to other things, and we were in a relationship. At least, I thought it was a relationship, even though we had to keep it secret because he was my boss. And an officer."

"How did he and Alexis happen?"

She ran the corner of her thumbnail back and forth against the pad of her index finger. "If I had to guess, probably the same way it happened with me. I knew I wasn't the only one, but I thought the other woman was the manager of a bar we always went to. I knew he and Lexi had hooked up before he and I did, but I didn't realize they were together the whole time."

Ash rose up onto an elbow. "Why would you accept that? You don't seem like a woman who would put up with a guy cheating on you."

Paige twisted her mouth. "I wasn't always the confident hard-ass you see before you. And there was something about Patrick that was…it's hard to explain. He had this hold on me that I couldn't break away from. It was toxic and destructive, and I soaked up every tiny bit of attention he gave me. No matter how many times I told myself to end it, I couldn't."

"I went into business with him. I think I understand a little of it."

"Yeah, I guess you do."

"But you did break away from him."

She met his probing gaze. "I deployed to Iraq for a year when he and Alexis announced their engagement."

"What does that mean?"

"I volunteered to go to a war zone to get away from the toxic situation I was in."

"Oh. Well. I mean…you could have done something worse."

She huffed out a breath. "Like what?"

"Murder?"

Paige grinned. "I didn't consider that a viable option at the time."

He smiled and rested his head on his hand. "What was Iraq like?"

Sighing, she looked back at the ceiling. The question, coming from Ash, didn't annoy her as much as it usually did, but it was still hard to answer. How did you describe war to someone who'd never been?

"It was hell…and salvation, all in one."

"Why salvation?"

"Denise was my roommate. I met Bree there. And Graham. I learned so much about myself and what I was truly capable of. I realized I couldn't let other people decide my life for me."

"And you became the badass woman you are."

"Yeah."

"Why do you say it like that?"

How had she said it? "Like what?"

"You sounded sad. Or maybe disappointed? I'm not sure, but it didn't sound like it was something you're proud of."

"Mmm. I don't usually show all sides of me to men I'm involved with."

"Which sides do you usually show?"

Paige rolled to face Ash and tucked her hand under her head. He rested his head on his arm and draped his other arm over her waist.

"The one you saw in the Virgin Islands."

"Why only that side?"

"Men like the pretty woman in the heels whose only interest is in keeping things simple. Most men can't handle the complicated side of me."

He grinned. "The side that can kick their ass?"

"Yeah." It had taken her a couple of encounters to figure out she needed to downplay her capabilities.

He picked up on what she didn't add. "Those men were stupid. I'd go as far as to say they weren't real men if you had to hide who you really are." He played with a lock of her hair, rubbing it between his fingers. "If I'm perfectly honest, you're intimidating as hell."

And this was where the kiss off came. She braced to roll away, but he tightened his arm around her and rose back up on his elbow to loom over her.

"And completely out of my league."

Paige blinked at that statement.

"I can see you're surprised. You're smart. You're beautiful. And yeah, you can kick my ass five ways to Sunday, but I'm *not* stupid. I know the likelihood of a woman like you looking twice at a guy like me is slim to none."

She frowned and shook her head. "I know you own a mirror because I can see it. Do you not use it?"

"That's not—" He shook his head. "I know women find me attractive, physically, but I'm a geek with hyperfocus ADHD. I like video games and computers, and have to set myself reminders for important things, like a date with my girlfriend or to eat."

"You forgot a date with a girl you were dating?"

He pressed his lips together. "More than once. But I'm not about to look a gift horse in the mouth. You're here. In my bed. Naked. And I… Not once in the last week have I had to set a reminder to remember I needed to be somewhere you are. In fact, I haven't been able to concentrate on my programming because I keep checking my watch to see how much longer I needed to work until I could leave without looking too eager."

A rush of pleasure coursed through her. She didn't think she'd ever been someone's distraction before.

"You like that you distract me," he said accusingly.

She bit the corner of her lip to keep from smiling. "Maybe."

Ash rolled on top of her. "That's okay. I like that you distract me too."

Paige smiled up at the ceiling as he kissed his way across her collarbone and down between her breasts.

"You called me a horse."

He paused and smiled against her skin before biting the sensitive flesh on the inside of her breast. "I called you a gift horse. One I'm going to take full advantage of."

She threaded her fingers into his hair as he moved lower. "Does that mean I get to take advantage of you as well?"

"I'm counting on it."

CHAPTER 23

Paige opened the hotel room door wider and let Angie in. "Hey."

"Heeeey." Angie grinned at her, flashing a wide, knowing smile.

"Don't." She knew this was coming but hadn't been able to devise a way to avoid it.

Angie set her computer bag on the farthest queen bed, then handed over the box of paperwork and the bag of donuts that sat on top of it. "Don't what?" she asked innocently.

Paige glared at her and set the box on the suite's small desk. "You know what."

"Fine. Spoilsport. Why are we meeting here instead of at Work Space?"

"I don't want anyone overhearing us," she said.

"Anyone specifically?" Angie asked.

"Kurt, the guy at the front desk."

"Any particular reason?"

"Not a particular one, no, but he gives me a bad vibe."

Angie shrugged. "Okay. I packed up all the paperwork you left with me yesterday." She tilted her head and gave Paige a look. "I finished scanning all the financial documents—receipts, invoices, mileage logs, all that—and sent them to Samara."

"Perfect. Samara is dialing in in a few minutes."

"Cool. Donut?"

"No thanks."

Angie set the bag next to the bed and sat on the edge, folded her hands together, and looked anywhere but at Paige.

In three...two...one...

"Okay, I can't stand it!"

Paige smiled.

"Did you find Ash?" Angie asked.

"I did." She didn't intend on withholding the basic details from Angie, but she was going to enjoy teasing her a little bit. It was the least she deserved for trying to play matchmaker.

"And?"

"And what?"

"And! And, and, and! Tell me there was an *and*!"

Paige laughed. "Yes, there was an and."

Angie squealed and kicked her feet and punched the air. "Are you like, together? Are you a couple?"

She hesitated. "I wouldn't go that far."

"Why not?"

"Well, for one, because we're investigating his company for potential embezzlement, and he could be an embezzler."

"Pfft." She waved a hand. "Neither of us thinks that."

"We still have to eliminate him as a possibility, Angie."

Her shoulders sagged. "Ugh. Fine, but it's not him."

Paige rolled her head back and forth. "Probably not, but we still need to do the work."

Her computer dinged, indicating an incoming call and she pressed the trackpad to answer. Samara appeared on the screen, the large conference room behind her.

"Hey, Samara. How's your family?" Paige asked.

"They're good and send their thanks for letting me come back to Charleston to help them out."

"Of course. You ready to get started?"

"Yes. I went through all the paperwork Angie scanned yesterday, and combined it with the information we scanned Monday and what I already had."

"Great," she said. "I want to focus on each person involved with the company individually first."

"Let's start with Ash so we can get him out of the way so he and Paige can be a couple," Angie said.

Paige hung her head and pinched the bridge of her nose.

"Hey, Paige."

If possible, her head fell even lower, and Angie whispered "oops" behind her.

"Fuck." She lifted her head and looked at the screen, smiling flatly. "Graham."

Thankfully, he appeared more amused than angry. "Give me a call when you're done."

"Yup."

"Okay...starting with Sebastian Moreno," Samara said, discomfort evident in her voice. "He bought his house seven years ago, significantly below market value, then took out a home equity loan of thirty thousand. Judging from the charges on his credit cards, it was to fix up the house. He still has about two years left on it and makes double payments on time.

"Other than the mortgage and the loan, he doesn't have any debt —at least not in his name. He has an IRA worth over two hundred and a little more than forty between checking and savings. Eighteen months ago, he transferred sixty thousand to the business account of M.A.G. Security. He receives twenty-four hundred a month in salary from M.A.G. Security, and that's him in a financial nutshell."

"Has he reported any additional income in the last eighteen months?" Paige asked.

"Last year, he reported $31,432 in self-employed income. As far as I could tell, it matched deposits in his bank accounts," Samara said.

"How many accounts does he have?" Paige asked.

"One checking account. He has two savings accounts—one appears to be solely for his mortgage and loan. And his IRA. That's it." Samara flipped through a couple of pages on her desk. "Unless he has a hidden offshore account, he lives within his means."

"See?" Angie asked from the bed.

Paige threw her a glare before turning back to the computer. "Okay. Did you have a chance to look at Natalie?"

"I did. She is employed by a financial firm in Garden City, Georgia. She was subcontracted by M.A.G. Security to perform the review of their finances. She provided a copy of the contract she has with them, and I found the original in the pile of paperwork yesterday before I left."

"Has she been paid yet?" Paige asked.

"Not that I can see," Samara said. "Nothing sticks out in her finances. She even provided her husband's banking information. I did a quick glance, and nothing there either."

"What about their wedding and honeymoon?" Paige asked. "It was a destination wedding to the Virgin Islands—that couldn't have been cheap."

"There were several charges to their credit card from the hotel, which they paid off with their joint account. They opened it a year ago. They each have automatic deposits from their personal accounts. There were also two large deposits a few months before the wedding, which came from both sets of parents.

"Other than that, there are no extravagant expenses. They rent a two-bedroom apartment. Their cars are paid off. They file their taxes on time and maximize their 401(k) contributions."

"So they're boring, money-wise," Angie said.

Samara laughed. "Pretty much."

Paige grinned. Nothing wrong with being financially boring. "All right, let's move on to Patrick and Alexis."

Her gut told her it was one of them. If she had to guess right then and there, her money would be on Alexis, but it wasn't out of the realm of possibility that it was Patrick. When she'd known them neither one had ever been shy about bending, or even breaking, the rules if it benefited themselves—even at the expense of others. Still, they had to go through everything objectively. She couldn't let her personal feelings get in the way.

She'd told Ash she would turn him in if he'd stolen the money. That also meant she would exonerate Patrick and Alexis if they were innocent.

"According to M.A.G. Security's business accounts, he draws a $75,000 annual salary from the company," Samara said.

"Wait," Graham said. "He pays himself twice the amount he pays his partner?"

"Correct," Samara said.

"What a tool," he muttered.

Yeah. "What about his spending?" Paige asked.

"He writes off a lot of dinners and drinks as business expenses —it's honestly almost a fifth of M.A.G.'s expenses," Samara said. "Theoretically it's all aboveboard. He either scans the receipts or shoves them in the drawer in the Work Space office, and they all have the names of the people he met and what they spoke about."

"While it's crappy he pays himself more of a salary than Ash, it's not too extravagant," Paige said. "What about savings or investments? Any large deposits?"

"No. He has a decent IRA, but hasn't contributed in almost two years, and a government Thrift Savings Plan account that has been sitting for a few years. Between savings and mutual funds, he has fifteen thousand and some change."

Paige paced back and forth in front of the table. Movement helped her process information. "Okay, so he hasn't contributed to his IRA since he stopped working. The TSP could be a holdover from when he was in the Air Force. He can't touch those without paying a penalty. What's his debt look like?"

"A lot of credit card debt, more than twice the national average, and a monthly car payment."

"No mortgage?" Paige asked.

"They rent for thirty-six hundred a month," Samara said.

"What?" Angie asked. "That's outrageous."

No doubt Patrick and Alexis lived in a house they felt suited their social status…with the rent to match.

"Otherwise, there are no unexplained deposits or withdrawals, or anything indicating he had a $150,000 windfall?"

"Nothing."

Paige stretched her neck to one side. "All right. What about Alexis?"

"Outside the joint debt she has with Patrick, she has twenty thousand in student loans plus a couple of personal credit cards with a combined balance of three thousand."

"How much is her salary from M.A.G.?" Paige asked.

"She doesn't report any income."

Paige stopped pacing and faced the computer. "What? Patrick said she took care of all the administrative work. She isn't drawing a salary?"

"Not one that's paid in her name. For the last three years, she and Patrick have filed their taxes jointly. Prior to that, they filed married, but separately, and she reported fifty-five thousand a year," Samara said.

"Doing what?"

"Uh…" Samara flipped through a stack of papers next to her and pulled a sheet out. "She was a fitness instructor."

Paige rolled her eyes. Of course she was.

"Fitness instructors make that much money? Shit."

Paige turned and looked at Angie. "You know you make more than that, right?"

"Yeah," she said around a mouthful of food. "But I have to actually work for that money."

Paige looked at the donut in Angie's hand, then back at her. "Yes. We're slave drivers. You should get a much easier job."

"Right? I could totally be a fitness instructor." She took a huge bite of donut.

"All right, so everyone's financials are copacetic? No one is drowning in unmanageable debt; no one's making payments to an online gambling site; no one has any unexplained large cash withdrawals to pay off a loan shark named Four Finger Freddie?" Paige asked.

"No." Samara shrugged and shook her head.

"What about the business accounts?" Paige asked.

"Nothing stands out immediately, but I'm going to go line by line and match each transaction up with the appropriate expense."

"Okay." Paige rested her hands on her hips and dropped her head back, staring at the ceiling. Shit. Why couldn't anything ever be easy? One helpful deposit or withdrawal pointing a big neon sign at the guilty person.

Moving on.

"Angie, you've been looking into their digital lives, right?" she asked.

"Yeah. I started with Patrick and Ash since they're the owners of the company. Ash has very little presence, which I honestly expected since he's a programmer. He either knows how to cover his tracks or erase them."

Her gut told her it wasn't him, but she was glad Angie was being diligent. "And Patrick?"

"Oh, he's all over the place. Facebook, Twitter, Instagram, Snapchat. He even has a Kik account." She curled her upper lip and wrinkled her nose. "Oh, and at least three different Tinder profiles. It's actually harder to nail him down because he's literally everywhere and has multiple profiles for every platform."

Paige sighed and sat on the corner of the bed. "What about Natalie and Alexis?"

"I have searches running, scraping for information on them, but I haven't had a chance to look at the results yet."

"I don't think Natalie took the money, but just in case, take a look at what you've…scraped…so far to definitively rule her out."

Her phone chirped, and she picked it up. A text from Ash flashed on the screen.

> Can you talk? It's important.

She frowned and thumbed in the passcode. "Hang on a second," she told them and called Ash.

It rang once. "Hey, can you come here?"

"Here, where?" she asked.

"Work Space," he said.

"Sure. What's wrong?"

"Someone was killed in our office."

CHAPTER 24

*A*sh faced Detective Martin Gander, his arms crossed.

"You said you normally work from home?" Detective Gander asked.

"That's correct," Ash replied. For the third time.

"What brought you in today?"

"We hired a company to look over our financials—I thought they were going to be here this morning."

"And you hired this company because your company is missing money." Detective Gander tapped his pen against the small notebook he held.

"Correct." Did everyone feel guilty when they were questioned by the police? He'd never even been pulled over. He knew he wasn't guilty, so why did he feel guilty when he had nothing to be guilty about?

"Where is your partner this morning? Mr....Greene?"

Ash sighed. "I don't know. I haven't seen him since yesterday afternoon."

"When you punched him?"

"Correct." Okay, he was guilty of that.

"And you punched him because...?"

"Because he was assaulting me," Paige said as she approached from the side.

Despite the circumstances, Ash couldn't stop a smile from forming at seeing her. She'd left his house early that morning, and he'd counted the minutes, anticipating when he'd see her again. His whole body grew lighter as if a huge weight had been lifted. Except for one part of him. It grew heavier as blood rushed lower, stealing all the oxygen from his brain.

Was it possible to be whipped this quickly? Who the fuck cared?

The detective shifted his stance to face Paige. "And you are?"

"Paige Davis. Chief Operations Officer of The Leonidas Corporation." She handed him two business cards. "My contact information and our lawyer's contact information."

The detective's eyebrows rose as he took the cards. "You're already giving me your lawyer's information?"

Paige tilted her head and gave the detective a baleful look. "Someone was killed in my clients' office. Of course I'm giving you our lawyer's information."

"How do you know the person was killed?"

Paige glanced around slowly, then back. "Well, Detective...?"

"Gander. Martin Gander."

"Detective Gander, I don't think Savanah PD would send this many cops for a heart attack. And Ash said 'someone was killed in our office' when he called."

Gander glared at him and he shrugged. No one told him he wasn't supposed to say anything.

"And this is the part where you tell me any further questions go through your lawyer?"

"Not at all," she said. "Ask away."

The detective raised his eyebrows before he was able to school his features. Ash grinned. Fuck, she was fabulous. He was also ecstatic to know he wasn't the only one Paige managed to keep on his toes.

Detective Gander cleared his throat. "Mr. Moreno, where did you go after your altercation with Mr. Greene?"

"I went home."

"Can anyone confirm that?"

He opened and closed his mouth.

"I can," Paige said.

Detective Gander's pen paused, and he looked up. "You were with Mr. Moreno?"

"Yes." She opened her tote on her shoulder and pulled out her phone, looking at the screen with a frown.

"What were you and Mr. Moreno doing?"

Her thumbs flew across her phone screen. "We were having sex," she said, absently.

Ash swallowed wrong and coughed. Holy shit, she just said that out loud. Not that he wouldn't have admitted it if pressed, but he probably wouldn't have come right out and offered it.

Paige said it with no shame, just put it right out there. Bluntly. As if discussing what they had for dinner.

So out of his league.

She looked up. "You okay?"

He nodded. "Yup."

She nodded and continued typing.

"You admit to sleeping with your client?" Detective Gander asked.

"I was sleeping with him before he was my client." She frowned at her phone, then looked up sharply. "Who was killed?"

"Why does that matter?" Detective Gander asked.

"I don't know that it does," she said.

"It was Kurt, one of the employees," Ash said. Something in her voice told him there was a reason she asked.

"Kurt?" she asked. "Front desk Kurt?"

"You knew the victim?" Detective Gander asked.

Paige shook her head. "I met him two days ago. We spoke

briefly when I first arrived. You need to look into what access he had to Work Space's records and client accounts."

"Why do I need to do that exactly?"

"Because Work Space has been overcharging at least one client by a thousand dollars every month," she said.

"Which client?" Detective Gander asked.

Paige looked at Ash, two small lines between her narrowed brows. "M.A.G. Security."

~

*A*sh watched Paige speak to the attorney her company's counsel had recommended. They'd been directed to the police station to continue the questioning, the police's goodwill thinning upon learning the victim had been stealing from M.A.G. Ash was now a murder suspect. If Patrick ever showed up, he'd be one as well.

Paige broke off from the lawyer and joined him. "Don't answer any more questions unless John is with you."

"John?" he asked.

"John Toller—your lawyer."

She was already on a first-name basis with his attorney. Of course she was. She was handling all this for him. He had a feeling she was going above and beyond what she normally did for the average client. When Detective Gander had looked at him suspiciously, he'd understood what Paige had felt when he'd done the same to her—angry, upset, determined to prove his innocence.

Her warning not to say anything had barely prevented him from telling the detective he didn't do it. But it also made him wonder.

"Paige, you don't think I had anything to do with this, do you?" he asked in a low voice.

"Of course not."

"Then why did you tell me not to say anything else to the detective? Especially when I was with you when it happened."

"Because it doesn't matter what you say at this point. It's just my word that we were together. There's no actual proof. If you say something they interpret the wrong way, it puts all the attention on you," she said.

He looked over her head and inhaled deeply. Fuck. How was he supposed to...? What did he do...? Shit. Maybe he should have watched more procedural dramas on TV.

"Or on me," she said.

He looked at her. "What? They think you're a suspect?"

"It's a murder. Everyone is a suspect."

"That's...ridiculous."

She smiled, obviously amused for some reason. "I love that you think I'm incapable of murder."

He shook his head. "It's not that I don't think you're capable. It's that I don't think you would resort to murder."

He leaned forward to kiss her, but she pulled back.

"I think it's best if we cool things off for now. Until we're both cleared."

Disjointed thoughts tumbled through his mind—all of them bad. They both knew they were innocent, so what did it matter if people saw them together? If they *were* together? She'd already told the police they were sleeping together.

"It's perception," she said as if reading his mind. "It doesn't matter if we're cleared or not. Both of us have motive and opportunity. Once it gets out that TLC is involved in this investigation, we're going to get a lot of attention. The court of public opinion is nasty, and neither of us wants *that* kind of attention right now. We need to go back to keeping it completely professional until the murderer is found."

She'd warned him last night, and everything she said now made sense. She always made sense—Paige was practical and methodical about everything. Well, almost everything. She hadn't been calm yesterday. She'd admitted he made her lose control, and this was her way of regaining it.

He took a small step back. "Of course."

"Ash," she whispered.

"I get it, Paige. It's fine."

She stopped herself from saying more when the lawyer joined them.

He glanced between the two of them. "Everything all right?"

She nodded.

"Sure." Ash held out his hand. "Ash Moreno. Murder suspect."

He laughed and shook his hand. "John Toller. Attorney. You're not a murder suspect, just a person of interest in a murder investigation."

"Isn't that the same thing?" Ash asked.

"Not always. Sometimes it just means you have information germane to the investigation. They're going to question you together."

Ash frowned and glanced at Paige, who seemed as surprised as he was. "Is that usual?"

"No," John said. "But like I said, you're not a murder suspect."

John led them to the conference room and took a seat between them. Detective Gander joined them with another man.

"This is Detective Eric Smith," he said.

Detective Smith nodded but didn't offer to shake hands. The two men sat across from them.

"All right," Detective Gander said. "Let's start with you, Mr. Moreno. When was the last time you had contact with the victim?"

Ash shifted in his seat. "I spoke with him yesterday morning when I arrived at Work Space, I think."

"And what did you speak about?"

"I said good morning, I guess."

"That was all you said?" Detective Smith asked.

"I might have said hey…?" Ash shrugged.

"What was the deceased's connection to your company?" Detective Gander asked.

"Other than running Work Space, where we rented an office, he had no connection to M.A.G. Security. At least as far as I'm aware." He let out a defeated sigh.

"Why would you be unaware whether he had any involvement with your company?" Detective Smith asked.

Ash pressed his lips together. "I've discovered I don't know a lot about what's actually going on in my company."

"This missing money?" Detective Gander asked.

"Yes."

"And you hired Ms. Davis and…" He flipped through his notes. "The Leonidas Corporation to look into it."

"Yes."

"Ms. Davis, why did you suggest we look into the deceased's access to Work Space's financials?"

"I received information from one of our investigators that Work Space had been invoicing M.A.G. Security more than a thousand dollars a month over what they should have been paying. Our cyber technician found that Work Space was overcharging several of their tenants."

"How did you find that information?" Detective Smith asked.

Paige leaned toward John and whispered something, then sat back.

"Ms. Davis isn't comfortable answering that question at the moment, but is willing to provide a list of tenants who are affected by the excess billing," John said.

Detective Gander looked at Paige but asked his question to John. "Why isn't Ms. Davis comfortable answering the question?"

Ash leaned forward slightly so he could see Paige out of the corner of his eye. The corners of her lips tilted up in a placid smile, but she said nothing.

"Ms. Davis will provide all the information you need to figure that out on your own," John said.

The detective blinked. "Yeah. Fine. We'll go from there."

Shit. She'd just stared down a murder detective and made him back down.

"Can you both verify your whereabouts between six a.m. and eight a.m.?" Detective Smith asked.

Ash looked at John, who nodded. "I was at my house, working on the program for our company."

"And you, Ms. Davis?"

"I left Mr. Moreno's house a little before six and went straight to my hotel," she said. "I left for Work Space at ten-forty, after I received the call from Mr. Moreno."

"Do you always call the men you have sex with by their last names?" Detective Smith asked.

Ash's hackles rose and he leaned forward. The detective was out of line. It was none of his business who Paige slept with, much less what she called them.

Before he could say anything in her defense, Paige said, "It depends." The tone of her voice had dropped—now it was husky and sultry. "Sometimes I call them Daddy."

Detective Smith turned bright, tomato red, and Detective Gander choked on air.

He could hear the flirty wink in her voice. She'd defended herself and put the detective in his place by owning their relationship without responding to his insinuation.

Ash should have known she didn't need him to defend her honor—she was more than capable of doing it herself.

CHAPTER 25

Paige pushed into her hotel room and barely stopped herself from slamming the door closed. Tossing her bag onto the desk, she kicked off her heels into the closet. Bracing her hands on her hips, she paced back and forth in the small space and concentrated on controlling her breathing.

What the fuck was going on? Kurt's murder was connected to this case. She knew it, but now she needed to figure out why and who.

Some of her anger reflected inward. Getting involved with Ash was a bad idea, but for some damned reason, she couldn't stop herself. He was just so…real. He didn't play games or try to feed her lines or impress her with…anything. There was no pretense. No posturing. He didn't try to one-up her or prove he was more manly or capable or knowledgeable. It was…

Fuck. It was sexy.

If she had a checklist for her ideal guy, he'd check two of the boxes. He was tall. He loved the water. He was good in bed.

Okay, three. Three boxes off her list of qualities and yet…he came along and basically said, "That's nice. Have you seen this?"

Handed her a completely different list and then checked every single item on it. Things she didn't even know she wanted.

Gentle. Intense. Sweet. So fucking sweet. He was awkward and a nerd and thought every facet of her was as impressive as the next. Not once since he'd shown up at TLC had she needed to pretend to be anything other than who she was—she hadn't been able to control which version of her he got. He saw *her*. *All* of her. And he'd accepted all of her.

He was too good for her. And she didn't care. She was selfish enough to risk breaking him to have him look at her like she was everything he'd ever wanted in life.

And this morning, she'd pushed him away. It didn't matter that her reasons were sound—that they needed to provide as little fodder for gossip and speculation as possible—she'd hurt him, and it had felt like she'd taken a physical blow.

Fuck.

She blew out a breath and pulled her hair away from her face. Marching into the bathroom, she twisted her hair into a bun, securing it with a hair elastic.

She changed into leggings and a thin, long-sleeved shirt. Angie was going to be there soon with more equipment so they could teleconference with Samara on more than just Paige's laptop. They'd work through this as long as it took to figure out who took the money and, maybe, killed Kurt.

~

"*L*et's focus on the transactions between Work Space and M.A.G. and see if we can track where some of the money went."

Sitting cross-legged in the middle of one of the beds, Paige sifted through the stack of papers in front of her. She looked up at the monitor where Samara sat in her office back at TLC.

"M.A.G. signed a two-year lease with Work Space, and the first payment was half of what the advertised monthly payment is, so my guess is some kind of incentive to sign a long-term agreement. But I can't find a contract with Work Space, so I can't be sure," Samara said.

"I can't find anything on their website indicating they offer any kind of incentive package either."

Paige glanced over her shoulder at Angie sitting on the other bed. "Can you—?"

"Yup." Angie's fingers flew across her laptop keyboard. "It looks like they offer a ten-percent discount for the first month if you sign a six-month lease, twenty-five percent off for a year lease, and fifty percent for eighteen months or more."

"That explains the first month, but six months into their contract, M.A.G. started paying a thousand dollars more every month," Samara said. "I don't have any communication indicating they increased their rates. Are you able to see if any of the other renters had an increase in their rates?"

"It looks like three other companies with long-term contracts began paying an increased rate around the same time," Angie said.

"Other than long-term contracts, what do those companies have in common?" Paige asked.

"Hang on..." Angie said. "All three companies made payments to a company called Magnolia Management."

"Are you hacking the other companies' financials?" Samara asked.

Angie looked up at the screen, wide-eyed and projecting innocence. "No?"

Paige smirked. "Try being more confident when you answer that question."

"No," Angie said firmly.

"Who is Magnolia Management?" Paige asked.

"According to their website, they are an executive administrative firm," Samara said. "I show a few checks written out to them but no regular payments."

"Who signed the checks?" Paige asked.

"Alexis."

Paige looked at Angie on the other bed. "Is Magnolia Management an LLC?"

Angie typed on her laptop for several seconds. "It is."

"Who's on the board?"

"It's a sole proprietor."

"Who's the proprietor?"

Angie looked up from her screen. "Kurt Tuttle."

Holy shit.

"Who is Kurt Tuttle?" Samara asked.

"The guy that was killed," Angie said.

"His last name was Tuttle?" Paige needed that confirmed.

"According to this, yes," Angie said. "Why?"

Paige looked at Samara. "Tuttle is Alexis Greene's maiden name."

"Hang on." Angie typed furiously on her laptop. "They're cousins."

"Alexis and Kurt?" Paige asked.

"Yeah. Their fathers are brothers."

"Holy shit. They stole the money together."

"But how?" Samara asked. "Other than the checks, I can't find anything connecting Magnolia Management to the missing money or Work Space, and there's nothing exorbitant about the amounts of the checks."

"Give me a bit," Angie said. "Now that I have the dots, I can connect them."

"Airtight, Angie," Paige warned. "I don't want her getting away with this on a technicality."

"Do you think she killed Kurt?" Samara frowned.

Paige closed her eyes and shook her head. "I don't know."

The Alexis she used to know, the one who went by Lexi and was more worried about scoring free drinks at the bar—she didn't think so. But this Alexis….

"Samara, were M.A.G.'s payments to Work Space automatic?" Angie asked.

"Yes," Samara said. "Automatic payment on the third of every month."

"Were the payments withdrawn *from* M.A.G.'s account by Work Space or was the payment set up to pay *to* Work Space?"

"Let me see… It's an automatic payment set up within the bank's bill pay software to pay to Work Space. Why?"

"Can you read me the routing and account numbers the payments were sent to?" Angie asked.

Samara rattled off the numbers.

"Bingo." Angie smirked. "That isn't Work Space's business account information."

"The payment info says Work Space, and it's their address as well," Samara said.

"I don't doubt the payment info in the bill pay system is set up to say Work Space on that end. What I'm telling you is that is not Work Space's official business account. That account doesn't belong to Work Space at all."

"Then who does it belong to?" Paige asked.

"Magnolia Management," Angie said.

Paige sucked in a breath, the picture forming in her mind.

"Holy shit. They funneled the payments through Magnolia and skimmed off the top," Samara said.

"That's exactly what they did. Then Magnolia paid Work Space the correct amount on behalf of M.A.G.," Angie said. "I bet it's the same setup with the other companies as well."

"Okay, that explains some of the missing money, but that wouldn't come close to a hundred and fifty thousand." Samara's gaze was focused downward, possibly staring at her desk as she matched up puzzle pieces. "That wouldn't be enough to kill someone over, would it?"

Angie shrugged. "Guess it depends on how badly you need the money."

Paige wasn't so sure. Something Samara said earlier tugged at the tendrils of thought in her head. "Samara, you said Patrick was meticulous about scanning his receipts, right?"

"Yes. Religiously for the last thirteen months. It's the only thing in all their files that's consistent."

"Huh." Paige nibbled at the corner of her bottom lip. How much money was enough to kill someone over?

"Huh, what?" Angie asked.

Paige shook her head. "When we were stationed together, Patrick never filed his vouchers on time. It was like pulling teeth to get him to file them. I have a hard time believing he's going to religiously file for reimbursement."

"People change," Angie said.

"Maybe, but something feels off. Samara, can you put some of the receipts up on the screen?"

"Sure. Just a second."

Five credit card receipts appeared on the TV. Paige rose from the bed and leaned closer to the screen, peering at them. "Are these all from one month?"

"Yes."

"Can you pull up the last six months of receipts and put them all on the same screen?"

"Yep." Samara loaded the documents and spread them out on the screen.

Paige scanned the credit card receipts, looking for anything out of the ordinary.

"Well, butter my ass and call me a biscuit," Samara said.

Angie dissolved into a fit of giggles. "What?"

"They duplicated receipts and changed the dates," Samara said.

Paige stopped chuckling. "How?"

"Here." Samara used her cursor to circle numbers on the receipts. "See this transaction number? It's the same as this one and this one. This transaction number"—she circled another—"is the same as this one, this one, and this one. I bet if I go back through all of them, there will be a lot of receipts that are copies."

"You're right," Paige said. "How didn't anyone notice that?"

"Why would they?" Samara asked. "The only reason I noticed is because all the receipts were on the same screen. Technically, the money isn't missing. He filed vouchers for his expenses and was reimbursed for them."

"So he's in on it as well?" Angie asked.

"I don't know." Paige shook her head and pinched her bottom lip. "Samara, how much was he reimbursed in the last year?" Paige asked.

"Hang on."

They waited while she ran the information.

"Between five and fifteen hundred every month. Almost twenty thousand dollars in total." Samara looked at them, her eyes so wide her long lashes brushed her sculpted eyebrows.

"But that's not close to what's missing," Angie said. "There's still over $100,000 unaccounted for. Where is it?"

Samara shook her head. "I can't see anywhere else the money could have come from."

Paige looked at Angie. "Okay, let's focus on the reimbursements for the moment. Did they end up in the Magnolia account?"

"They did not. The only transactions between Magnolia and M.A.G. are the checks that Alexis wrote. To herself."

"Check Patrick's accounts," Paige said.

"Looking at what we thought were legitimate reimbursements," Angie said, "most of the money went in and went right back out again."

"Can you see the routing information for the transfers?" Paige asked.

"Yeah, let me..." Angie's keyboard clicked. "The money was transferred to a different account owned by Kurt and Alexis Tuttle."

"How would Patrick not realize what was going on?" Samara asked.

Paige shrugged. "He said he turned over all the financials to Alexis. He was happy to spend the money and let her handle everything. Guarantee it was the same for their personal accounts."

"You got to hand it to her," Angie said. "It's kind of an ingenious situation."

"Until her cousin got killed," Samara said.

"Well...there's that. Do you think it was because of the money?"

"How much is in that account?" Paige asked.

Angie looked at her laptop. "I mean...I wouldn't kill for it, but who knows."

"How much is it?" Samara asked.

"A little more than $53,000." The corners of her mouth turned down.

"I know a few people that would kill for that much money." Samara shook her head. "But where did it all come from? Because it didn't come just from M.A.G."

"I don't know," Paige said. "Right now, we know where some of the missing money is. We know Kurt and Alexis had multiple accounts that have a decent amount of money in them."

"What do we do now?" Angie asked.

"We turn all the info over to the police so they can act on it," Paige said.

"Ugh. That's no fun. I thought there was going to be a night-time raid. Fast-roping down the side of a building and kicking through a window in a shower of glass." Angie made karate chopping motions with her hands.

Paige grinned and shook her head. "Angie, what is it you think we do?"

CHAPTER 26

Detective Gander met Ash and John Toller at the reception desk and held his hand out to Ash. "Mr. Moreno, thank you for coming. Alexis Greene was brought in for questioning regarding the money missing from your company as well as the murder of her cousin, Kurt Tuttle."

Ash's eyebrows shot up. "They were cousins?"

"Ms. Davis didn't tell you?" he asked.

"No. We haven't spoken since yesterday."

"Oh. Uh…yes, Mrs. Greene and Mr. Tuttle were paternal cousins. From the information Ms. Davis and her team provided, it appears they were skimming off the top of lease payments made to Work Space from your company as well as at least three others. Your company appears to have been the first, and then they expanded their reach to other companies that employed Mrs. Greene to manage the administrative aspects of their business."

Ash ran a hand through his hair, letting the information soak in. Why hadn't Paige told him any of this? He mentally shook his head. He knew why. Optics and professionalism. He just wanted all this to be over.

"As far as the falsified expense reimbursements, we don't know if it was only your company involved or if it was the other companies as well," Detective Gander said.

"What expense reimbursements?" He was getting really tired of being blindsided with information.

The detective looked over Ash's shoulder and tilted his chin. "I'll let Ms. Davis explain all that to you."

Ash turned and found Paige approaching their small group. Faint dark circles under her eyes and the stress lines around her mouth belied her calm appearance. How was it that he, who could never read what someone was thinking or feeling, was so tuned in to her? His nerves twitched with the impulse to wrap her up in his arms and hug her and tell her it would all work out.

Paige's gaze dropped and he realized his fingers were tapping against his thighs. He clenched his hands into fists to stop.

She met his gaze and smiled faintly. It was small, but it was enough.

"Gentlemen," she said when she reached them.

"Ms. Davis." Detective Gander cleared his throat. "Thank you for coming in and thank you for sending the information over to us. Our cyber team is going through the process of obtaining warrants so we can legally gather the information."

"Hopefully it won't be too late to actually obtain the information," John said.

Paige smirked. "I wouldn't worry about that. The accounts might be frozen due to a random IRS audit."

"Random, huh?" Detective Greene asked.

"Very random," she assured him.

"Good to know," he said. "Detective Smith is signaling to me. We're going in to question Mrs. Greene. We may have some follow-up questions for you, if you don't mind sticking around."

"Of course not," she said.

"I don't have anywhere to be," Ash added.

"You can wait in the lounge, just there." He pointed at an open door, across the room from them.

"Thank you," Paige said.

"I'm going to step out to make some calls," John said.

For the first time since the night they'd met, Ash was unsure what to say. A thick, awkward silence fell between them. He cleared his throat. "Do you want to see if they have any coffee in there?"

"Sure." Her voice was too high and too bright, but she spun and headed to the lounge.

Ash took in the worn leather couch and three round tables. "One of the tables?"

"Yes." She pulled out a plastic chair and sat, setting her tote on the floor next to her.

"Why didn't you—?"

"I'm sorry I didn't—"

They both stopped speaking as quickly as they'd started.

"You first," he said.

She licked her lips. "I'm sorry I didn't speak to you before passing the information to the police, but we needed to get it to them as quickly as possible. They needed to bring Alexis in for questioning before I could give you all the details. I didn't want there to be any perception that we were protecting you or trying to hide any information. As it is, we broke more than a few laws getting it, which they're overlooking for the sake of expediency."

"That answers my question," he said.

"Why I didn't call you?"

He nodded. "Basically, yes."

She wrapped her hand over his fist. "I'm sorry, Ash. You may think I'm erring too far on the side of caution, but this is the first time I've crossed a line with a client, and I have to make sure you and I both are protected."

"I understand. I just want to be done with all this."

It was like a light dimmed in the room, casting a shadow over her face. She pulled her hand away. "Of course."

"No. That's not—"

"Ms. Davis?"

They both looked to the door, where Detective Gander leaned into the room.

"Yes?"

"Mrs. Greene is asking to speak to you," he said.

"Me? Why me?" she asked.

The detective shook his head. "I don't know, but she said she would only cooperate if she could speak to you first."

Paige shrugged. "Okay." She stood and slung her tote over her shoulder. A few steps short of the door, she stopped and looked over her shoulder at him. "Are you coming?"

Her gaze was shuttered and the light, teasing lilt he'd gotten used to hearing in her voice was gone. She'd obviously taken what he'd said out of context. He just needed a minute to fix it—to explain what he meant. Why couldn't he ever find the words he needed when he needed them?

"Yes." He didn't care if it was awkward or embarrassing or weird—he had to take any moment to make her understand.

She nodded and followed Detective Gander out of the lounge, and he jogged to catch up. "Paige."

The small tilt of her head was the only indication she heard him.

"We should talk after this."

"Of course," she said with a single nod.

The tight feeling in his stomach didn't go away with her agreement.

~

*P*aige focused on Detective Gander, waiting for them in front of an open door leading to a hallway, instead of the ominous presence of Ash just behind and to her left.

"We're going to monitor your conversation," Detective Gander said.

"Understood," she said. "She and her lawyer are aware?"

"Yes. She told her lawyer she wanted to speak to you alone." He stopped in front of a door marked *Interview Room 2.* "Nothing she says to you is privileged."

He held the door open and stepped aside for her to enter. Through the doorway, she could see Alexis seated at a table, speaking to an older woman.

"I don't care," Alexis said.

The other woman, presumably her attorney, drew her shoulders back and stood, snatching her bag from the back of the chair. She turned and looked at Paige. "This is against my advice."

"Noted," Paige said. "Would you like to stay?"

"No!" Alexis said. "Just you."

Her lawyer closed her eyes and exhaled audibly, then stalked out of the room.

Paige waited for the door to click shut before hooking her purse on the chair across the table from Alexis. "You know they're listening and watching, right? Your lawyer could have stayed."

Alexis crossed her arms and tossed her head. "I don't care if they're watching—I'm innocent."

Paige raised her eyebrows at that but remained silent.

"I didn't kill Kurt!"

"Ah. That. Then who did?"

"I don't know." Her voice caught at the end, and she cleared her throat while looking at the side wall, blinking rapidly.

Paige tilted her head and studied Alexis. She was pale, for all her makeup, her hair messy rather than artfully arranged, and stress pulled at the corners of her mouth.

"Why did you want to speak to me?"

"I want to hire you."

She blinked. That got her attention. "You want to hire…me?"

"Your company," Alexis said. "Leonidas…whatever."

"Why, exactly?"

Alexis leaned forward. "Because I don't trust the police to find

Kurt's killer. They'll pin this on me because we were embezzling the money together, but I did not kill him."

"Alexis—"

"P.D., please," Alexis whispered. "I need your help. I know you probably hate me, but I don't have anyone else I can trust."

No one had called her P.D. in a very long time. Paige sighed.

"Walk me through the embezzlement." Although they knew the basics of how, they still didn't know why.

Alexis looked at her hands and began picking at her cuticles. "Before Patrick met Ash, he kept a tight hold on all our finances. He was stingy and controlled everything I spent, right down to the penny. If I went grocery shopping, I had to look up the prices online and figure out how much everything was going to cost, including tax. I couldn't even substitute a product because it might be more than what I told him."

"You had a job—why couldn't you use that money?"

"Patrick made me deposit it in our joint account. Joint, except I didn't have access to it. I had to ask him for my own money. Then he made me quit because a fitness instructor didn't fit the image he was trying to project as a serious businessman." She huffed out a half laugh. "Then, when I figured out a way to access the accounts and leave his sorry ass, we had nothing. Barely five thousand dollars. Everything was being put on credit."

Paige tilted her head. "But you had access to the corporate accounts."

"*After* Patrick and Ash started their company. When he had so much damn money just pouring in from investors, it didn't matter how much he spent or on what. And he didn't hand it over to me because he thought I could handle it, he pushed it off on me because he's lazy and too cheap to hire a professional."

She looked at the table and grew quiet for a moment.

"Kurt knew what was going on. He suggested skimming off the top so I could leave Patrick. We figured twenty-five thousand would be enough for me to get a fresh start and file for a divorce, but we needed a way to hide what we were doing. Kurt set up the fake Work Space account to send the monthly payment to, then paid the real bill from there.

"But it was taking too long, so he suggested doing the same thing with some of the other companies that had long-term contracts with Work Space. Companies that would hire out their administrative work and not pay too much attention to what was going on as long as they had receipts."

"What about the duplicate voucher receipts?"

"We only did that with Patrick. He used networking"—she made air quotes with her fingers—"as an excuse to party and cheat on me."

"So why didn't you leave? You had over fifty thousand dollars."

"I was going to, but it was so easy. We got greedy. If twenty-five thousand was enough, why not more?" Her voice dropped to a whisper. "If I had just left when I originally planned to, Kurt would still be alive."

A commotion at the door drew their attention.

"I want to see my wife!" The door burst open, and Patrick stumbled in, Alexis's lawyer and Detective Gander in the doorway behind him. He paused upon seeing Paige, then rushed to Alexis, knelt next to her, and took one of her hands in his.

"Alexis…why? Why would you do this to me? To…to us?"

Alexis snatched her hand away and shoved up from her chair, away from Patrick. "As if you don't know."

He stood slowly. "I don't. Help me understand."

"Because it was the only way I could get away from you and hurt you where you'd feel it the most—in your wallet. Money is the only thing you care about."

"That's not true. I love you, Alexis." He took a step toward her, and she countered with a step back.

"That is such bullshit. You never loved me. You just wanted a trophy wife. Someone to parade around with on your arm and show off. It took me a while to see that. To be honest with myself.

When Kurt suggested cleaning you out, I was just going to empty the bank accounts and take off, but we had nothing. We were living on credit, and you were spending the rest of it in strip clubs and bars.

"Then Ash stupidly fell for your scammy sales pitch and agreed to go into business with you. We had money coming in hand over fist, and your lazy ass turned it all over to me. It was almost too easy."

She looked at Ash hovering in the doorway with the detective and her lawyer. "I'm sorry you got dragged into all this, Ash."

He shrugged and shoved his hands in his pockets.

"I would have given you a divorce," Patrick said.

"What? And tarnish your dazzling reputation? Right."

"But why kill Kurt if he was helping you?" Patrick asked.

Alexis fisted her hands at her sides. "I didn't kill Kurt!"

Her attorney marched into the room. "We're done until I have time to confer with my client. *Alone.*"

Paige nodded and grabbed her bag from the back of the chair, slinging it over her shoulder. Something about that whole scene felt staged. Not on Alexis's part, but why bring up Kurt in a room full of people unless Patrick wanted to trip her up?

She stopped just inside the doorway and turned. "Alexis?"

Paige caught the slight tilt of her chin before Alexis turned to face her. "Yes?"

"I can't guarantee the outcome you're hoping for," Paige cautioned.

"But you'll help?"

"Yes."

Alexis closed her eyes and exhaled softly. "Thank you."

CHAPTER 27

"So we're investigating a murder?" Graham asked. He'd driven down from Charleston earlier in the day while she'd been at the police station.

"I wouldn't say we're investigating a murder so much as trying to prove Alexis didn't *commit* the murder." Paige sighed and tilted her head back against the desk chair.

They were waiting for Samara and Angie to join them, and then they'd move to a small conference room they'd arranged with the hotel. As nice as her suite was, it was too small for all of them.

"What's our rate for this?" he asked.

She lifted her head and stared at Graham, her mouth a flat line.

"You know, we're never going to make any money if we keep doing this shit pro bono."

She dropped her head back again and closed her eyes. "I know."

"Why are we doing it?" he asked softly.

With a sigh, she lifted her head. "Because at one time, I considered her a friend. I don't think she did it."

"But she did steal the money from M.A.G. Security as well as other companies?" he asked.

"Oh yeah. She admitted to that in front of the police and her lawyer."

"And you don't think it's possible she killed her cousin for it?"

Paige shook her head. "There's something off about that, but no. She was really shaken up about his death."

"Could she have been putting on an act?" Graham asked. "She wouldn't be the first person to use crocodile tears to gain sympathy."

"That's the thing though—she wasn't using tears. She was fighting them. Fighting to maintain her composure and not lose it in front of the cops. I don't think she was faking her pain. Plus…"

She stood to pace, replaying the scene from the interrogation room in her head.

"Plus what?" he prompted.

"The way Patrick burst into the interrogation room. It was super dramatic. 'I want to see my wife.'" She lowered her voice to repeat his words.

"It was so over the top. Like, made-for-TV dramatic. Everything he said to her felt rehearsed, and then he asked her why she killed Kurt. Why would you ask your spouse why they killed someone in front of the police and a room full of people?"

Graham followed her movement around the room. "You think he killed the cousin and is trying to pin it on her?"

Paige stopped, hands on her hips, and squinted at the far wall. "But that's too obvious. Right? I mean, after Alexis, the next logical person is Patrick."

"Or the partner," he said. "You can't discount him because of your relationship."

She shifted her gaze to him. "That's not what I'm doing."

Was it though? Was she too close to this?

Graham leaned forward and rested his arms on his knees. "Paige, you're one of the smartest people I know. You look at problems like a puzzle. You've always been able to look at *all* the pieces and see where they fit in the big picture. I never question your judgment or your decisions."

She waited. There was a "but" in his tone. She thought she knew what the but was, but...she didn't know if she could admit it to herself.

"Right now, you're hesitating," he said quietly. "And you're questioning yourself. I have never, not once, not even when you were a brand-new HUMINT analyst, seen you question yourself. Not even when everyone told you you were wrong about an assessment. The fact that you're doing it now tells me you're too close to this."

She dropped into the chair, shoulders slumped forward, and sighed heavily. "What do you suggest I do?"

"Take a step back. I asked Addison to come down and take a look at this with a fresh set of eyes, starting with the missing money."

Paige let her head fall back and closed her eyes. It made sense. She was missing something. Some key element of information. Graham was right. She couldn't figure out the big picture because she was so focused on the smaller pieces.

Addison had a background as an analyst, and in six months, she'd be defending her dissertation for her psychology degree. She'd bring a fresh perspective to the whole problem.

"I feel like I'm failing," she said quietly.

"Bullshit," Graham said.

Paige turned her head, still resting on the chair, and gave him a confused look.

"You're not failing," he said. "For once, you don't have all the answers. It's honestly kind of refreshing."

"What?" She lifted her head to give him a full glare.

"It's kind of nice to know you can mess up. I was beginning to get an inferiority complex."

Paige gave him a baleful look. Now who was bullshitting?

Graham laughed. "I'm kidding. There's nothing inferior about me."

"There's nothing wrong with your ego at least," she said dryly.

"Seriously, Paige. Step back. Give it a day or two. Don't think about it. Just clear your head and come back with fresh eyes and a fresh perspective."

She sighed. "I'm not going to be able to stop thinking about it."

He pushed up from the chair and headed to the door. "I know. But if it's not staring you in the face while you think about it, you might figure out what you're missing. I don't want to see you for two days, Paige. Two *full* days."

"You're not the boss of me!"

"Yes, I am," he replied as the door to her suite closed behind him.

Paige stuck her tongue out at the door for good measure. Yes, it was childish, but she felt like she'd been grounded and sent to her room.

She also felt defeated. It wasn't like her to miss something in a case. She was the one who usually had the answers because she could look at things objectively. Even in the middle of jungles and kidnappings, she was the one who kept a level head and didn't let her emotions get the best of her.

But now…now her emotions were all over the place. She knew deep down that Alexis hadn't killed her cousin. That sliver of hurt and pettiness from years ago was big enough, if she'd felt even a hint that Alexis had done it, Paige wouldn't have offered to help her. Their former friendship wasn't driving her gut feeling that Alexis was innocent. Of murder, at least.

But Patrick and Ash? She didn't know. She didn't know if her current feelings for Ash and her former feelings for Patrick prevented her from seeing the truth. That one of them could be the murderer.

Her cell phone rang, and she spun the chair to pick it up from the desk, smiling when she saw Denise's name.

"Did Graham tell on me?" she asked by way of greeting.

Denise chuckled. "He did call and say you could use a friendly ear. What's going on?"

She caught Denise up on the situation, from Ash showing up at her work with his partner, her former lover, to her former friend being arrested for embezzlement and possible murder.

"Wow," Denise said. "You've had a busy few weeks."

"You could say that."

"What's really eating at you?"

Paige hesitated. If she admitted it out loud to Denise, she'd be admitting out loud to herself. There'd be no going back after that.

"Paige?"

"It's something Ash said today at the police station," she said quietly.

"What did he say?"

"That…that he just wanted to be done with it all."

"Done with what?"

She shrugged even though her friend couldn't see it. "I'm not sure. I mentioned needing to cool things off while the murder investigation was going on, and he said he just wanted to be done with it all."

"And you took that to mean he wanted to be done with you too?"

"Maybe."

"I have two questions. One, do you think you could have read more into what he said than what he meant? And two, why do you think you need to cool things off?" Denise asked.

"Because I don't want anyone to question my professionalism or impartiality. You know how people are in security and the military or law enforcement. It doesn't matter how good you are at your job—as soon as you sleep with someone, you're the Whore of Babylon, and the only reason you're where you are, doing the job you do, is so some guy can use you as a cum receptacle."

"I totally forgot about you being called the Whore of Babylon."

"I'm pretty sure it was the same week you were called a FOB-hopping whore," Paige said.

"That was a sucky deployment."

"For a multitude of reasons."

"Is Graham giving you shit about it?" Denise asked. "'Cause I'll come down there and kick his ass."

"Nope. Graham hasn't said anything."

"One of the other guys who work for you? Because you know you can fire them, right?"

Paige chuckled. "No one has said anything. But perception is reality. I don't want to destroy everything I've worked toward for the past ten years just because I like a guy that happens to be a client."

"And now we circle back around to the first question. Which I notice you conveniently skipped. Is it possible Ash misunderstood what you meant? Or could you be reading more into what he said than he meant?"

"Of course I could have. This is why I don't do this." Frustration forced her out of the chair, and Paige began to pace again.

"Do what? Investigate embezzlement and murders?"

She pressed her lips together, knowing Denise was being purposely obtuse. "Relationships. Romantic entanglements."

"Love?"

Paige closed her eyes and pinched the bridge of her nose. She said it. Denise had actually said it.

"Paige? You there?"

"I'm here."

"Did you hear what I said?"

"Fuck. Yes. Love. I can't trust myself when I think I love someone. Are you happy?"

"Do you *think* you love him or do you love him?" She was like one of her dogs with a bone—would not let it go.

"I don't know, Denise. It's way too fucking soon. And the only other time I thought I loved a man, he lied to me, strung me along for almost a year, and then asked someone else to marry him."

"Do you really think Ash would do something like that? From what little interaction I had with him, and from what you told me, he doesn't seem the type of guy to play games. Or murder someone, for that matter."

"I don't think so either, but it's not him I don't trust. It's me. How much of that belief is me thinking with my heart instead of my head? How do I make sure I don't lose myself if things continue?"

"Paige, you are not the same person you were back then. You're not going to let yourself be anything other than what you're meant to be, and he wouldn't expect you to be anything else. If he did, then he's not the right guy for you."

"And what if I get so entangled, I don't realize it's happening? What if bit by bit I lose pieces of myself until I don't recognize me anymore? That's what happened the last time."

"Then I'll come and beat some sense into you and kick his ass," Denise said.

Paige laughed.

"Sometimes you have to take a leap of faith and trust that the person you love is going to be there to catch you."

"Fuck." Paige flopped onto the bed.

"Yeah, pretty much."

"How'd you get so smart?"

"I had no choice. I've got a pre-teen in my house that's seriously driving me to look up all-girl boarding schools."

Paige chuckled.

"In all seriousness. Take the time, like Graham said. Don't obsess about the problem, and come back to it in a couple of days."

She sighed. "You're right. You're both right. But don't tell Graham I said that."

"Absolutely not."

"Thanks. I did need a friendly ear."

"Always," Denise promised. "Come up and see us soon. We're going to have puppies in a few days. Puppies make everything better."

CHAPTER 28

*A*sh flipped, turned, pushed off the wall with his feet, and porpoised through the water until the fire in his lungs forced him to the surface for a breath. He'd gone to the pool instead of staring blankly at the final code edits at home. He hadn't been able to focus or concentrate, all the letters and numbers blurring together.

What was even the point? The code wasn't going to go anywhere. Not now, with the missing money and a freaking murder. Who in their right mind would invest in M.A.G. Security after all that? Even if they found the money and the murder was solved, they were done.

He reached the end of the lane and stopped at the wall, braced his arms on the ledge, and pulled off his goggles.

But that wasn't the only reason he had to leave his house. He couldn't stop thinking about Paige. Couldn't stop seeing her in his bed, on his floor, standing in the kitchen wearing his shirt while they ate ice cream out of the carton.

Muscling out of the pool, he wiped water off of his face and stalked to his gym bag. He pulled out his towel and wiped it over his head before quickly drying off the rest of his body.

He couldn't even swim without getting distracted.

He hated it. He hated not knowing if it was because he had true feelings for Paige or if it was his hyperfocus targeting her. It had happened to him a lot in high school. He'd like a girl to the point of obsession until something else distracted him and he fixated on that.

His phone rang and he dug it out of the side pocket of his bag. Natalie's name appeared on the screen.

"Hey," he answered.

"Hey. What are you doing? I've called you three times."

"Swimming." He tucked his phone between his ear and shoulder and wrapped the towel around his waist before sitting on the metal bleacher. "What are you doing?"

"Conor and I were supposed to go to the movies, but he got called in to the trauma center. Do you want to come over for an early dinner?"

"Depends. What's for dinner?"

"Nothing fancy. Baked chicken, couscous, and salad."

Fancy or not, it sounded better than the leftover takeout he had in his fridge. "Sure. I need to shower first."

"Okay, but make it quick. I feel like we haven't spent any time together since the wedding."

"I just saw you two weeks ago. What's going on, Nat?"

"I'm worried about you," she said quietly. "With everything going on with the embezzlement and the murder."

"I'm fine, Nat."

"You're not, Bash. I know you."

He inhaled deeply and ran a hand through his wet hair. "You know it's supposed to be my job to take care of you, right?"

"We take care of each other. Come over for dinner. I'll make s'mores milkshakes," she said in a singsong voice.

"Fine. Twist my arm."

"Yay!"

Thirty minutes later, Ash let himself into her apartment and found Natalie standing next to the sink, chopping vegetables for the salad.

He tossed his keys in the bowl beside the door and joined her in the kitchen, bending down to kiss her on the cheek.

"Hey. You still smell like chlorine. Do you want to shower before we eat?"

He straightened. "Nah. I rinsed off at the pool, but I'll take a longer shower when I get home."

She scraped the carrots off the cutting board into the salad bowl and took it to the small table in the nook next to the kitchen. "Do you want wine or a beer?"

"I'll just have water."

"Ugh. You're seriously going to make me drink by myself?"

He grinned at her. "I'll have a beer."

"Atta boy."

He grabbed the beers, she fixed their plates, and they sat across from each other at the small dining table.

"So…how's married life?" He took a bite of food and waited for her to gush about how great it was.

Instead, her nose wrinkled a little. "Honestly, it's not that much different than it was before."

"Really?"

"Yeah." She pushed her couscous around on her plate before scooping some up and eating it.

Ash lowered his fork and really looked at his sister. Something was off.

"What's wrong? I thought you'd be happier."

His eyes widened as her eyes filled with tears.

"Nat. What is it? You're worrying me."

She shook her head quickly and picked up her napkin, dabbing at her eyes. "It's stupid."

"I'm sure it's not stupid," he said.

"I just…I thought things would be different after we were married, but it's exactly like it was when we were engaged."

Ash blinked. That wasn't what he'd been expecting. He thought either she or Conor had received bad news—an irregular medical exam, a surprise bill, an infected filling. Not that things were…normal.

"Isn't that a good thing? I know I'm not the pinnacle of experience, but it tells me that you guys were solid to begin with."

"I guess." She shrugged. "It's just that we came back from our honeymoon, and we both jumped right back into work and our ordinary lives. There was no 'yay, we're married, let's do awesome married stuff.' It was 'cool, that happened, better get to bed early because I have a meeting in the morning.' I expected to feel different."

Ash swallowed his chicken and took a sip of beer to help it go down. He was so out of his element with this conversation. "Different how?"

"I don't know…different. More adult. I told you it was stupid."

When all else failed, resort to humor. "I mean, if you want to feel married, you could wear matching shirts like Nonna and Nonno."

Natalie lowered her beer bottle and glared at him.

"I especially like it when Nonno wears black socks and sandals. Doesn't Conor have a pair of those hiking sandals? I bet he could pull it off. Ooh, I know!"

He pointed his fork at her while she glowered at him.

"What if instead of black socks, he wears bright patterned socks? Isn't there a website where you can order custom socks? You can get socks with each other's faces on them and wear those with your sandals and matching shirts."

He put up a hand to dodge the lettuce she chucked at his head.

"You're horrible," she said.

"You're lucky, Nat. A lot of people would kill to have the kind of normalcy you and Conor have." He looked down at his plate because his thoughts immediately shifted to Paige.

"Have you talked to her lately?" Natalie asked.

He didn't pretend to not know who she was talking about. "Not since the other day at the police station."

"Have you tried calling her?"

He shook his head.

"Why not?"

Ash placed his fork very precisely near his knife on the table, then took a long drink of his beer. He set the bottle down and turned it until the label faced him. "I'm not sure she wants to hear from me."

She leaned forward. "Why do you say that?"

"Because she said we needed to cool things off while the investigation was going on."

"But…it's over. They know who did it, don't they?"

"They arrested Alexis, but she said she didn't kill her cousin." He raised his gaze and met Natalie's. "And she asked Paige to help clear her."

His sister stared at him blankly. "And Paige agreed?"

Ash nodded.

"That's…" Natalie shook her head. "Why would Paige agree to help her? Alexis stole from you. From your company."

Ash shrugged. "She must believe that Alexis didn't kill him."

"But she thinks Alexis embezzled the money, right?"

"As far as I know. Leonidas turned over all the information they had to the police. They've taken over the investigation."

"Then you should call her." She laid her hand on his. "Bash, you like her. And she likes you."

"Are you sure about that?"

Her brows pinched together. "That you like her or that she likes you?"

"Both."

"Do you…not like her?"

"I do. I think I more than like her," he admitted.

"Just more than like?" Natalie asked.

"I've never been in love before." He pushed his plate away. "How do I know if I am? I've known her for what…a month? Isn't that too soon?"

"I knew I was going to marry Conor on our second date," she said.

"Really? Did you love him that soon?"

She shook her head. "No. But I knew I would eventually."

"How? How did you know?" This was the information he needed. He could take what Natalie told him and break it down to apply it to his own situation.

"I just knew." She looked up and shook her head a little. "He centered me. Made everything clearer. I could see our life together."

That was less than helpful. "It's the exact opposite with Paige. I can't focus on anything except her, and I don't know if it's because my feelings are real or if it's my ADHD zeroing in on the bright new shiny object."

"Everyone focuses on their partner in the first few months of infatuation. When I started dating Conor, I wanted to know what he was doing, where he was, what he was thinking."

"Really?" That was exactly what he was experiencing with Paige.

"Yes, it's perfectly normal. Wondering all those things about Paige doesn't make you special, and it doesn't mean it's because of your ADHD."

"That's not what you said in high school when I had a crush on Amy Miller."

Natalie cocked her head and gave him her are-you-kidding-me look. "You memorized her class schedule."

He shrugged. "So?"

"Including when she went to the bathroom between classes."

"I wanted to have a chance to talk to her."

"Bash, all she did was lend you a pencil, and you decided she was the love of your life."

Okay…he saw it.

"You have a connection with Paige. A *real* connection. If you want to explore that and see where it goes, then you need to *talk to* her."

"All right. I'll call her when I get home."

"Good." She stood with a satisfied smile and gathered her plate and empty bottle.

He picked up his plate and followed her to the kitchen, setting it in the sink. "So…about those s'mores milkshakes."

Natalie grinned. "You wash. I'll shake."

Full and thinking he should have swum more laps before going to Natalie's, Ash pulled into the narrow driveway on the side of his house. His renters used the larger driveway that led to the single-car garage at the back of the property.

He shouldered open the side door into the kitchen, reminding himself for the millionth time to plane it down so it wouldn't stick, and flipped on the light just inside the door.

Silence echoed back at him as he kicked off his shoes. He really should get a dog. He tossed his keys on the counter and filled a glass with water. It wasn't late and he had time to work on the code and perform a dry run on one of their initial clients. A client who hadn't canceled their agreement to test the program after hearing about the embezzlement and murder.

Ash didn't bother with the lights as he walked through the house to his office, muscle memory guiding him.

Something stabbed into his foot.

"Ow! Shit." He jerked his foot up and rubbed the sole on his other leg. What the hell had he stepped on?

He reached around the doorway and flipped on the light.

"Shit. Shit, shit, shit."

His office was trashed. Papers everywhere. His monitors smashed. Absentmindedly, he set the glass down on top of a small bookcase and went to the small rack on the side of the room that held his server.

Gone. The hard drive was gone. All his work. All his code. Gone. Whoever had stolen it had smashed the server components for good measure.

He ran his fingers through his hair and fisted handfuls.

"Fuck!"

CHAPTER 29

*P*aige stared at the ceiling from her spot on the floor, moving her feet back and forth like windshield wiper blades. Rather than twiddle her thumbs at the hotel in Savannah, she'd driven home. Knowing she wouldn't get anything accomplished at work, she decided to use her two days *stepping back* as personal days.

She'd started and given up on three books. She'd weeded her front yard. She'd even gone to the beach.

That had been a disaster. Bound and determined not to think about Ash at all, the sound of the ocean brought back all the memories from their time in the Virgin Islands. Instead of brown sand and water, she'd seen crystal clear blue water and Ash's muscles bunching as he swam. Remembered the way his tongue felt when he licked the salty ocean water from her skin.

She'd returned home less than thirty minutes after arriving and started and deleted four different texts to him.

What could she even say that made sense? *I miss you? I want to see you? I shouldn't have pushed you away? I'd really like to sit on your face?*

The ceiling fan blades needed dusting.

She blew out a breath and turned her head. Huh. How long had it been since she'd gone through the storage space under the stairs? She flopped over to her stomach, rose up to her hands and knees, and crawled over to the half door.

It protested being opened after so many years of remaining closed. Thankfully the light clicked on when she pulled the cord, so she didn't have to rummage around in the dark.

She pulled out a large gray plastic tote. There was no way she was going through it in there. Spiders. A shiver racked her shoulders at the thought.

"Bleh."

Clearing the small door, she plopped down on her butt and lifted the lid, revealing stacks of books.

"Aww…my books." She leaned over the tub and hugged it.

She'd forgotten all about them. They were all the books she'd insisted on keeping when she'd joined the Air Force. They'd been collecting dust in her parents' attic until they decided to sell their house five years ago so they could downsize to a Class A camper and travel the U.S. They'd threatened to donate them all if she didn't get them.

Maybe she could find something in there to read. She'd probably have more luck rereading something she was familiar with.

She pulled out five or six books at a time and looked at the titles before setting them aside. More than twenty years later, she couldn't remember why she'd been so adamant about keeping them. It probably had something to do with the fact she'd been nineteen when she'd joined the Air Force and wanted to hold on to the things that had been important to her.

The next book on the top was *Alice in Wonderland*. She grinned and lifted it out. It had been her favorite book as a child, and she'd insisted her parents read it to her every night, no matter how many times they'd read it before, no matter how much her parents pleaded with her to please let them choose another story. They'd been more than willing to let her read it as many times as she wanted when she could do it by herself.

The cover was faded, the glue on the spine deteriorated to the point that some of the pages had separated and come loose. She gently flipped through the pages, scanning the story.

We're all mad here. She should get that tattooed. It definitely described her life. She flipped to a section where several pages had separated and gently pushed them back in place.

It was the trial of the Knave. She'd loved the ridiculousness and confusion of it all as a little girl. Now she understood the book was deeper than the fantasies and adventures of a little girl. Turning the page, she started to read from where she'd opened the book, understanding Alice's frustration with the whole proceeding.

A line jumped out at her, and she read it again. *Begin at the beginning, the King said gravely, and go on till you come to the end: then stop.*

Paige lowered the book to her lap. "Begin at the beginning," she said out loud. Something clicked and the pieces she had missed began to take shape in her mind.

What was the beginning? Not when they were first presented with the problem of the missing money. Natalie told them the money was missing, so they went looking for it.

She grabbed her phone from the coffee table and called Samara, who answered on the third ring.

"Hey," Samara said. "Is everything okay?"

"Yes. I'm going through some boxes at home."

"Okay. Um…did you have a question?"

"Yeah. Several, actually. All the documents from M.A.G. were scanned, right?"

Samara repeated the question away from the phone's mic. "Angie says yes."

"Including any we got from Natalie?"

"I don't think Natalie gave us any documents. Let me check. Hang on."

Paige stood and went to her small office to log on to her work laptop. If Angie had scanned them, they'd be on the TLC server. One benefit of having a computer wizard was being able to access everything securely from a remote location. Another benefit was a computer wizard who insisted on standardized naming conventions for all files.

Pulling up the M.A.G. investigation files, she scrolled through the list of documents but didn't find anything that would indicate they were the original documents provided by Natalie.

"Paige?"

"I'm here," she said.

"No one remembers getting any documents from Natalie," Samara said.

"Is Addison there with you?"

"She is."

"Put me on speakerphone," Paige said.

"Sure. Hang on. Okay, you're on speaker."

"Paige? It's Addison. What's going on?"

"Hey, Addison. I was cleaning out my storage closet and got distracted by a book."

"Okay." Her voice held a note of amusement.

"One of the lines in the book was 'begin at the beginning.'" She slipped on her flip-flops, grabbed her keys from the hook by the front door, and headed to her car.

"Okay?"

"How did we know M.A.G. Security was missing money?" Paige asked.

A jumble of words came over the phone, until finally one voice said clearly, "They told us the money was missing."

"But Samara didn't initially find any accounting errors, right? As far as you could tell from the documents we had and the bank records, there was nothing wrong."

As soon as Paige started her car, the Bluetooth picked up her cell phone, and she set the phone in the cup holder.

"That's right," Samara said. "It wasn't until Angie accessed their accounts that we actually found any discrepancies."

"Exactly," Paige said. "We never found any money missing. We found money that was being skimmed off the top, but it didn't add up to $150,000."

"But we did find that account with the fifty in it," Angie said.

"We did, but we weren't supposed to. We were never supposed to find any money missing."

"I'm confused," Addison said.

"I'm sorry. The timeline and details are still jumbled in my head. I'm on my way back to Savanah—I should be there in about two hours depending on traffic."

"There's a whiteboard here," Angie said.

Paige laughed. "Awesome. I'll be there soon and draw you guys a picture."

She ended the call and took the opportunity at the next red light to find Natalie's contact information in her email. There was no answer when Paige tried to call her. It was a little after six, according to the dash clock. Paige decided to swing by Natalie's apartment on the way to the hotel on the chance she would be home. Then she could see if Natalie still had whatever documents led her to think money was missing.

The drive down Highway 17 was uneventful and flowed smoothly until she hit traffic on I-95 two miles before the exit she needed to take to get to Natalie's. Those two miles added almost thirty frustrating minutes to the drive. As soon as the traffic cleared, she gunned it off the exit ramp, impatiently drumming her fingers on the steering wheel.

The whole drive, she replayed the events of the last few weeks in her head. Starting with the initial meeting with Natalie, Ash, Patrick, and Alexis, trying to remember every word, every gesture, every nuance of the key players.

Unfortunately, that also meant she replayed every moment with Ash. Every touch. Every whisper. Every moment she wanted more and stopped herself from taking it.

She finally pulled into the apartment complex and followed the small signs around to Natalie's building. So late in the evening, there were few open parking spots, but she found one on the back side of the next building. Natalie's apartment was on the ground floor, the door decorated with a colorful wreath. Paige knocked sharply.

The door unlatched as if it hadn't been closed properly. She waited a few seconds before gently pushing the door open further.

"Natalie?" With no response, she opened the door fully and called out louder. "Natalie? Conor? Are you home?"

She didn't think they were the type to leave their door unlocked and unlatched unless they were in a hurry to leave. A prickle of unease crawled across her skin, making the hair on the back of her neck stand up. She gently slipped her keys into a pocket. Not that it mattered. If someone was in the apartment, they would have heard her call out.

The entryway didn't afford a clear view of the apartment. All she could see from her vantage point was the small room to her left, either a laundry or utility room, the edge of a couch farther down in what must be the living room, and a refrigerator to her right.

She eased closer to the corner of the kitchen opening and slowly peered around it. Natalie was sprawled in the middle of the floor on her side.

"Shit." All caution left as she rushed to her side, quickly scanning what little of the apartment she could see over the open countertop.

It had been ransacked. Papers strewn across the floor of the small dining area. Seat cushions removed from the couch and chair.

Kneeling by Natalie's head, Paige moved her hair from her face and found the pulse point on her neck. Strong and steady. There was no obvious blood, so hopefully she was only unconscious.

A noise in the living room drew her attention. A person in dark clothes, wearing a black ski mask, was running for the back door.

"Hey!"

Paige leaped up and body-checked them, knocking them into a small table as they reached for the handle of the back door. Judging by the breadth of shoulders and the solidness of their chest, the attacker was a man. He caught his balance before he hit the floor and came up swinging.

She dodged his well-telegraphed punch.

Her training with Dani, their hand-to-hand combat instructor, kicked in. Although she was about the same height as the intruder, she didn't have the strength to take him down with a punch. She needed to distract and disorient him in order to get the upper hand.

She stepped in and swung her elbow up, striking him on the underside of his chin with the hard bones of her joint. His teeth clacked together, and he grunted as he stumbled back. Before she could strike again, he kicked out, hitting her on the upper thigh, just above her knee.

Sharp pain buckled her knee. She saw his fist coming and barely had time to turn her head and throw her arm up. It wasn't enough to deflect the blow, and he caught her on the side of the head, on the edge of her orbital bone.

"Natalie? Babe, I'm so sorry. This is the last—Natalie!"

The attacker looked toward the sound of Conor's voice and shoved Paige. He ran at the door and slammed his shoulder into it, breaking one of the panels of glass and splintering the door-frame before disappearing into the night.

"Hey! Stop!" Conor rushed around the counter but hesitated

when he saw Paige. The indecision between going after the assailant or helping her was plain on his face.

Paige shifted to her butt and swiped at the corner of her eye, her hand coming away with blood. "You won't catch him. Check on Natalie and call an ambulance."

Given the direction he needed, Conor raced back to Natalie, his phone already in his hand.

Fuck. Her knee wasn't dislocated, but he'd probably done some damage. She'd definitely be limping for a few days. Pulling her phone from her back pocket, she grimaced at the cracked screen. She scrolled through her contacts until she found the number she needed.

"Detective Gander."

"Detective, this is Paige Davis." She wiped more blood away before it could trail into her eye.

"Ms. Davis, what can I do for you?"

"Can you send a car to Natalie Mills's address? Someone broke in and attacked her."

"Natalie Mills…? That's Sebastian Moreno's sister, isn't it?"

"Yes."

"The Moreno family is having one hell of a night," he said.

Frowning pulled at the corner of her eyebrow, sending a fresh rivulet of blood down the side of her face. "What do you mean?"

"Sebastian Moreno's house was broken into earlier today. His laptop and server were stolen."

CHAPTER 30

$\mathcal{A}$sh exited the elevator and strode down the short hall to the nurse's station. "Natalie Mills? She was admitted about thirty minutes ago."

The nurse glanced up at him, peering over the top of her glasses. "Name?"

"Uh…Natalie Mills?"

"I got that. What's your name?"

Heat crept up his neck. "Oh. Sebastian Moreno."

She checked a piece of paper on the desk. "You can go back. Take the first right, then the first left. You can wait back there."

"Thank you." He walked quickly down the hall, following the nurse's directions. The small waiting room had a dozen or so chairs placed around the walls and Conor paced back and forth between them. When Ash entered the room, his brother-in-law pulled him into a tight hug.

"I never should have answered the call," he said into Ash's shoulder. "If I hadn't gone to the trauma center, I would have been home to protect her."

"You can't blame yourself. I had dinner with her. If I had stayed until you got home, I'd have been there to protect her.

Neither of us imagined something like this could have happened." He slowly backed out of the hug. "How is she?"

Conor shook his head. "I'm not sure yet. The EMTs said she had a nasty bump on her head. They took her for a CT scan and sent me up here to wait."

"What happened?" Ash asked. All he'd been able to get out of Conor during his frantic phone call was that there had been a home invasion and Natalie was at the hospital.

Conor scrubbed his face and sat down heavily in one of the chairs with the best view of the corridor. "I'm not sure. Paige said the door was open when she got there, and she found Natalie unconscious in the kitchen. The burglar was still in the apartment. She tried to stop him, but he got away."

Ash's stomach flipped and he sat down next to Conor. "Wait. Paige was there?"

"Yeah. She's here at the hospital. Whoever it was clocked her pretty good. She was getting looked at in the ER when I came up here."

"Is she still down there?" Ash asked.

"I think so. She was giving her statement to the police while they checked her out."

Nervous, unfocused energy jittered through him. He needed to move, but didn't have anywhere to go. He paced back and forth in the waiting room, frustrated with the small, confined space. He wanted to go down and find Paige. They probably wouldn't let him back with her in the ER, if she was even still there, and he didn't want to chance missing her.

Voices carried down the hall, and Conor popped up, worried anticipation on his face. But then his shoulders slumped, and he sat back down. Ash followed his gaze. Paige and Graham walked slowly down the hall, carrying to-go trays of coffee, Paige limping slightly. Graham passed him with a chin lift and handed a coffee to Conor.

Paige stopped in front of him. "Hi. I didn't know how you took your coffee so it's black, but there's cream and sugar if you want it."

Ash ignored the coffee, too focused on the narrow white bandage on the corner of her eyebrow and the dark purple bruise forming along her temple and cheekbone.

He gently pushed a strand of hair away from the side of her face. "What happened?"

She stepped to the side and set the coffees on the nearest table. "I went to talk to Natalie on my way back to the hotel. When I knocked on the door, it opened like it wasn't latched all the way. I called her name, but she didn't answer. When I went in, I saw her lying on the floor in the kitchen. I was going to call an ambulance when I saw the thief. I tried to stop him, but he got away."

"Why would you do that?"

Paige's eyebrows pinched together and the corners of her mouth turned down.

"I wouldn't go there if I were you," Graham said. "She already chewed my ass for asking the same thing."

Ash looked at him, then back at Paige. The image of her running down a wall face-first popped into his mind, and he remembered who she was. More importantly, he remembered what she could do.

"You're right," he said. "I'm sorry."

Paige nodded, accepting his apology. "What about you? Detective Gander said your house was broken into as well." She moved to the chairs and eased down while keeping her leg as straight as possible, leaving an empty spot next to Graham. Ash took the seat on the other side of her.

"I had dinner with Natalie earlier. When I got home, I went into my office, and it was trashed. The monitors and server were smashed, and the hard drive and laptop were gone. Best the police could tell, they climbed in through a window in the spare room."

"I don't think it's a coincidence both your and your sister's houses were robbed on the same night," Graham said. "Someone is trying to tie up loose ends."

"Natalie isn't a loose end," Conor ground out.

"Conor, I know you're upset, but Natalie was the first person to notice the missing money. She has information neither we, nor the police, have."

"What information can be so important someone would want to hurt her?" He gripped the sides of his head and rested his elbows on his knees.

Paige moved to the seat next to him and placed a hand on his arm. "Conor, we can't figure out how Natalie knew there was money missing. Nothing in the paperwork we got from Patrick or Ash indicates anything was amiss. The only reason we discovered the embezzlement was because we were looking for where the money went."

"Okay, but you discovered it," Conor said.

"We didn't," Graham said. "Paige and her team found an embezzlement scheme and an account with a lot of money in it, but they never found the money that Natalie said was missing."

Conor leaned back and rested his head against the wall behind him. "I'm so confused. Do you think Natalie knows who took the money?"

"Probably not," Paige said. "But she may hold the key to figuring out who did. We think that's what whoever broke into your apartment was looking for. Was Natalie supposed to be somewhere tonight?"

Conor shrugged. "We were supposed to go to the movies, but I don't think anyone else knew that."

"They could have been watching the apartment," Graham said. "They saw you leave and assumed she was with you."

Conor closed his eyes and shook his head. "Fuck."

Ash knew this was going to haunt Conor for a long time to come.

Conor opened his eyes and sat forward, his attention zeroed in on something down the corridor. He stood and met a dark-haired woman wearing a white coat and light pink scrubs in the middle of the room.

"How is she?" he asked.

"She has a mild concussion and a broken wrist." The doctor glanced at them all, but focused on Conor. "We're going to keep her overnight to monitor her, but she should be able to go home tomorrow."

Conor's whole body slumped, and he covered his face with his hands, mumbling something quietly.

Ash joined him at the doctor's side. "Can we go back and see her?"

"One of you can go back and sit with her. She's in and out of consciousness. Some of that is the head injury and some of that is the medication we have her on to help reduce the swelling."

Ash nodded and squeezed Conor's shoulder. "Go on. I'll see her tomorrow."

Conor hugged him, slapping him on the back, and followed the doctor out of the waiting room.

Graham stood and looked at Paige. "You good?"

"Yeah," she said. "I'll see you back at the hotel."

Graham shook Ash's hand. "I'll see you later."

Ash wasn't sure what to think of that. He hadn't had much interaction with Graham.

"Have you talked to the police already?" Paige asked.

Ash nodded. "I gave my statement at my house. The officer said they might have some follow-up questions for me. What about you?"

"I'm going to get a ride share back to the hotel."

"I can take you." His heart pounded in his chest. He really didn't want her to say no, or that they needed to continue keeping their distance from each other.

"I'd appreciate that."

He didn't think it was possible for his heart to beat any faster, but it picked up its pace at her acceptance. He didn't want to read too much into it, but he hoped it meant more than a ride—that he was more than a convenience.

"Can we stop by your sister's apartment first?" she asked.

"What for?"

"Well, their back door needs to be secured. I don't know if the apartment management knows about the break-in yet. You can also get some clothes for her and Conor for the morning."

"That's a good idea."

"And I'd like to see if you can tell what the thief took."

"Oh." She didn't accept the ride to spend more time with him —it was just to access Natalie's apartment.

She put a hand on his upper arm. "That's not the only reason I want to go with you, Ash. I could have gone to Natalie's apartment alone."

"I'm that easy to read?" he asked.

"You're not, actually, but I'm learning your tells. I'd like you to stay at the hotel tonight."

It was a good idea. He probably wouldn't sleep well, knowing someone had invaded his space. "That makes sense. I'll see if they have a room."

"With me," she said softly.

His mind blanked. "Oh. Okay. What about keeping our distance?" he blurted out. Why had he brought that up?

Paige inhaled deeply. "At this point, I don't think it's going to make a difference one way or the other and I can't worry about it. I don't want to possibly miss out on something special just because I'm concerned about what other people might think."

"So we're not keeping our distance anymore? I'm not trying to be difficult, but I don't read between the lines well, and I function much better if people just say what they're thinking."

She smiled. "I don't want to keep my distance from you. I like you. A lot. And I would really like to explore what this could lead to."

"'This' meaning us and a relationship?" He needed her meaning to be very, very clear. He didn't want there to be any questions or ambiguity about what they were doing.

"Yes. As long as you don't want to keep your distance."

Ash closed the small space between their bodies and slid an arm lower around her waist. He cradled the side of her face that wasn't bruised.

"I don't want to keep my distance."

He lowered his head and kissed her softly, brushing his lips over hers. He wanted to deepen the kiss, but knew if he did, he'd lose himself in it.

Pressing his forehead to hers, he said, "I like you a lot too."

A throat cleared. They both looked up and toward the corridor. An older nurse glared at them. "Unless you two have a reason to be here, could you like each other somewhere else?"

Ash smiled at Paige, and they stepped apart. "Yes, ma'am," he said.

"Natalie's apartment?" Paige asked.

"Sounds like a plan." It was the start of a plan. They could figure the rest of it out tomorrow.

CHAPTER 31

Someone had already replaced the broken window panel with a piece of plywood and done their best to lock the door at Natalie's apartment. Ash found the broom and dustpan in the laundry room and told Paige where to find the furniture spray and a dust rag to clean up the fingerprint powder. Most of it was on the door handle and desk.

He appreciated Paige's suggestion to stop at Natalie's apartment. She wouldn't want to come home to this mess.

Paige straightened the couch cushions. "I've never understood why people look in the couch for things. No one hides shit in their couch."

"Natalie wouldn't have hidden it anyway. She thought it was normal paperwork."

Paige glanced through a handful of papers, then tapped them on the desk and set them in the corner. "Would she have kept it here or taken it to work with her?"

"I don't know honestly. Except for this, we don't really talk about work."

"Can you ask her tomorrow?"

"Sure."

"Thanks."

Ash pulled his phone from his back pocket and opened up his reminder app.

"You don't have to ask her right now," she said.

He glanced at her. "I'm setting a reminder for myself, otherwise I'll probably forget."

"Oh. Okay."

He slid his phone back into his pocket and grabbed the broom, sweeping up broken glass now that all the papers, cushions, and other things had been picked up from the floor. The main bedroom was trashed as well, clothes pulled out of drawers, the sheets pulled off the bed and the mattress askew, as if someone had tried to flip it. Paige helped him push the mattress back in place and made the bed while he picked up clothes, placing them on the end of the bed.

Finding an overnight bag was easy since it, along with shoes and other bags, had been tossed out of the closet. He grabbed a shirt, boxers, and pants for Conor. Paige handed him some of Natalie's clothes, and he put those in the bag. She came out of the bathroom with a makeup bag that she tossed on top of the clothes.

"What's that?" he asked.

"Makeup remover, toothbrushes, and toothpaste."

"Thanks. I wouldn't have thought of that."

She shrugged. "The hospital probably has soap and toothpaste, but I thought she'd like to have her own."

He zipped the bag closed and slung the strap over his shoulder. "After you."

Outside the apartment, he pulled the door shut tightly behind him and pushed on it a few times to make sure it was locked. Paige stood at the end of the short corridor, scanning the parking lot.

"What is it?" He tried to see what she might see, but in the middle of the night, everything was quiet. The parking lot was full, and only a few lights shone through some of the apartment windows.

She shook her head. "I'm just trying to get a feel for where someone would have parked to watch the apartment. When you came for dinner, did you park where you're parked now?"

"Yeah. It's closer to their apartment than the front parking lot, and it's usually empty."

"So no one would have seen you arrive if they were sitting out there?"

"Probably not. Natalie parks back there as well. She said it's easier to carry in groceries, but I think Conor parks in their assigned spot. His car is the white one, third from the end of the row."

She nodded and turned. "Ready?"

Ash gestured toward the exit at the back of the short hall. "Lead the way."

~

*P*aige handed Ash the key card to swipe at the entrance of the hotel's underground parking garage. They had to drive down to the last level before he finally found an empty spot, halfway between the vehicle ramp and the elevator. She did a quick scan of the area while he stowed the duffel bag in the trunk.

"Do you always do that?" He locked the car with the fob.

"Do what?"

"Scan parking lots. Look for threats."

She thought about it while they waited for the elevator. "Habit."

"Occupational hazard?"

The elevator dinged, and they entered the car. She pressed the button for her floor and tapped the key card against the reader. "That and parking garages are one of the most frequent locations for a woman to be attacked."

Paige glanced at him when he didn't say anything else. His mouth was tight, and anger shone from his eyes. Perhaps she shouldn't have mentioned women getting attacked since Natalie was in the hospital for that very thing happening.

"Sorry."

"What are you sorry for? You're the one that has to spend life with eyes in the back of your head because you can't do something as simple as walk through a parking garage without having to think about someone attacking you."

That was unexpected. She assumed he was thinking about Natalie, but instead he was angry on her behalf. For something she did without consciously thinking about it half the time. A blossom of warmth spread through her chest as the elevator doors dinged and opened on her floor.

When they reached her room, she set her phone and the key on the dresser. Angie had picked up her car from Natalie's earlier since Paige had gotten a free ride to the hospital in the ambulance. The go bag she always kept in her car was on the bag stand on the other side where Angie said she'd leave it, and her car keys were under the TV.

Paige sat on the end of the bed and rubbed her good eye.

"Are you okay?" Ash sat next to her.

"Yes, just tired, and my head is swirling with everything that's happened."

"Do you want to talk through it?" He yawned hard.

She covered her own yawn, then smiled. "Not right now. We can go over it this afternoon with everyone else."

She stood and her thigh muscle protested. "Right now, I need to get some ice on my leg and go to sleep."

"What happened to your leg?"

"I got kicked."

"You got kicked and punched?"

"Yeah."

"Take your pants off and lay down." Ash went into the bathroom and plastic rustled. He came out carrying the ice bucket and grabbed the key from the dresser.

"Pants. Bed." He left the room.

"Bossy," Paige said quietly. It was kind of hot.

She grabbed a T-shirt from her suitcase and took it into the bathroom with her. Her leg protested distinctly as she pulled off her jeans and assessed the damage in the mirror. The dark blue and purple bruise covered a large portion of the outside of her right thigh above her knee.

She heard the door open and close while she scrubbed her face. After changing into the T-shirt to sleep in and folding her clothes, she grabbed a hand towel and took her clothes back into the room.

Ash was spinning a bag of ice before twisting the end into a knot.

She held her hand out for the bag. "Thanks."

He walked around to the side of the bed farthest from the door and pulled the covers down. "Lie down."

She frowned but walked around the side of the bed, the side she normally slept on anyway, and lay down on her left side facing the window. He took the towel from her and placed it gently on her leg, then settled the bag of ice on top of it.

Paige hissed out a breath. The bag wasn't heavy, but he had to move it back and forth to get the ice cubes to settle in a way that it wouldn't roll off her leg.

"Sorry." He let go of the bag. "Is that okay?"

She nodded.

He leaned down and kissed her on the temple. "Be right back."

She followed him with her eyes until she couldn't see him anymore. Why had her fight or flight response kicked in? She felt restless. It was different from when she was fighting the thief—she'd just jumped in and tried to stop him—but now she felt jittery and nervous and wanted nothing more than to get up and pace.

Ash returned from the bathroom wearing nothing but boxers that hugged the lean muscles of his lower abs. He set a glass of water down on the table next to her and held out his hand. "Here."

"What's that?" she asked.

"Ibuprofen, in case you haven't taken any."

She hadn't. "You just had some in your pocket?"

He smiled. "I grabbed some when I grabbed Conor's shave kit."

She smiled back and held out her hand, taking a sip of water to wash them down. "Thank you."

"You're welcome." He walked around the bed and turned off the overhead light before getting into the other side of the bed.

Unable to see him with her back to him, she could feel the heat from his body as he moved around to get comfortable.

As tired as she was, she wasn't falling asleep anytime soon.

"Are you okay?" he asked.

"Mmm-hmm."

He shifted, his presence hovering over her.

"Are you sure? You haven't moved since you laid down."

She squeezed her eyes closed and debated lying. But she hadn't lied to him about anything yet, and it didn't feel right.

"I'm uncomfortable," she said softly.

"Is it your leg?"

"It's the entire situation."

The bed bounced when he pushed away, and she blinked when the lamp clicked on.

She twisted her upper body to look at him as he leaned toward her. He stared at her for a heartbeat, then rolled the other way and got out of bed. He walked around to her side and flipped the covers back.

"Scoot that way." He motioned toward the side he'd just vacated.

Paige shifted backward to the warm spot on the bed, giving him enough room to slide into her side. He made sure the ice bag was still positioned properly on her leg and pulled the covers back over them.

He rested his head on his hand, facing her. "What entire situation?"

"This." She gestured to her leg. "This." She gestured to him.

He pointed at his chest. "Me?"

"Yes. No. Kind of." She took a deep breath. "It's what you're doing."

"What am I doing?"

"You're taking care of me."

"Am...I...not supposed to take care of you?"

Fuck. She had no idea how to do any of this.

Paige rolled to her back and dug the cold ice bag out from under her leg, then threw back the covers and got up to pace.

Ash adjusted the pillows behind his head to prop himself up and watch her. "Paige. Talk to me."

"I take care of people." She pointed to herself. "I take care of everything. I don't need to be taken care of."

"Bullshit."

That one word pulled her up short. "What?"

"Bull. Shit." He sat up. "Everyone needs to be taken care of at some point, Paige. Everyone *should* be taken care of by the people they matter to. I admit, it's not something I'm always great at because I get lost in my own shit. I forget to feed myself sometimes, much less someone else. But right now, this minute, you had a shitty fucking night, you're injured, and you need to be taken care of."

He glared at her. "So get back in bed, put the damn ice pack on your leg, and let me take care of you."

Her mind went blank. She had no witty, sarcastic, put-an-egotistical-man-in-his-place comment because Ash wasn't being egotistical. He was being caring.

Fuck me.

All she could think to do was follow instructions. She went to the wrong side of the bed, turned off the lamp, and got in. Before she even settled, Ash was laying the towel on her leg. She found a comfortable position on her side, and he gently placed the bag of ice over her thigh once more. Then he pulled the blanket up to her lower chest and slid his arm under her pillow so she could rest her head in the hollow of his shoulder.

"You good?" he asked.

She nodded.

"Good. Let me know if you need anything."

"You're kind of bossy."

"Only when I need to be."

Paige smiled. Maybe she did need it. If she was honest with herself, it felt nice to be taken care of. She couldn't even remember the last time someone had put her needs ahead of their own, had made sure she had what she needed instead of assuming she had it covered.

Her eyes stung and she blinked rapidly to keep any tears from falling. She was tired. That was why it affected her so much.

Like Ash said, she'd had a rough fucking night.

CHAPTER 32

When they exited the hospital elevator on Natalie's floor the next morning, Ash saw Tinker, the guy who'd offered to let Ash crash at his place the night he'd played video games at Leonidas, sitting next to her door, reading a magazine with a motorcycle on the cover. There seemed to be a lot of nurses walking back and forth in the hallway, slowing down as they passed Natalie's room.

Tinker looked up as they approached. "Hey, boss lady. Heard you got salty about my assignment in Yemassee."

"Fired," Paige said.

His grin was lopsided when he winked at her. Ash guessed Tinker didn't take her threat seriously because he went back to reading his magazine.

"How long have you been here?" she asked.

He looked at his watch. "About two hours. Got here around seven this morning. Boss man caught me before I'd opened the garage."

"Is Levi covering for you?"

"Yeah. He's working out pretty well. Good with his hands, knows what he's doing, and pretty much keeps to himself."

"Why are you here?" Ash asked.

"Graham asked me to come down and hang out, keep an eye on your sister."

"Because of the attack?"

"Yeah. Could be the attacker timed the break-in wrong and surprised her, but we didn't want to take any chances. They probably wouldn't try to do anything in a hospital, but better safe than sorry."

She nodded. "How's the situation here?"

Tinker shrugged. "No issues on my front, but a lot of nurses have been going into her room. Don't know what that's about."

"You don't know…really, Tink?" she asked.

He grinned again.

"What did I miss? Is something wrong with Natalie?" Ash asked. Why else would nurses be going into her room?

Paige huffed out a short laugh and shook her head. "I guarantee there's nothing wrong with Natalie. If I had to guess, all the nurses are women, and they're going into Natalie's room so they have an excuse to check out Tink."

Ash took in the man's tattooed and muscled forearms, short dark blond hair, full beard, and his general air of "don't give a shit, but don't fuck with me," and the tension left his shoulders. "Oh. Right."

"Did any of the nurses happen to mention when Natalie might be discharged?" Paige asked.

"Yeah. Later this morning. They said probably before lunch."

His shoulders relaxed even more. If they were letting her go home, her injuries weren't that serious. "I'm going to go in."

Paige ran a hand down his arm. "I'll be in in a sec."

He nodded and kissed her temple absentmindedly before knocking on the door to Natalie's room and opening it.

Conor sat on the far side of the bed, holding Natalie's hand against his face. They both glanced in his direction.

Natalie smiled. "Hey."

"Hey." He closed the door and approached the bed, setting the duffel bag on the table at the end. "How are you feeling?"

"I've been better. I've been worse."

She wore a neon green cast on her right arm from her hand to just below her elbow.

Following his gaze, she lifted the cast from the pillow it rested on, then lowered it. "They let me pick the color. I figure if I have to wear it, I may as well be obnoxious about it."

He pulled a chair over to the bed. "I'm so sorry, Natalie."

"For what?"

"For not protecting you. For dragging you into this whole mess in the first place. If I hadn't asked you to look at the financials, none of this—"

"Stop it. None of this is your fault. You did exactly what you should have done. You had no way of knowing any of this was going to happen."

He ran a hand through his hair. The sensible part of him knew she was right, but it didn't stop him from feeling like shit that his little sister had been attacked, and she'd been attacked because of him.

"They'll find who did this, Ash," she said.

"I know. But it doesn't change what happened to you." He touched the tips of her fingers sticking out from the bright cast. "It could have been so much worse than it was."

Natalie curled her fingers into his. "It wasn't, so like Mom always says, don't go borrowing trouble."

"I had all the same thoughts you did while I was sitting here last night," Conor said. "She told me the same thing. I didn't take it any better than you are."

Ash smiled across the bed. Natalie could tell them she was fine and everything would be okay, but it wasn't going to stop them from being mad that they weren't there to protect her.

The door opened behind him. Ash turned in his chair as Paige slipped inside.

"Hey, how are you feeling?" She stopped at the foot of the bed.

"Probably about as good as you look," Natalie said.

Paige smiled. "That bad, huh?"

The corners of Natalie's mouth tilted up, which he took as a good sign. "Conor told me you caught the guy in the apartment and tried to stop him."

"Tried. Wasn't able to."

"I don't know whether to thank you or yell at you."

Paige shrugged a shoulder. "Eh, you can do both. I'm used to it."

"Thank you," Natalie said.

"You're welcome."

No one said anything for several moments, and Natalie looked at him, widened her eyes, and twitched her head in Paige's direction. She wasn't subtle about what she was doing, but that didn't mean he understood why she was doing it.

"Well, it's getting suitably awkward in here," Paige said, "so I'll cut to the chase. Natalie, do you have the original documents you used for the financial review?"

Natalie scowled at Ash before answering. "They're at my office."

"What was in the documents that made you realize there was money missing?" Paige asked.

"The amount on the conversion notes didn't match what was deposited in the business accounts," she said.

"What conversion notes?" Paige asked.

"What *is* a conversion note?" Ash asked.

"It's kind of like a loan document," Natalie explained. "Early investors give a business money in exchange for equity in the company once the company has a valuation. They get a certain number of stocks based on the value of the stock at a given time, usually for more than the amount of the initial investment. That way investors get a return on their money."

"Hang on a second." Paige pulled out her phone, typed on it, and held it out as it started to ring.

"Hello?" a husky, feminine voice answered.

"Hi, Samara. It's Paige."

"Paige! Oh my god . How are you? Are you okay? We heard about the attack. Is Natalie okay?"

"We're both good. I'm with her now actually. Do you recall any conversion notes in the paperwork we got from M.A.G.'s files?" Paige asked.

"I don't," Samara said. "I would have made note of those because I would have looked at the investors."

"Okay. Thank you."

"You're welcome. Let us know if you need anything—we're still at the hotel."

"We will. Bye."

Paige pressed her thumb to the phone and disconnected. She looked at Natalie. "Any chance we can grab those papers from your office?"

"Of course. We can go as soon as I'm discharged."

"No," Ash said.

"You need to go home and rest," Conor said.

"You don't need to be involved in this any more than you already are."

He and Conor talked over themselves, explaining all the reasons Natalie was not going to go to her office and why she needed to go home and take it easy.

He should have known better. Natalie was too stubborn for their own good.

❧

*A*sh exchanged looks with Paige as she tried to hide her grin. They were in the front seat of Ash's car on the way to Natalie's office while Natalie and Conor argued in the back seat about why she refused to sit on the sidelines like a sheltered princess.

They pulled into a little shopping center of six businesses. A kid's play place promising hourly drop-off rates and Natalie's office, Heritage Financial Planning, bracketed a pizza restaurant, a nail salon, a hairdresser, and a small café serving hot breakfast and lunch. It was a good location for all the businesses, attracting a wide variety of customers.

They waited for Tink to park his bike a few spots down from theirs, then everyone followed Natalie into the office as she gave Conor one final "Shush."

A tall, slender man with spiky brown hair stood up from the reception desk to the left of the door. "Natalie. Oh my god . We heard what happened. Are you okay?"

"Hi, Victor. I'm okay. You know Conor." She put her hand on his shoulder. "This is my brother, Ash, and my friends Paige and, uh…" She hesitated over Tink's name.

"Christian." He stepped forward and shook Victor's hand.

"Right, Christian. They picked me and Conor up from the hospital. I just need to grab something from my office really quick."

"Oh. Yeah. Sure." He dragged his nervous gaze away from Tink. "Do you want me to let Mr. Miller know you're here? He was asking about you."

"I'll poke my head into his office on my way out," she said.

"Is everyone going to wait out here?" His wide eyes telegraphed that he hoped the answer was no.

"Well…" Natalie glanced around. "My office is kind of small. I don't think we'd actually all fit."

"I'll go with you," Paige said.

"Can I use your head?" Tink asked.

Victor blanched. "My what?"

"He means the toilet." Paige glared at Tink, who just smirked.

"Oh. Of—of course. It's down the hall on the left."

Tink tilted his chin up as he passed Victor and followed Natalie down the hall. "Thanks."

He broke off at the men's restroom, and Paige followed Natalie into an office two doors down and across the hall.

Natalie flipped on the light and went to a wide filing cabinet on the left wall. She pulled open the bottom of the two drawers and squatted next to it as she flipped through tabs.

"Here it is." Natalie pulled out a long, brown file folder and shut the drawer.

A single gunshot rang out. Natalie flinched and jerked her head toward the door.

"Stay there," Paige ordered and closed the office until just a crack remained for her to look both ways down the hall. Victor stood at the end of the hall, his hands in the air, fear visible even in profile.

Too many panicked voices in the reception area spoke at the same time, but one was louder than the rest, though she still couldn't understand the words. A woman with graying brown hair stepped into the doorway of her office diagonally across from Natalie's office and looked down the hall, then at Paige.

Paige held up her hand, telling her to stop. Over her shoulder, she said, "Natalie, come here."

Natalie joined her, crowding close. "What's happening?" Her voice trembled when she whispered her question.

"I'm not sure. I want you to go across the hall with that woman, lock the door behind you—barricade it if you can. If there are windows and they open, get out of the building and call 9-1-1. Go now."

Paige swung the door open enough to push Natalie through while keeping an eye on the entrance to the hallway. Natalie crossed in four quick steps, pulling the woman back into her office, and closed the door quietly. Smart girl.

A man stepped out of the office at the end of the hall. "What's going on?"

Paige didn't have time to motion for him to get back.

"Where is she?"

Disheveled and sporting a week's worth of beard, Patrick entered the hall, holding a gun. What the hell?

Paige stepped out of the office and pointed at the man at the opposite end. "Sir, get back in your office and lock the door."

"No," Patrick shouted, pointing with the gun. "Stay where you are."

Paige positioned herself in the middle of the hall, facing Patrick, hands raised slightly out. Her heart pounded in her chest, and her stomach roiled, but she needed to remain calm and get the civilians out of the building.

"Sir," she said firmly, "get back in your office."

"I will shoot him, Paige. I will shoot everyone in here." Patrick emphasized his words by gesturing at her with the gun. "Tell me where she is."

"Where who is?" She needed to stall for time and get him farther down the hall, in front of the bathroom.

"Don't act stupid—Natalie. Where is she?"

She took a small step back. "She's not here."

"Bullshit! I followed you from the hospital. I saw her come into the building."

Another step. "And I got her out as soon as I heard the gunshot. Who did you shoot?"

"Fuck! Don't. Move."

For a moment, she thought he was talking to her, but he shifted to look past her at the man at the end of the hall. She moved back into Patrick's line of sight.

"Who did you shoot, Patrick?" There was no way to hide the

worry in her voice. Were one of the three men in the foyer bleeding out? Why didn't she hear sirens?

"No one. It was a warning shot." He ran his free hand through his hair.

"What are you doing here, Patrick? What is this about?" Soft voice. Encourage him to talk. Keep him moving down the hall. Distract him long enough for the police to show up. Don't get anyone shot. That was the plan. It was a good plan. He just needed to cooperate.

"I can fix this. I just need to fix it, and everything will be okay."

He was talking out loud to himself, not to her, but she answered anyway. "Fix what?"

"The money! I need the documents Lexi gave her. That stupid bitch set me up. It wasn't enough that she and her fucking cousin were stealing from me. No, she had to put me in the line of fucking fire."

"You're not making any sense, PJ."

He took two steps forward, and she moved back, Ginger Rogers to his deranged Fred Astaire. "Then let me spell it out for you. I was laundering money for a drug cartel through the company. They gave me the seed money, which would convert into stocks. They sell the stock, and voilà—clean money."

Jesus. That was so much bigger than she had envisioned. Paige frowned as the implications of that kind of scheme tumbled through her mind.

"This was a test run. They were going to give me more money when we went into the next stage of funding. Then fucking Ash had to go and demand a fucking audit and hired his fucking sister. Fuckin' Alexis gave Natalie the loan notes, which showed them giving me the money."

High-pitched sirens wailed in the distance. Finally.

"The police are close. You need to let everyone out of the building and surrender."

"No." He stepped closer.

Paige backed up again, drawing even with the office Natalie had escaped through.

"Stop moving."

She stopped. "You're not going to kill anyone, Patrick. Set the gun down and back away from it."

He sneered. "Kurt proves that wrong."

Only years of practice kept her from reacting. "Why?"

"He figured out what was going on and tried to blackmail me on top of what he was already stealing. Said he'd tell you everything if I didn't cut him in. I said stop moving!" Patrick pointed the gun at the wall and pulled the trigger.

The blast echoed off the walls, and the sharp burn of the bullet hit her upper arm.

"Motherfucker!" She bent at the waist and grabbed her arm.

"Shit. I didn't mean to—"

Paige looked up just in time to see Tink tap Patrick on the shoulder, then coldcock him, sending him to the floor like a felled tree.

"What the hell took you so long?" she asked through gritted teeth.

Tink shrugged. "I wanted to let him get through his evil villain speech. Plus…I had breakfast burritos. You know what spicy food does to me."

Paige rolled her eyes as he stepped over Patrick.

"Let me see your arm."

"In a minute." She pushed passed Tink. "Tie him up please and check the rest of the offices."

"Do you have any restraints?" Tink asked.

"Get creative."

She wiped her hand on her jeans and gave her arm a quick look as she reached the end of the hall. Thankfully the black material of her shirt hid the blood quickly soaking the three-quarter-length sleeve.

Ash sat in the far corner behind Victor's desk. He and Victor had been handcuffed together around an exposed pipe. Quickly scanning him, she didn't notice any visible blood or swelling and his face didn't show any signs of pain. Her relief at seeing them unharmed was short-lived when she spotted Conor face-down on the carpet next to them.

"Shit. Is he…?" Had Patrick lied? She knelt next to Conor and searched his neck for a pulse.

"No." Ash shook his head. "Patrick hit him on the head with his gun. I heard another shot."

She let out a short breath. "It was another warning shot." No sense in worrying him—he'd find out soon enough.

"Are you okay? Where's Patrick?"

"He is also unconscious right now. Tinker is taking care of it."

Movement caught her attention, and she watched as the older man from the hall tried to push through the front door, smacking his face into the glass when it didn't open. He fumbled with the lock at the top of the door and finally escaped outside.

"Are you okay?" She scanned Ash's face.

"No! I am not okay!" Victor said. "I am handcuffed to a water pipe during an office shooting. Why would I be okay?"

He yanked at the cuff, and Ash winced when his hand hit the pipe.

"Uncuff me!" The high pitch of his voice and dilated pupils indicated Victor was close to a panic attack.

"I don't have any keys, so you're going to have to wait for the police to get here," she said softly. "But you're safe now. Tink— Christian—has the gunman restrained, and the police will arrest him as soon as they get here."

"How long is that going to take?"

"I heard sirens a few minutes ago, so any—"

"Show me your hands! Show me your hands!"

"Moment." She brought her other knee down and raised both her hands, wincing when the torn muscle of her arm pulled. "Let them see your hands."

Ash and Victor raised their free hands.

"Who else is in the building?" a black-clad Emergency Response Team member asked.

"At least two—my coworker and the gunman," Paige clenched her teeth as her hands were jerked down and tied with flex cuffs at the small of her back. "They're in the hall. There were two women in the third office on the right—I don't know if they got out of the building or not. I don't know about any of the other offices."

A hand under her arm pulled her to stand and guided her over to the four chairs in the waiting area, then pushed her to sit. "Stay there."

Ash and Victor were uncuffed and escorted outside. Ash looked over his shoulder, concern evident in the furrow between his eyebrows.

"I'll be fine," she mouthed. He responded with a short nod and left.

Grunting, she tried to position her arm in a way to relieve some of the pain caused by having them cuffed behind her back. Her thigh throbbed. Her arm burned *and* throbbed. An adrenaline crash was approaching fast, and she really needed some more painkillers.

An ERT entered the foyer with Tink and sat him down on the floor in front of Victor's desk, opposite her.

Tink tilted his head at the ERT standing over him. "They had restraints."

Paige chuckled and shook her head. She scanned the ceiling and wall, looking for the bullet hole. She found it high on the wall behind Victor's desk. The front door opened, and four EMTs rushed in, followed by Detective Gander. Two disappeared down the hall while the other two went to Conor.

Detective Gander sat in one of the chairs and let out a big sigh. "You know, these are the times I wish I still smoked."

Paige waited. Tink had his head back against the desk, pretending to sleep.

Gander gestured to the ERT member guarding them. "Uncuff them."

Tink raised his head, brought his uncuffed hands around to his front, and held out the flex cuffs for the cop to take.

The ERT guy looked at Tink, her, then Gander.

"No?" Tink tossed the cuffs across the room, landing them in the small trash can at the end of the row of chairs. "Three points. We good?"

Paige looked at Detective Gander, eyebrows raised.

He waved his hand at Tink.

"Later." Tink popped up, adjusted his jeans, and sauntered out the door.

The ERT guy looked at her. "When did he—?"

"As soon as he sat down," she said.

"And he just—"

"Sat there pretending to be asleep."

"Why?"

Paige wasn't sure which question the "why" referred to, but the answer was the same. "Because he could."

The door opened and Tink stuck his head and shoulders back in. "She's not going to mention it, but she was shot in the arm. Someone should look at it."

"Damn it, Tink."

"Knew you wouldn't say anything till you got outside. Later, boss." He disappeared back out the door.

Detective Gander stood and motioned to one of the EMTs. "You were shot?"

"Patrick fired a warning shot at the wall. It ricocheted and hit me in the upper arm."

The EMT reached over her back and cut the cuffs loose. She couldn't stifle the groan as she brought her arms in front of her.

"Do you always do this?" Detective Gander asked.

"Get shot? I've been shot *at*—first time I've actually been hit." She glanced away from the EMT cutting up the sleeve of her black T-shirt. "I don't recommend it."

Gander rubbed the center of his forehead and sighed. "I'll get your statement at the hospital."

"I can give it now," she said.

"No. You can't," the EMT said. "The bullet is still in your arm. Even if it wasn't, the wound needs to be irrigated, cleaned, and stitched up. You're catching a ride with us."

Paige dropped her head against the wall behind her. "Well, shit."

CHAPTER 34

*A*sh paced behind the police line, watching the front door of Natalie's office. What was taking so long?

He'd given a quick statement to the police while distractedly watching the door. With one eye still on the building, he'd found Natalie sitting safely in one of the police cruisers and assured her Conor would be fine, but they'd probably have matching concussions. Patrick apparently had a talent for knocking people out. Then he'd taken up position directly in front of the doors, waiting for Paige to come out.

He got a glimpse of her sitting in one of the chairs when Tink had exited, then turned on his heel and stuck his head back through the door. Ash asked what was happening, and he'd simply said, "It's all good."

As if that explained everything.

He felt a solid presence on his left and looked over to find Graham standing next to him, feet braced, arms crossed over his chest, a gray tweed newsboy cap perched on his head.

Graham caught his stare and adjusted the cap. "You like it?"

"Weirdly, it suits you. Not what I expected."

"What kind of hat did you expect?"

"Well, I wasn't expecting one, but if I had been...probably a cowboy hat," he said.

Graham nodded. "I have one of those too. Got it in Texas. It's a little too yeehaw for Georgia."

"What's that then?"

He appeared to think about it for a moment. "Cultured without being uptight."

"Huh. Are we having this conversation to distract me from worrying about Paige?"

"Depends. Is it working?"

Ash glanced at the door. "It was, but now I'm worrying again."

"She'll be okay," Graham said.

"What do you mean she'll *be* okay? Is she not okay now?"

"It's never okay getting shot, but Tink said it's superficial—nothing serious."

Ash stared at him. "What?"

Graham turned and faced him. "You didn't know she'd been shot?"

"No, I didn't know she'd been shot. Where was she shot?" His mind raced, playing back everything Paige had done since appearing in the hall. She'd said the second gunshot had been a warning shot, like the first one, and there was no reason to think otherwise. Nothing Paige had said or done indicated she'd been shot.

"Sorry, man. I thought you knew, and that's why you're so worried. Tink said she caught a round in the arm. Patrick tried to fire into the wall. It ricocheted and hit Paige. She's good, man."

"She's good?" Their blasé attitudes were driving him insane. How could they stand around and not be concerned at all? "She was shot and that's all you have to say?"

"Yeah. That's it. If it were more serious, Tink would have told me. He wouldn't have left her in there by herself. According to him, she wasn't even going to say anything until she got out of the building." Graham glanced behind him. "The rest of the team is here with the lawyer."

Ash looked over his shoulder to see John Toller, the lawyer TLC had retained for him, talking to Tink, Angie, and another woman he didn't recognize.

"Do we need a lawyer? Patrick is the one who took us hostage."

Graham smirked. "It's always better to have a lawyer at the beginning than need one at the end."

The building door opened, and Paige came out. Her shirt had been cut away from her arm and shoulder. The white bandage wrapped around it was already soaked through with blood.

Ash ducked under the police tape and met her halfway, enveloping her in a tight hug as soon as he reached her while avoiding her injured arm.

Bile rose in his throat, and his heart thudded behind his ribcage. The level of fear he'd felt when Patrick had gone down that hallway, knowing he was going after Natalie and Paige, was only slightly less than the amount of relief he felt now.

"It's okay," she said against his chest. "Conor's going to be all right, and you and Natalie are safe."

He pulled away and held her by her hips. "You think I'm worried about them?" Was she serious?

"Well…yes."

"I was worried about you!"

"Oh. I'm fine."

She was just as blasé as everyone else.

"You're fine? You were shot. You could have been killed. Do you have any idea what I was going through, knowing you were down that hall? I could hear you talking to him, Paige. I could hear you keeping his attention on you. And then I didn't even know you'd been shot. That's not 'fine.'"

"That's what I do, Ash." She stepped out of his embrace. "That's my job."

"Your job is to get shot?"

"Of course not. But protecting people? Keeping others from harm? That is my job. And sometimes that job can be dangerous."

She watched him intently, waiting for a response. For his acceptance of everything she'd just said. But he didn't know how to say what he was thinking, what he was feeling. The fear and relief and awe.

Watching her train at her job and knowing she would actually put that training to use were two separate concepts. He didn't know how to reconcile his conflicting feelings—he knew she was capable of doing what she did, but his heart insisted that he could have lost her.

"Ma'am." An EMT stepped up to them. "We need to get you and the other gentleman loaded before we bring out the gunman."

Paige dropped her gaze and took another step back. "Of course. I need to let Graham know they're taking me to the hospital."

Fuck. He realized he should have stumbled over the words. Any words would have been better than no words. "I'll tell Graham. You get taken care of. I'll see you at the hospital."

"I'll call you later." Her voice was soft. He'd never heard her voice that soft.

He ran a hand through his hair and glanced at Graham, Tink, and Angie talking to John Tolliver. Graham gave him an enigmatic look and shook his head, like he was disappointed with Ash.

Welcome to the club. He was disappointed in himself.

"Conor!" Natalie rushed past him and ran to the gurney carrying Conor to the ambulance.

Ash followed and stood by Natalie, watching as the EMT closed the doors.

"He's going to be okay," she said quietly. Her hands were folded under her chin, like she was praying, and he knew she was talking to herself.

"They'll both be okay."

He wrapped his arm around her shoulders and pulled her close to his side, hoping he and Paige would be okay as well.

~

As h bounced his leg and stared blankly at the TV on the wall across from him. He'd spent way too much time in the hospital in the last couple of days. First Natalie, now Conor and Paige.

They'd decided to keep Conor overnight. He'd jokingly asked if they could put him in the same room Natalie had been in and name it after them. At least Conor could see the humor in the situation—Ash was having a hard time finding it.

Paige was in surgery. The bullet had skimmed along her humerus bone and lodged behind it, so the doctors had to dig it out. Again, nothing humorous about it.

It seemed half of Leonidas was in the waiting room. Graham, Tink, Angie, Samara, and a woman who'd introduced herself as Addison were all there. Addison reminded him of Paige. She had the same quiet confidence. The same steady, assessing stare.

Angie had tried to talk to him, to distract him, but gave up after he'd only been able to give her one- or two-word answers. He'd apologize later. He just didn't have it in him to focus on anything except Paige's status.

The doctor entered the hallway, a blue paper cap still covering her hair. "Paige Davis's family?"

"Yes." Angie jumped up from her chair. "We're her framily."

"Framily?" the doctor asked.

"Friends that are as close as family. Found family. Picked family. We're family, just not by blood. Well, sometimes there's blood, like now, but not usually."

"I think she gets it, Ange." Tink slid an arm around her shoulders from behind and covered her mouth with his other hand.

The doctor smiled. "Framily. I like that."

Ash couldn't stand it anymore. "How is she?"

"She's fine. She's in recovery and we'll transfer her to a room shortly. We're going to keep her a day or two. She lost some blood and required a transfusion, but that's expected with a gunshot wound."

"Will we be able to see her tonight?" Ash asked.

The doctor checked her watch. "It'll be at least another hour before she's ready to be moved."

"I'll wait." He didn't care if he had to wait all night and all day tomorrow. He wasn't leaving until he saw her.

"Okay." She nodded. "I'll ask the nurse to let you know when you can go back."

"Thank you, doctor," Graham said.

"You're welcome." She turned and left the waiting room.

Graham turned to him. "You're not going to leave until you've seen her, are you?"

"No."

"Figured. We'll bring you some food before we head out. You have my number—please let me know when you get in to visit her. Text is fine. Call if anything major happens."

Ash nodded, staring intently at the clock, trying to calculate how many minutes it had been since the doctor looked at her watch and said it would be an hour.

"Ash," Graham said.

He blinked and looked at Graham. "Yeah?"

"Take care of her. Yeah?"

There was more in Graham's message than the words themselves. Graham was trusting him with someone he cared for deeply, and that trust was important. More than anything, it was a warning not to break that trust.

"I will."

<h1 style="text-align:center">CHAPTER 35</h1>

*A*sh frowned at the barely touched food on her plate. He'd be surprised if she'd taken even two bites. "Are you sure you don't want anything? You hardly touched your lunch."

He'd been trying to get her to eat all day. She'd picked at her breakfast and lunch. He'd offered to get her something besides hospital food, but she'd refused.

"Just some water." She reached for the cup, but Ash got there first and held it for her.

"Don't strain your arm." He handed her the cup, watching as she drank most of it.

She dropped her head down and held the cup out to him.

"Are you okay? Is your arm hurting?"

She shook her head. "No, it's fine. I just want to go home."

"I know, but the doctor said your temperature needs to be down for a full twenty-four hours before they'll release you."

"I know what the doctor said, but I don't like it." Her tone was short. "I hate feeling helpless."

"You're not helpless—you just need to rest and let your arm heal."

She lifted her head and glared at him. "Having someone wait

on you and hold your cup of water so you can drink is the very definition of helpless."

"I'm just trying to help, Paige. I didn't mean to make you feel like you couldn't do things for yourself. I only want you to get better."

"You're smothering me, Ash. I can't breathe with you hovering over me every waking minute. Have you even been home since I got here?"

He picked up the pitcher and refilled the cup. "I've been home. I just want to make sure you're okay."

"I'm fine." She leaned into the pillow and closed her eyes. "I just need you to give me some space."

He went cold and stilled.

With a deep, quiet breath, Ash slid the cup close to the edge of the bedside table. He'd heard those words before. In that same tone, with the same emphasis. *Some space* always meant the end of things. *Some space* started off as a day. Then a week. Phone calls being sent to voice mail and shorter and shorter texts until they stopped responding and answering his calls.

"Sure. I need to get a new computer. Today's as good a day as any."

He grabbed his keys from the sink counter in the corner and turned to say good-bye. Her head was slightly turned, her breathing even. Nodding to himself, he quietly opened the door and headed down the hall.

The nurse waved to him as he passed their station, and he listlessly gestured back. Static filled his head. All he could focus on was getting in the elevator, out of the hospital, and going home. He needed to be somewhere else before he contemplated the end of his relationship with Paige.

Would things have been different if he'd told her he loved her before she got shot? Would she have felt smothered if she knew how much he cared?

The elevator dinged and he waited for the doors to open. Angie stepped out of the car.

"Hey! You're finally leaving?"

He flinched at the question. He had been too smothering, just like Paige said, if Angie was asking him that.

"Yeah. I'm going to go home and get some sleep."

"It's probably a good idea. You won't be any use to Paige if you pass out. See you later."

"See you around, Angie."

~

It was so hot. Someone needed to turn the A/C on. Paige tried to push the covers down, but they were trapped under something. Who the hell had tucked her in?

Someone touched her forehead, the fingers cool against her burning skin.

"Ash?" Her mouth was as dry as the Iraqi desert.

"No. It's Angie."

Paige cracked her eyes open. "Where's Ash?"

"He said he was running home for a bit. I'm going to get the nurse—you're burning up."

"Need some water."

"You need more than that."

Ash had water. She just needed him.

~

Paige moved her parched tongue around, trying to work up even the tiniest bit of moisture. She blinked open crusty eyes and looked over where the table, and cup of water, should be. Graham sat in a low chair facing the bed, one leg crossed over the other with a book perched on his knee.

"What are you reading?" Her voice sounded as dry as her mouth felt.

Graham calmly placed a bookmark between the pages, closed the book, and looked up. "Don't fucking do that to me again."

His anger seemed a little misplaced. "I didn't exactly enjoy getting shot myself. Is there any water?"

Graham stood and set his book on the chair, went to the table at the foot of the bed, and poured water into a cup. He handed it to her and said, "I could give less than two shits about you getting shot, although I'm not entirely happy about it. I'm talking about you almost dying on me."

Even room temperature, the water was pure bliss. She drained the half-full cup before handing it back to him. "More. And what are you talking about? When did I almost die?"

"You were septic, Paige. You had a fever of a hundred and four. The doctors were talking about inducing a coma because you weren't responding to the antibiotics, and your fever wouldn't come down."

She frowned. "I don't remember any of that. How long was I out?"

"Almost three days." He handed her another cup of water.

"Shit." She drank that cup more slowly. "Where's Ash?"

"I haven't seen him," he said gently. "Angie said she saw him heading out when she came to visit, but he hasn't been back since. She said he wasn't answering his phone either."

Worry fluttered in her chest. What if Patrick had gotten to him?

"Is Patrick in jail? Are Natalie and Conor okay? When can I get out of here?"

"Slow your roll, hero. Patrick is in jail. Natalie and Conor are fine. You'll get out of here when the doc says you can. You just woke up."

"That doesn't mean I don't have things to do." Like figure out where Ash was and why he'd left without saying anything.

CHAPTER 36

"Thought I'd find you out here." Denise leaned over the half door of the old horse stall.

Paige looked up from the pile of puppies tumbling over and around her lap. She picked up one of the puppies and smooshed her face into the side of its face.

"It's my last day to cuddle them."

"You're going home tomorrow?"

She sighed and set the puppy down, where it was promptly pounced on by one of its littermates.

"Yeah. It's time. I want to be in court Monday and I need time to get my shit together."

Denise opened the door to the stall and closed it behind her. "Cool. Then I can ask, what the fuck are you doing?"

"Excuse me?" Why was everyone yelling at her lately?

Denise sat down across the stall from her. "I haven't said anything this entire time, but why the fuck have you been hiding up here the last week instead of tracking Ash down and beating some sense into him?"

Paige sighed again. So much for getting home without having to talk about Ash.

"I think his silence speaks volumes."

"Do you want to know what my biggest regret with Chris is?" Denise asked.

"That he's funnier than you?"

"That's a lie," Denise said. "That I wasted so much time. That I didn't fight harder for what I wanted. I was afraid if I let him in, I would end up getting my heart broken, and I let that fear stop me from taking a chance on someone accepting me and loving me for who I am. And you're doing the exact same thing."

"He left me in the hospital, Denise. I think it's pretty clear he realized he couldn't handle who I am or what I do."

"That's a bullshit story you made up in your head."

"You didn't see him after I was shot. You didn't see him look at me as if I was a stranger. As if I was someone he couldn't understand."

"Is it possible you misread his look?" Denise asked.

She cocked her head. They'd had the same interrogation training. "I'm pretty good at reading people's expressions."

"What did his expression emote?"

Paige thought about Ash's look when she'd come out of the building. "Relief. Worry. Shock. Disgust."

"I think you're probably right on the first three. You'd been shot. His brother-in-law had been knocked unconscious, and he'd been handcuffed to a pipe by his deranged partner. Of course he'd be worried and in shock and relieved you were okay. But you're projecting on the last one to hide from the truth."

She gave Denise a baleful look. "And what's that?"

"That you love him, and it scares the crap out of you, and it hurts that he left, and you don't know why."

Paige looked up and pressed her lips together. Denise never pulled her punches. She loved her, but sometimes she hated that she was so blunt.

"Loving someone and letting them love you doesn't make you weak, Paige," she said softly.

Paige wiped at her face. "What do you suggest I do?"

"Pretty sure I said that at the beginning—track him down and beat some sense into him."

"And what if I'm right, and he wants nothing to do with me?"

"Then you come back here and snuggle some more puppies, and we'll get drunk and talk shit about him."

Paige smiled even as tears filled her eyes. "But what if you're wrong?"

~

ash shuffled into the kitchen and rummaged through the cabinets, looking for a clean mug. Coming up empty, he grabbed one sitting on the counter, gave it a quick rinse, looked inside, and shrugged.

Good enough. He poured the dredges from the pot he'd made the day prior…maybe the day before that…and stuck the cup in the microwave.

For the hundredth time in the last week, he told himself he needed to get his shit together, find out what the hell was going on with Patrick and M.A.G., and get back to writing code. Even if the company tanked, someone would want to buy his program.

He just couldn't work up the motivation to do it.

When the microwave dinged, he took the cup to the living room, ignoring the stunning view of Blackbeard Creek outside the floor-to-ceiling windows. They were one of the many upgrades his parents had made to the small house his mother had inherited on a coastal island.

He eased down on the couch, traded his coffee for the TV remote, and started flipping through channels. He didn't have cable at home—he was always too distracted to sit for very long—but he'd found a show about two brothers who fought demons and ghosts that was pretty cool. He was contemplating whether he wanted to binge another season or drag a cooler down to the dock and drop a line, when something big and soft, but forceful, hit him in the back of his head.

He lunged up and spun to face his attacker.

Natalie stood behind the couch, a large decorative pillow in one hand while the other pressed her cell phone to her ear.

"Yeah, he's here. I'll call you back."

"What the hell, Natalie? How did you even get here?"

"I swam." The sarcasm was so thick he had no trouble picking it up. "I rented a boat, dumbass."

The best part about his parents' place was the inaccessibility—or so he'd thought. You needed a boat to get there from the mainland. Or a small plane, if you were a douchey McMansion owner who built their own airstrip next to their house.

That still didn't explain… "Great. *Why* are you here?"

"Why aren't you answering your phone?"

"It died."

"Why didn't you plug it in?"

He shrugged. "Didn't see a need to."

She smacked the pillow against the back of the couch. "Why aren't you answering the house phone?"

"I unplugged it. Stupid thing wouldn't stop ringing."

Natalie flung the pillow at his head, and he batted it away before it hit him.

"And you didn't think to answer it?" Her voice hit a pitch close to a screech.

"Who would be calling here?"

"Your lawyer, for one. Me, for another, you asshole." Her voice broke at the end, and she covered her face with her good hand, her shoulders shaking as she began crying.

Ash walked around the couch and pulled her into a hug.

"Hey. What's going on?"

Natalie wrapped her arms around his waist, her cast pressing into the side of his ribs.

"You could have been hurt or dead. You just disappeared, you jerk." She punched him in the ribs and he grunted. "Especially with Paige so sick."

He froze. "What do you mean, 'with Paige so sick'?"

Natalie pulled back and wiped her nose on the sleeve of his T-shirt.

He looked down at the slime trail. "Really?"

"Have you seen your shirt?"

She had a point. "Back to Paige. What do you mean she's sick?"

"She was. She developed sepsis from the gunshot wound. It was really bad for a couple of days. No one could get ahold of you."

His stomach plummeted. Fuck. He'd left her. She'd asked for space, but he'd left. "But she's okay now?"

"As far as I know. Angie said she was taking some time off work. You need to shower and put on clean clothes. Do you even have clean clothes?" She moved around the room, trying to pick up cups, plates, and trash.

"Give me those." He took everything from her, and she took the opportunity to pile more things in his hands on her way through the room.

"Why do I need clean clothes?" He followed her into the kitchen.

"And a shower."

"Whatever. Why?"

"Because you stink. Bad." She wrinkled her nose as he put the dishes in the sink.

"Then go away and stop smelling me."

"Aren't you listening? You have to go back."

Ash went through everything they'd said up to that point. "You haven't said anything about going back."

She huffed out a long-suffering sigh and turned. "You have a court date tomorrow. Which you would know if you had kept your phone charged and hadn't turned off the house phone."

Jesus. Was he being charged with something? Was there a warrant out for his arrest? Was he a—

"What's that look for?" Natalie asked.

"What's the court date for?"

"The judge is going to decide whether your personal assets will be frozen in addition to the business assets."

"What?"

She handed him her phone. "Log into your email. Your lawyer has been trying to get ahold of you for days."

Ash swiped up on the home screen and logged into his email through the phone's browser. There were at least ten emails from John Toller, informing him M.A.G.'s assets were frozen, the status of Patrick's arraignment—not that he cared—the charges against Patrick, and Ash's court date so the judge could decide whether Ash's assets would also be frozen until his role in the money laundering scheme could be determined.

What the hell? He was a victim of Patrick as much as anyone.

He checked the date. The hearing was the next day at three p.m. That meant he had time to get home, charge his phone, and confer with John before his hearing. He typed a quick email and sent it to John, letting him know he'd be at his office first thing in the morning.

"Give me thirty minutes." He handed Natalie back her phone.

"It's going to take me longer to clean up this mess. Did you use every dish in the house?"

"I wasn't really paying attention. Leave it—I'll come back and clean the house."

"It's fine. I have time. You need to shower and get back."

He kissed her on the cheek and rushed through a shower. Thankfully, he'd run out of clothes two days ago and everything was clean, if wrinkled, in the dryer. He threw all the clothes he could find in the duffel he'd brought with him and dropped it by the front door.

Natalie was closing the dishwasher when he returned to the kitchen.

"You're good locking up?"

"Of course," she said.

"I'll call you when I get my phone charged."

"Okay." She hesitated a moment. "Bash, can I ask you something?"

"Sure." Although he was unsure why she was so hesitant.

"Why did you leave without saying anything to anyone? Without saying anything to Paige? That's not like you. Especially after everything we talked about."

He pulled at his ear. "She said she needed space. In my experience, when a woman tells me she needs space, she means she doesn't want to continue seeing me."

"When did she say that?"

"The second day she was in the hospital."

"Bash...that was right around when she went into septic shock. I think you should call her. She doesn't know why you left."

He folded his arms. "She told you that?"

"Angie did."

"She told Angie she didn't know why I'd left?"

Natalie nodded. "Yeah."

He didn't know what to think. Paige wouldn't lie about something like that.

"I'll call her after the hearing." That would give him time to think about what to say.

CHAPTER 37

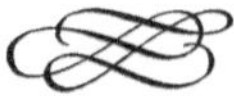

Paige slid into the back row of chairs in the courtroom. She'd given her deposition after being released from the hospital, before going to visit Denise, so she wasn't required to be there. The hearing was the one location she knew Ash would be. Asking him in person to talk felt better than calling him or showing up at his door. Hopefully, if he rejected her, the public setting would keep her from making a complete fool of herself.

Alexis was seated on the stand, testifying about her and Kurt embezzling money, although she had no idea about the money laundering. She had just turned over all the forms that looked like they were part of the company to Natalie like Patrick had told her to.

Paige took what she said with a grain of salt. Alexis was a lot smarter than people gave her credit for.

"Ash never had any idea about what was going on. That was one of the reasons it was so easy to skim money from the accounts—Ash left the business portion of the company to Patrick, and Patrick handed it off to me. As long as there was money to spend, he didn't ask any questions."

"Thank you for your assistance today, Ms. Greene," John Toller said.

Alexis left the witness box and walked down the center aisle of chairs. Pausing next to Paige, she whispered, "Thank you."

Paige nodded and turned her attention back to the front of the room.

"Mr. Moreno," the judge said.

Ash and John stood.

"Based on your earlier statements, the testimony of witnesses today, and the submitted depositions of the employees of The Leonidas Corporation, it is this court's decision not to freeze your personal assets. Any assets related to the company M.A.G. Security will remain frozen and inaccessible until such time as the investigation is complete and those assets are released by the legal authorities."

"Thank you, Your Honor," Ash said.

"On a personal note, Mr. Moreno. I would caution you to take a more active role in any future business ventures you enter into."

"I will, Your Honor."

"Case dismissed."

Paige breathed a sigh of relief. John had indicated he believed Ash would have no issue, but nothing was ever one hundred percent given.

Ash shook John's hand. She couldn't hear what they were saying, but Ash smiled.

She stood as they turned to the exit. Ash hesitated and her stomach flipped. Was that a good pause or a bad pause?

"Paige, you didn't need to be here. We submitted your deposition last week," John said.

"I know. I'm here for moral support and I wanted to hear the verdict myself."

"It went in our favor—which I never doubted."

"Thank you for all your help," she said.

"Of course. Thank Jocelyn for the referral."

"Will do."

John shook her hand and left the courtroom. She took a deep breath when Ash was in front of her.

"Hey. I was going to call this afternoon to let you know how it went."

Paige smiled stiffly. "I wanted to be here for you."

He nodded. "How's your arm?"

"It itches."

"About—"

"Why—"

They both stopped.

"You first," he said.

"Why did you disappear from the hospital?" She hated the neediness in her voice. Hated the rush of blood to her cheeks and the tightness in her belly.

He slid his hands into his pockets. "Do you remember what you said to me?"

She shook her head. "I don't remember anything from right after the surgery to waking up to Graham yelling at me."

Ash raised his eyebrows. "He yelled at you?"

"I apparently scared him."

"I understand the feeling."

Paige laced her fingers together and squeezed them tightly to keep them still. "What did I say to you?" Afraid to know the answer, she needed to understand why he walked away.

He inhaled and looked over her head. "You told me I was smothering you, that you couldn't breathe, and you needed space."

Shit. It was so much worse than she imagined. She blinked hard. "Ash, I had a fever. I didn't know what I was saying."

He looked back at her, his pain reflected in his eyes.

"I know. But some part of you meant it. Some part of you felt it."

"Ash, I don't. I don't want or need space from you. I know things have been crazy, but I care about you. A lot." Holding back the full strength of her feelings was a defensive mechanism, but she couldn't turn it off. It was too hard to take that last step off the ledge.

He took one of her hands in his and brushed his thumb over her knuckles. "I care about you too, but it's more than what you said. It's everything that has happened up until this point. You are smart and capable and one of the strongest people I have ever met. You need someone who can support everything you are and everything you do."

He squeezed her hands gently. "Maybe if we'd met again when people weren't dying or trying to shoot you, it would have been different. But I will never not worry when I know you could be hurt, and I know that makes your job harder. If you're worried about me worrying, you won't be able to focus on what you need to do, and I will never ask you to change who you are."

"Ash—"

"The judge didn't freeze my accounts, but I need to figure out what I'm going to do with the program and the business, and how I'm going to afford it all, or if any of that is even possible at this point. I'm sorry, Paige, but I think it's for the best if we go our separate ways."

Her chest was caving in on itself, making it nearly impossible to pull in air without sobbing. But she refused to break down in the middle of an empty courtroom.

"Of course." It came out as a harsh whisper.

"I really am sorry, Paige. I wish things could have been different." He kissed her on the cheek, then rested his forehead against hers. "You were right though. I should have fired you."

Eyes closed tightly, she clenched her jaw as he brushed a kiss against her forehead.

"Take care, Paige," he whispered.

And then he was gone, leaving a gaping void of numbness in his wake.

~

"Ma'am?"

Paige looked up from her phone, which she had been flipping end over end on her knee. "Yes?"

"Are you all right? Are you waiting for someone?" A bailiff stood in front of the bench she was sitting on, frowning down at her. The kindness in his eyes showed his questions came from concern and not because she'd been loitering on the bench for close to an hour.

She tilted the corners of her mouth up into a partial smile. "I'm okay, thank you."

"You sure? You look like you have the weight of the world on your shoulders. It's not an unusual look in this building, but I don't recall seeing you in any of the courts today."

"I'm sure. I was just trying to make a decision, and I'm not sure what to do."

"Mind if I join you?" He pointed at the empty space next to her.

"Not at all."

He sat with a sigh and leaned back against the wall. Paige shifted toward him slightly, giving him her attention.

"Long day?" she asked.

"They're all long days. Some days are longer than others."

"They're probably never boring."

He chuckled. "No, they're never boring. I'm Byron."

"I'm Paige." She shook his outstretched hand.

"What's this decision you're trying to make?" He raised his white-gray eyebrows, which stood out against his dark skin.

He reminded her a lot of Graham Senior. The kind of gruff, older man that would pat your shoulder while you cried, then tell you to rub some dirt in it when you were done.

"I hurt someone and I think I have a way to apologize, but I don't know if they'll appreciate it. Or even accept it."

"When you say 'hurt'…?"

"Emotionally, not physically," she assured him.

He nodded sagely. "Well, I don't know how you hurt this person, but I believe it's always best to apologize if you're wrong. And sometimes even when you're not wrong."

She smiled. "You're married?"

"Yes, ma'am. Thirty-two years and still going strong."

"Congratulations."

"Thank you. It hasn't always been easy, but one of the things we learned early on was it's important to say you're sorry when you mess up."

"What if you say sorry, and they don't accept your apology?" she asked.

"You can only control your actions, not someone's reaction. If you think you did wrong and you think there's a way to make it right, you should do it."

She pressed her lips together and nodded. "I just don't know if it will fix things."

"You can't always fix things after they're broken. You just have to accept they're broken."

Paige took a deep breath and blew it out slowly. "Yeah."

They sat quietly for several minutes until he raised his hand to acknowledge another bailiff standing in the doorjamb of one of the courtrooms.

"I have to get back to work." He pushed up from the bench. "Good luck, Paige."

"Thank you, Byron."

She watched him amble over to the courtroom and speak briefly with the other bailiff before both walked through the door. Taking another deep breath, she unlocked her phone and called Graham.

"Hey," he said. "You back in town?"

"Not yet." She crossed one arm under her breasts. "I need a few more days. Maybe a week."

He didn't say anything for several seconds. "Am I going to lose you, Paige?"

"Not anytime soon. You're stuck with me for a while. I am going to need your help with something though."

"Whatever you need."

"Thanks. I'll see you in a few days."

Ending the call, she pulled up the internet browser app and booked her tickets.

CHAPTER 38

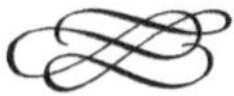

$\mathcal{A}$sh pulled on the inner door of The Leonidas Corporation's office, wondering, for the umpteenth time, why Graham wanted to see him in person instead of just talking to him over the phone.

A sense of déjà vu swept over him, seeing Graham Senior sitting at the desk in the lobby, sipping on a mug while reading a magazine. He glanced up when Ash walked in.

"Welcome back," he said.

"Thanks. I have an appointment with Graham. The other Graham."

Graham Senior chuckled. "I figured since I don't have an appointment with you. You remember the way?"

"I remember." Ash headed down the hall, waving to the older man as he passed. When he reached the open office area, he realized he didn't actually know where Graham's office was. He'd only been to the conference room and Paige's office. He glanced at her door, but it was closed. Not sure if it was relief or disappointment churning in his gut, he headed to Angie's desk.

"Hey, Angie."

She whipped around in her chair. "Ash!" She launched herself at him, wrapped her arms around his waist, and squeezed tight.

"Oh my god ! I thought I was never going to see you again. I never even got to say good-bye." She let him go. "I wanted to call you so many times, but I didn't know if you'd want me to, so I didn't. I've been fiddling with your program. I hope you don't mind, but the code is so beautiful, I couldn't help it. I'd love to show you what I've done with it."

"Uh…sure, but first I have an appointment with Graham."

"Oh. Okay, make sure you stop by before you leave."

"I actually don't know where his office is," he said.

"Down the hall, past the conference room where we had game night—it's the last door on the right."

"Thanks, Angie."

"You're welcome. And I mean it—don't leave without saying good-bye."

"I won't," he assured her. He held his breath the entire way down the hall, half hoping and half dreading he'd see Paige. What would he even say to her if he saw her?

She hadn't left his mind in the two weeks since he'd left her standing in the hall of the courthouse, her face etched with pain. Every minute of every day, he second-guessed his decision. Could they have made it work?

He'd been so sure he made the right choice, ending things when he did. Paige would have realized sooner or later they weren't suited. It had only been a matter of time. Right? Then why did her pain-filled face haunt his dreams?

Graham's door was open, but Ash knocked anyway to get his attention.

"Hey, come on in." Graham gestured to a chair in front of his desk. "You can close the door. Have a seat."

Ash closed the door, then sat down.

"How have you been?" Graham asked.

"Staying busy. The cops found my hard drive and laptop at

Patrick's house when they searched it, so I've been working and trying to find new investors." He left out the part about spending a good portion of every day brooding over Paige.

"That's actually why I asked you to come by today, and I appreciate you taking the time to meet with me in person. I have a proposition I'd like to present to you."

That got his attention. "What's that?"

"We want to expand Leonidas and form a cybersecurity branch of our company. Angie is on board with helping get it established, but she doesn't want to run it. She said, and I quote, 'If I'm in charge of it, I won't get to do the fun stuff.'"

"So what? You want me to head it up?" He didn't know if he could work with Paige and not lose his mind.

"Kind of. We want to invest in M.A.G. Security. You'd be a subsidiary of Leonidas, but you'd still be your own business and your own boss. We'd bring in the customers and work closely with you, especially when we need more cyber help on other cases —more than Angie can support on her own."

Ash tried to imagine what that would look like.

"Partners?" he asked.

"In a sense, yes." Graham shifted some papers around on his desk and pulled a check from underneath a folder. "Fifty thousand dollars initial investment into M.A.G. Security for Leonidas to buy in. From what Angie has said, your program is genius and I'd be stupid not to invest. Again, her words."

Ash stared at the check Graham held out to him. It would solve a lot of his problems. Not just the money, but having a partner like Leonidas, one that was established with a ready-built customer base and the connections to the businesses he'd built the program for in the first place. He wouldn't have to think about investors or shares or going public.

But partnering with Leonidas meant partnering with Paige. And right now, today—hell, next year—was just too soon. He was too raw.

"I appreciate the offer, but I need to give it some thought."

"Understandable. Why don't you take the check as a good-faith gesture?" Graham held the check closer.

Ash shook his head. "I can't do that."

"You've gone through a lot of shit in the last few weeks. I know your personal accounts weren't frozen, but I also know you're trying to get your company back up and running on your own. That's going to take some capital. Think of us as an early investor."

"Really, I appreciate the offer, but I'm not comfortable doing that."

Graham set the check on his desk, then ran his hands back and forth over his bald head. "Here's the deal. The check is from Paige. For some reason, she's blaming herself for what happened. She wants you to have the money so you can get back on your feet, but she doesn't want you to know that it came from her."

Ash blinked as Graham's words sunk in. "Then why are you telling me it's from her?"

"Because I am not cut out for this clandestine shit."

*A*sh wasn't sure what shit Graham referred to. "So the offer to be partners wasn't real?"

"Oh no. That's absolutely real. I want you to be part of Leonidas. Angie's right—your program will be a huge asset. Whether I hire you or we contract with you, I want you on the team."

"I can't rope down a wall." He didn't know if that was ridiculous to point out or not, but that was what his brain latched on to.

Graham chuckled and leaned back in his chair. "Neither can Angie. Dani probably could, but she doesn't."

"I haven't met her."

"She's been training for a fight the last few weeks."

Fingers tapping on his thighs, Ash considered everything

Graham had revealed, categorizing and filing away the pieces of information. "Why doesn't Paige want me to know the check is from her?"

Graham shook his head. "You'll have to ask her."

More tapping. "Is she in her office? Her door was closed."

"She's downstairs in the shooting range." He pulled open a drawer, grabbed something, and held it out to Ash.

He took what appeared to be a key card, like the type hotels gave guests. Printed on one side was a gold and black circle with the profile of a Greek battle helmet in the center and two crossed swords behind the circle. The other side was blank.

"Go back out to the lobby—there are elevators on the far side. Take it to the basement and turn right," Graham said. "The card will get you into the armory and shooting range. Follow the sounds of gunshots. Jayne should be down there observing."

"Thanks." Was Graham sending him to a literal firing squad?

"Hey, Ash?"

He turned in the doorway. "Yeah?"

"I hope you consider joining Leonidas, whatever happens."

"Thanks." That…meant a lot. Graham was very selective about the people who worked for him. He treated them like family and protected them like family. For Graham to invite him into that inner circle? Yeah. It meant something.

Angie wasn't at her desk to tell her he wasn't leaving just yet. In the foyer, the elder Graham saluted him with his coffee mug, one side of his thick mustache higher than the other like he was smirking. Not that Ash could see more than the bottom half of the man's mouth.

His mind conjured vivid images of what he might find in the basement. The light gray concrete walls were somewhat disappointing after imagining sleek metal walls with mysterious corridors leading off to secret rooms.

He looked left before going right and searched for a card reader since none of the doors were labeled. The third door on the left looked promising, and he waved the card over the raised panel next to the handle. It beeped and a loud click indicated the door unlocked.

He entered a room with a long counter, behind which were cages of guns. More guns than he'd ever seen outside of a movie. That and the muffled sound of gunfire from the next room told him he was in the right place.

Jayne looked up from the computer. "Hey. Ash, right?"

"Yeah. I'm looking for Paige."

He pointed to large monitors mounted on the wall over his head. "She's on lane five. Hang on and I'll buzz you in." He leaned to the side, close to a stand microphone, and pressed a button on the base. "Cease fire. Cease fire."

On the monitor, Paige set her gun on the ledge in front of her and turned to the camera. She spread her hands and mouthed, "What?"

"Stand by." Jayne released the button and rolled back over to the desk. "Go on in."

A buzz sounded and the door to the right unlocked. Taking a deep breath, Ash pulled on the handle and went to face his personal firing squad.

CHAPTER 39

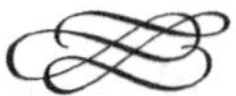

$\mathcal{P}$aige stared at the camera and waited for whatever Jayne told her to stand by for. The door buzzed and unlocked.

Ash was the last person she expected to walk through the door.

She took the hearing protection off while her heart kicked up a notch and nervous flutters spread from the center of her chest. What was he doing there? Had something else happened?

Shit. It hit her—Graham dimed her out. The jerk was getting an AARP subscription for Christmas.

Ash stopped a few feet in front of her and shoved his hands in his pockets. "Hey."

"Hey. What are you doing here?"

"Graham tried to give me a check for fifty thousand dollars," he said.

Paige nodded.

"From you."

She nodded again.

"Why, Paige?"

She set the earphones on the ledge next to her gun to give

herself time to think of an answer that sounded plausible. She hadn't expected to see him this soon and thought she'd have more time to formulate a speech and plan.

"I feel responsible."

"Why? Most of this happened long before we ever met."

"I can't explain why." She fiddled with the headband of the earphones. "I just do."

"It's a lot of money, Paige. Where did it even come from?"

"I sold my property in Costa Rica." That was why she'd needed more time off. Thankfully, her realtor had been able to find a buyer quickly. The fifty thousand was only the earnest money.

He took a step closer. "But why? That was your retirement. Your special place."

Emotions tumbled through her mind and heart. How did she explain that she felt like Patrick was her fault? With twenty-twenty hindsight, she knew Patrick had always been douchey, but would he have been less of a douche if she hadn't gone to Iraq? If she'd stuck it out and been the other woman? Could she have tempered his behavior in a way Lexi hadn't been able to?

None of that made logical sense. If she'd never gone to Iraq, she'd never have met Graham, she never would have helped start Leonidas, and she never would have met Ash. And she knew if she'd stayed, Patrick would have destroyed her. She would have become a shell of herself and never accomplished anything she had.

But in some small way, he'd done that anyway. The pain of learning about him and Lexi so long ago still echoed in her heart. That pain allowed her to build a defensive wall around herself that no one had been able to get through.

Until Ash. He'd snuck in and started tearing down that wall, piece by piece, until there was nothing left. Even if it didn't work out with Ash, if he was just here to tell her to pound sand, he was responsible for opening her heart again. He'd shown her that loving someone didn't mean she had to lose herself and that even though it might hurt, it was still worth it.

She owed him for that, but it wasn't like she could tell him, *it's a thank you for teaching me to love again.*

Instead, she said, "Because I know having your program be a success will make you happy. And I want you to be happy."

He stepped even closer. "Do you know what made me happier than I remember being in a long time?"

She shook her head, still unable to look directly at him. Of course this was the moment in her life she acted like a coward. She had nothing left to hide behind. Her usual methods of resting bitch face and fake-it-till-you-make-it weren't going to work— she couldn't pretend with him.

"You."

That got her attention. She finally looked at him. "Why?"

He laughed. "Because you accept me for who I am. You threw a book at me when I got in my own head. You're so far out of my league that I have a hard time wrapping my head around the fact that you even wanted to be with me, but you did. And every time I got to be with you or see you or hear your voice, I was just happy that I got to spend even that little bit of time with you."

"I'm not out of your league." A tiny little bean of hope sprouted in the void of her chest. She felt like the Grinch with her heart expanding three sizes.

"You are. I'm okay with that because, as crazy as it is to me, I think I make you happy too."

He was close enough now that she could smell his aftershave. She nodded. "You do."

"I'm in love with you, Paige. Every strong, kick-ass inch of you."

A laughing sob escaped, and she stared down the lane at her target.

"I don't think you're supposed to cry when someone says they love you."

The caution in his voice made her turn to him. Fully. Defenses down. Nothing hiding her feelings.

"You do when they make you happy because you love them too."

"You do?" he whispered.

Paige nodded. "I'm in love with you."

He slid his hand around the nape of her neck. "Thank god ."

"Kiss her!" Angie's voice called over the intercom.

They both started and looked at the camera bubble on the ceiling behind them.

Paige grinned and turned back to Ash, his grin just as wide and blinding as hers felt. He kissed her, still smiling, and she wrapped her arms around his waist.

Cheers and claps erupted, and they broke their kiss. Ash's arms wrapped around her good shoulder and lower back, holding her tightly.

"Is that a clown?" he asked.

She pulled back and looked down the firing lane at the paper target. "Yes."

"Why?"

"Because clowns are terrifying."

He looked at the camera, then at Paige. "I'm so glad you guys are weird."

"Me too. You fit right in."

The End.

DRINK RECIPES

Bushwacker

    1 oz Dark Creme de Cacao

    1 oz Dark Rum

    1 oz Kahlua

    2 oz Creme de Coconut

    2 oz Milk

    8 oz Ice

    Blend

    Enjoy

Lick My Pussy Shot

    1 oz Pineapple Juice

    1 oz Coconut Rum

    1 oz Melon Liqueur

    Splash of Grenadine

    - In a shaking glass with ice, combine rum, melon liqueur, and pineapple juice.

    - Shake well

    - Strain into 3 shot glasses

    - Add splash of Grenadine

ACKNOWLEDGMENTS

As always, I want to thank the readers who have stuck with me, waited me out, and supported me.

My awesome editor, Jessica, who walked me through I don't even know how many coaching sessions trying to figure out how to torture Paige and Ash.

My Sister Scribes—Anna, Freya, Taryn, and Maddie—who have supported me for the last three years and understood when I disappeared every now and then. I'm so glad to have you in my corner.

Suzanne Brockmann. That's right. Suzanne freaking Brockmann. Way back in 2020, I bid on a critique from her for Romancing the Vote. I won! And Suz (she told me I can call her Suz) read my draft. Holy cannoli, Batman! I still pinch myself. Receiving feedback from that caliber of an author was invaluable. Worth way more than I bid. I looked at my characters from such a different perspective after talking to her. I'm so thankful for her feedback and for the experience.

And finally, my family. My kids, who constantly ask, "Are you writing again?" My sister, who asked, "Are you still writing?" And my mom, who brags about me to all her friends. I love you.

ABOUT THE AUTHOR

Tarina is an award winning author who has spent her entire life in and around the military - first as a dependent and then as an enlisted Air Force member. She uses her life as inspiration for many of her stories, because truth is stranger (and funnier) than fiction.

Tarina is retired Air Force and a single mom of rambunctious twins. Her favorite hobbies are traveling and naps. You can find her trying to find the perfect writing spot with a cup of coffee next to her.

Stay Connected
Website
Email
Newsletter

ALSO BY TARINA DEATON

The Combat Hearts Series

Stitched Up Heart

Half-Broke Heart

Locked-Down Heart

Rescued Heart

Imperfect Heart

Holiday Heart (only available to newsletter subscribers)

The Jilted Duet

Make Me Believe

Believe In Me (Coming Soon)

The Leonidas Corporation

Found in the Lost

Truth in the Lie

Flaw in the Defense

Day in the Knight (coming soon)